DEAL WITH THE DEVIL
BOOK TWO

the DEVIL'S PLAYGROUND

CARIN HART

For those who like to roll the dice, take a chance, and fall in love with the wrong sort of man who might be oh, so right...

FOREWORD

Thank you for checking out *The Devil's Playground*!

Each book in the **Deal with the Devil** series is an interconnected standalone with a different couple, no OWD (though OMD from the heroine's past is a crucial plot point in this book), and a guaranteed HEA by the end. The heroes are protective, possessive, and as members of the aptly-named Sinners Syndicate, they don't just break laws, these heroes act like they don't exist.

Royce is the underboss, second-in-command to Devil. A much more lighthearted character, he still has his own demons—and his obsession with a seemingly innocent waitress who works at the Sinners' nightclub, aptly named the Devil's Playground.

Of course, I say 'seemingly' because Nicolette has her own baggage, her own past, and trouble following closely at her heels... plus an attraction to the charming boss who hired her on to sling drinks at Springfield's premier club.

Will they find happiness together? Considering this is

a Carin Hart novel, of course they will—and I hope you enjoy reading it!

The Devil's Playground includes: murder (on and off-page); threats of rape, noncon/forced blowjob, and domestic violence (not by the MMC); mentions of prior DV/sexual abuse; grooming; dubcon; cockwarming; praise kink; guns; drugs/drugging; sex work; kidnapping; and some light (and not-so-light) stalking.

xoxo,
Carin

Roll 'em...

A♥ A♣ A♦ A♠

PROLOGUE

THREE YEARS AGO

ROYCE

It's moments like these that I understand why no one else wants the gig as Devil's second: it's a pain in the ass to be responsible for the man.

Case in point? He's missing.

Again.

With Lincoln 'Devil' Crewes being one of the most powerful players in Springfield, I know that while ordinary civilians passing him by on the street probably won't see the dark-haired, dark-eyed brawler and recognize who he is, anyone with ties to the seedy side of the city definitely would. Hell, if a Dragonfly caught him off-guard without a Sinner to have his back, good chance he'd end up with a bullet between his wide shoulders and, somehow, it would be all my fault.

1

I'm his right-hand man. The underboss for our syndicate, my job is mostly as a liaison between the mafia leader and the rest of our guys. I do more than that, obviously, but as I'm cruising toward the quieter part of downtown Springfield, I can't help but think that my most important task is babysitting our volatile boss.

Link would put a bullet in *my* back if he ever knew that's how I think of it, but what can I say? The man's five years older than me, the head of the Sinners Syndicate, a fierce bastard who is icy cold during a business meet with our suppliers, then raging hot whenever he gets wind that our main rival is stepping foot on our turf. I know his moods better than most and, over the years, I've learned to avoid the minefield that might end with him blowing up and reaching for his trusty Sig Sauer.

Those are all reasons why he probably gave me the underboss title when he first cobbled the syndicate together all those years ago—and the fact that I've kept it despite my age just proves my point. None of the other Sinners *want* it.

Sometimes I'm not so sure I do, either, but then I remember how he had my back that summer when everything went to hell and *shit*. Devil already had my loyalty. Now Link Crewes has my total devotion, and my honest friendship.

There isn't anything I won't do for the boss after he saved my ass—including keeping his secrets for him.

I don't know for sure where he is tonight. If it wasn't for a problem we have with one of our gun runners, I'd let it slide, but Romeo will only deal with the Devil of Springfield. That means I've got to track him down or lose our next supply of weapons if Romeo decides to peddle his wares on the East End instead. It would trigger World War Three between us and the Libellula Family if he tried since guns belong on the West Side, but Romeo's only loyalty is to the almighty dollar.

I'd call the boss if I thought that would do anything. I gave it a try earlier after the message from Romeo's crew came in. No surprise: he didn't answer. And despite knowing that Link carries a second phone on him that never seems to ring, the one time I asked to have the number, the cold look he gave me had my breath catching in my throat.

Right. One phone for business. The other for... well, it can't be personal. Devil doesn't *do* personal, not like so many of the rest of us.

And I'm one of the few Sinners who know the reason —which is exactly why I'm coasting my nondescript two-seater down a deceptively suburban street on the edge of our big city.

It's a hunch. Normally I'd ignore it, leaving Link to the ghosts of his past. Lord fucking knows I have my own; in my case, that's literal, too, since Heather is dead. The woman who haunts Link?

She's very much alive.

Ava Monroe is a schoolteacher. First grade at Springfield Elementary, if I'm getting the details right—and I am. Of course I am. That's my job, to know details like that. Just like I know that she grew up in the same tenement that Link did, his childhood sweetheart and first love back when he was still Lincoln Crewes and not quite the Devil yet. That was about twelve or so years ago now.

3

The night he committed the kill that earned him his nickname was the same night he walked away from the woman he once affectionately called Saint Ava.

He doesn't talk about her anymore. It took years of me wondering if he was gay or just the type of guy who won't get involved with any of our products—guns, gambling, or girls—because he thinks it's a conflict of interest. Could be. He always carries the same weapon, hasn't gotten laid in all the time I've known him, and refuses to make a sneaky bet in our nightclub-slash-casino-slash-brothel that the Sinners call home.

So, basically, he's the opposite of me.

I swap out my piece whenever we get a new shipment. I don't shit where I eat, so the girls upstairs are off-limits, though the ones who visit the Playground aren't. And when it comes to gambling... well, they don't call me 'Rolls' for nothing. You might think it's because of my hoity-toity given name—haha, Rolls Royce, get it?—but, if so, you've never seen me at the craps table in the back of the Playground.

Link has his reasons for the way he is, same as me. And maybe I've gotten worse since Heather, but can you blame me? Nah, just like I can't blame the boss for the way he turned out.

It all started when I got wind of Ava and dug a little deeper. That eventually led me to realize that Link's not gay, and while he runs our business with an iron fist, he doesn't use his position as mafia leader to get women because—in his mind—he already has one.

She just doesn't know that.

He's the boss. As his second, I support him. If that

means I try to hook him up with one of our waitresses or a clubgoer just to work out some of his repressed need, I will, even if he's refused every last girl I put in front of him. One of them might snag his attention away from the timid teacher who moved on and is currently in a long-term relationship with one of her colleagues—and if Link decides to make a move on her at last and take out his competition, I'll help him with that, too.

I'm not just his babysitter. I'm a fixer, and one hell of a clean-up guy.

Link's Catholic. He's big on this penance thing. I might be agnostic myself, but I get the gist of it. He thinks he fucked up big, breaking some imaginary rule back when he was a hotheaded twenty-year-old, and keeping his distance from Saint Ava is his way of making up for it. Me? I've never pulled the trigger on any of my guns—at least, not at a living target—but I have blood on my hands regardless. Penance or whatever, if cleaning up other Sinners' messes after Link cleaned up *mine* allows me to get some closure over what happened with Heather, I'll fucking do it—just like I'll sneak around this quiet neighborhood so that Devil knows I've got *his* back.

I purposely park my car two streets away from Ava Monroe's house. If Link's out there, I'd rather not draw attention to either of us by pulling up alongside him.

My black suit blends into the shadows. My blond hair doesn't, and I keep my head bowed, hands in my pockets in case any of Ava's neighbors are out and about at this hour.

I recognize the black car at the end of the block. As basic and unidentifiable as the one I use, whenever the boss doesn't have one of the guys driving him around, he uses a car just like that. He swaps the license plates frequently, so that's no help, but as plain as it is, the compact two-seater sticks out in a sea of minivans and SUVs.

It's not parked directly in front of her house, but at an angle that would allow the driver to see right into her bay window with the curtains not drawn tight; dark as it is out now, the light in her home gives the impression that she's in a fishbowl. As I stride past on the opposite side of the street, I catch a peek of her delicate profile. She's sitting on a couch, probably watching television, completely unaware that someone is watching *her*.

For a moment, I'm so sure that, as consumed with spying on his ex as he is, Link doesn't know I'm standing outside his car. But then I grab the door handle on the passenger side, and it isn't locked. I yank on the door, sliding into the empty seat. The fact that the Devil of Springfield allows that, and all I get is a tight-lipped nod instead of his gun to my temple for intruding on him, is a sure sign that I'm not as sneaky as I think I am.

I wasn't really trying to be. At least, not with the boss. It's the rest of the neighborhood I was trying to avoid.

Here's hoping I did.

I jerk my chin at Link, grinning over at him. "Hey there. You come here often?"

"Fucking smart ass," he mumbles, fingers curved around the steering wheel despite the engine being off. He gives me a side-eyed glare. "Better not be hitting on me with a weak ass line like that."

"Nah. Just pointing out the obvious, boss."

To that, I get a grunt. Probably because it's not supposed to be obvious—and that he thought he'd done a better job of keeping the Sinners in the dark when it came to Ava despite making it clear to each and every one of us that this one particular teacher in town was off-limits.

We just weren't supposed to interfere, and he reminds me of that with a dark look as he works his jaw, then spits out, "What are you doing here, Royce?"

Royce... in the syndicate, so many of us go by nicknames, it's rare for me to hear someone call me 'Royce' without 'Rolls' being attached to it. It's like how nearly everyone in Springfield calls him 'Devil'... except me. Years ago, I shortened 'Lincoln' to 'Link' and nearly got a fat lip for it. I had no idea it was because Saint Ava used to use that name for him, but after I proved myself to him —after *Heather*—he became 'Link' to me, I stayed 'Royce', and even if someone else decided to take over as his underboss, they'd have one hell of a fight from me first.

Even if nights like tonight are part of the job, it's mine. So he likes to stalk a teacher, watching her from the shadows. So he has a secret.

Don't we all?

This isn't the first time I've wondered where he went when I couldn't find him. It's just the one time I actually followed my gut, headed downtown, and found him watching her from across the street.

Shit. If I could march over there, walk through that front door, and drag the unsuspecting woman out here to give her to Link, I would in a heartbeat. But I can't. He'd

7

never let me since he's so stuck on believing he doesn't deserve her, and I have to sit here knowing that there's no way in hell I can convince him that he does.

So, instead, I'll do what I've been doing since I learned about his Ava: I'll keep throwing other women at him, hoping he'll either get over this one or realize at last that she's the only one he wants—and maybe decide he's done with this penance bullshit for once and for all.

For now, though, we've got other things to worry about—which is exactly why I'm here.

"It's syndicate biz. One of our gun runners has an issue with the latest batch of nine-mils. He wants to meet with you."

"Which guy?"

"Romeo Valdez. When he couldn't get through to you, he stopped by the Playground. Jessie's entertaining him now, but he's ready to walk on this deal if he doesn't get that meet."

I could've handled it. As Devil's second, I'm thrown into a lot of the bureaucratic BS that you wouldn't think you'd get in organized crime. I guess that's just the 'organized' part of it because, half the fucking time, the boss is meeting with someone about one of our specialties; it's a wonder he can find any at all to come to downtown Springfield to sit in a car and watch his Ava.

But while I *could* have handled it, when one of our biggest suppliers wants Devil, it's my job to give them Devil.

Even if I have to track down our leader first.

His eyes are back on the light in that open window. For a moment, I expect him to completely ignore what it was *he* was doing here... but he doesn't, and I realize I should've known better.

I'm his second. He has my loyalty, and I have his trust.

"Tanner told me that Ava finally ended things with that teacher prick," he says, still staring at her house. "I guess I just wanted to see for myself that she was alone again."

I don't ask how Tanner knows that. Our resident tech whiz, he's as good with all that computer shit as I am with a pair of dice or a pack of cards. I wouldn't be surprised at all if Link has Tanner run Ava Monroe the same way every Sinner gets scanned before they're welcomed into the syndicate.

I'm not as good, but my research into Saint Ava said something similar: that she was in a committed relationship with another teacher at Springfield Elementary. It seemed like it was heading toward marriage—and I was already coming up with ways to distract the boss if that happened—but now... seems like one less worry for the both of us.

I open my mouth, ready to point out that this might be the time to make his move. But, as though he can sense me getting ready to prod, his head snaps my way.

"Romeo Valdez, yeah? That's what you said?"

I nod.

"Romeo." Link turns the car back on, scoffing under his breath as the engine turns. "Of course it has to be fucking Romeo."

I'm the smart ass, but I like to put the emphasis on *smart*. I know when it's open season to crack a joke—and when to keep my fucking mouth shut. In this case, when I get that Link's mood has more to do with Romeo's name than his relationship with the syndicate, I keep the comments to myself.

Pulling away from the curb, he asks, "Your car nearby? Or do I need to give you a ride back to the Playground?"

Because unless he has work for me, that's usually where I spend my nights. Either at the tables or working my way through the female patrons with a hard-on for a lucky gambler, if I wasn't already the underboss, I'd expect the Devil's Playground to be my domain instead of his.

"I parked about two streets away. I wasn't sure if I would find you here, but if I did, I didn't want to cause a scene."

"Good," he grunts under his breath, taking the first turn off of Ava's street.

As he pulls up behind my ride, a *click*-ing sound echoes throughout the car. It takes a second for me to understand that he was engaging the locks, trapping me inside. Sure, I could disengage them, but he made his point.

Link's hands stay on the steering wheel, a relaxed pose. He's not pulling out his Sig Sauer, another sign that he's not pissed, though that can change if he doesn't like the way our conversation goes.

I don't take any offense to that. This is Devil, after all. There's a reason he believes in that penance of his, and after everything he did to create the Sinners Syndicate, if he decided to shoot me now, the only thing he'd regret is losing his right-hand man—and the mess I'd make to the upholstery in his car.

"How long did you know?" Link asks me.

Just in case I'm wrong... "About?"

"Ava."

Figured. He mentioned her, but only because I tipped my hand by showing up here tonight.

"A while," I tell him. It's a safe answer. "I mean, I knew she existed. I knew you were still keeping her under your protection. But if you're asking about me knowing I could find you here tonight? That was a guess."

"A good one," Link says. "I come by here at least once a week to keep an eye on her. It's not Sinners business, so I kept it to myself. Looking back, I probably should've told you. Or," he adds, "kept my phone on."

His business phone, I think. He has no problem turning that one off or ignoring it when it suits him. But that other one...

I don't ask. After tonight, I don't think I need to.

I do shrug, though. "Don't worry about it, Link. I mean, maybe I don't get why—" I pause, not sure I want to finish that sentence right now. Last thing I need is to set Devil off when it's obvious just how defensive he can get over the topic of Ava Monroe.

He narrows his dark eyes. I didn't finish my sentence —but he does it for me.

"Let me guess... you don't understand why I'm mooning over a woman who spent the last two years banging another guy. Something like that?"

Bingo. "What? Nah. It's not like that."

"You're such a fucking liar," Link says, though there

isn't any heat in it. To prove it, he jabs the automatic lock button again so that I can get out of the car.

I hesitate. Something about that haunted look on his face... I've known Lincoln Crewes since I was eighteen, he was twenty-three, and we were both trying to avoid getting snagged by some of the more questionable gangs. With his rep—and my willingness to do anything to get a leg up—he created the Sinners Syndicate, and I was right there with him.

That was nine years ago. I probably know him better than most... and, shit, how well do I really know him?

"Link?"

He shifts in his seat, looking right at me. "Just thinking about what I said and what you didn't. 'Cause, fuck me, I am a sap. A killer and a cold-hearted bastard, but when it comes to *her*? I get more pleasure watching her live her life without me than all the half-dressed whores dancing down at the Playground you're so fond of."

I give him a half-smile. "To be fair, you shouldn't knock it until you try it."

Link's scowl tells me he doesn't appreciate my comment.

My hand inches over to the door handle right as his voice drops as he speaks again.

"One day, you might find the only woman who'll make you lose your head *and* your damn heart. Someone who you love with every last piece of you, enough that you'd carve that same fucking heart out of your chest and let her stomp on it with her pretty little feet if it made her smile. Because, goddamn it, the only thing worth *anything* in this Godforsaken world is that fucking smile."

His gaze never once leaves mine as the last of my smile slides off of my face.

That's when he adds one last shot before I pop open the passenger-side door: "I look forward to seeing it happen to you, Royce."

That makes one of us.

One day… right. Because it hasn't happened yet. Not to me, at least, no matter what the seedy underworld of Springfield believes. No matter what the various women I take to bed hope for until I set them free. They all want to be the one to capture my heart, to make me love them, to tame the wild gambler with the wicked grin.

But they can't.

Fall in love? Not going to happen. Obsess over one woman the way that Link's been doing for half my life? Nope.

Give my heart away to someone else?

Yeah, no.

Kind of impossible when I realized I was heartless that night three years ago when I watched Heather Valiant die in my arms.

But I don't tell Link that. I don't have to. He's the only one in Springfield who knows the truth about what really happened that night, which is why he said 'one day' the way he did.

I just hope that day never comes—even as I give the boss my trademark grin and say, "Wanna bet?"

Roll 'em...

ONE
SNOW

ROYCE

I've always hated the snow.

It's cold. Wet. Damn inconvenient, too. Springfield gets its fair share of it, but there was no such thing as snow days in the city when I was a kid unless we were talking feet instead of inches, and I'd bet part of my dislike stems from way back then.

Two decades later and I still curse under my breath when I see the first flakes fall—and for a totally different reason than when I was a ten-year-old icicle, tromping my way through the eight blocks it took me to get to my elementary school.

The snow makes clean-up duty a bitch.

Countless footprints crunch the crusty, icy, day-old layer. Some of the snow melted through the day, turning into a solid sheet once the sun went down and the February temperature dropped. I'd prefer the fluffy shit.

At least, then I could kick aside the prints and no one would know we were here.

Instead, to mess up the scene, I instructed Marco and Case to add even more steps around the back of this empty lot while Killian searches for any shell casings we missed on our first sweep.

While I supervise, I stamp my feet, trying to get some feeling back in them. I can just hear Devil's low growl as he mutters that I should've grabbed boots before I set out. My insistence on wearing my Italian loafers out to the scene meant I slipped once already on a patch of black ice I thought was a safer bet than the unplowed lot. One of the guys snickered. Too busy trying to keep from busting my ass, I don't know which one it was, but they were all conveniently doing their tasks when I looked around before.

We're a well-oiled machine. There are five of us that Link calls on when there's body duty, and All-Thumbs is back at the van, laying out the tarp so we can bag up the DB and store him until we can bury him.

If it wasn't a syndicate-related hit, I'd leave him here. Good riddance. For the last six months, Garrett Fink's been a pain in my ass. An informant who traded his info for free drinks down at the Playground, he kept hinting that he was going to spend more time over on the East End. It was his heavy-handed way of saying that he thought he'd get better perks informing for the Libellula crime family, and that the Sinners needed to step up.

I didn't bother Link with that. I gave Garrett a couple of 'sure's and 'maybe's before eventually telling him that, if he wanted to see what being a Dragonfly was like so bad, go right ahead. He didn't have Devil's mark on his skin. He wasn't a Sinner. He wasn't a prisoner of the Devil's Playground, either. He could leave whenever he wanted.

Garrett must have, too, since we got the call in earlier that his body was found in neutral territory, just a shade closer to the East End Damien Libelulla rules than the West Side where us Sinners have our turf.

It would be so much easier if the boss hadn't gone along with the idea of a truce between us and the Dragonflies. I understand why he did. When his rival had his gun to Ava's head, Link was willing to sacrifice anything to keep his wife safe. If that meant finally giving in to Damien's insistence that his Family and the Sinners didn't have to be constantly at war, fine. He would've done anything to get Ava out of danger.

Did I expect that he'd follow through with it once she was locked up tight, safe and sound inside of their penthouse? No. Last August, I had every one of our guys on guard, ready to retaliate.

Link had us stand down. First, because he was distracted by the big church wedding he was throwing for Ava. Then, because he found out that he was getting that heir he wanted after all. He'd knocked Ava up, and suddenly, the idea that there wouldn't be a firefight between the two main players in Springfield seemed a lot more attractive to the father-to-be.

Or maybe the friendship he once had with Damien meant enough to Link that it was worth seeing if we could have a little peace.

Not like I could say anything. The other Sinners

wouldn't dare, but as Link's second, I technically *could*— but when I remember that I'm the reason the big divide between Sinners and Dragonflies really began to grow six years ago and... yeah. He wants peace?

I'll do whatever the fuck I have to to get that peace for Link. And if that means standing here when it's twenty degrees out, just about freezing my nuts off, I'll do that, too.

There's gotta be at least four inches of snow behind the warehouse from yesterday's storm. That icy layer is cracked beneath the weight of Garrett's body, the blood shimmering against the unbroken plane of ice next to him that cradles the former informant's chest. And while the snow makes it easier to find the shell casings, that's about the only thing it's good far.

Snow tracks prints. Vivid red blood spatter stands out against the white.

It's a clean-up nightmare, and we're out here longer than I want to be.

Killian's the one who found the baggie of Breeze during the first sweep. Doesn't take a true crime genius to figure out that while Garrett had a rep for being a snitch for the Sinners, there was a reason he drifted this close to the East End—and it wasn't for intel. The Libellula Family is responsible for the drugs in Springfield, and this seems like a buy gone bad.

"Okay, fellas," I call out once the body's been moved and Case used a shovel to disturb any bit of bloody snow he could find. "Let's finish up and get the fuck out of here."

18

My hands are numb as I cup my mouth, letting my voice carry on the winter wind. There's no one besides us back here, and even if there was? The locals ignored a man being shot and left for dead in the snow. In Springfield, they couldn't care less about a crew of guys cleaning it up after the fact.

Especially since, even if they called the cops, odds are they'd be on the phone with someone on Link's payroll—or Damien's.

There are two cars parked next to the van: a basic, boring black sedan and a basic, boring silver one. The van itself is white, blending in with the snowy backdrop, so long as you don't see the city grime turning the edges of it black and slushy.

Garrett's body is loaded up in the back of the van with All-Thumbs getting the shit end of the stick, sitting back there with it. Marco's got the wheel, Case sitting next to him. Like me, Killian drove to the scene in his own ride. His is silver. Mine is the black one.

As the head of the crew, I'll be the last one on the scene. I wait for the three younger soldiers to get situated in the van first, then for Killian to start up his car before I even think about heading for mine.

No matter how much my toes feel like rocks in my loafers.

Once Marco turns on the engine, he rolls down the window and raps the top of the van. Case bitches about him letting the cold air in, but he ignores his partner.

"Hey, yo," he says instead, talking to me and Killian. "We're heading to the Playground once we put Fink on ice again." We have our own quasi-morgue storage where we put bodies when the ground's too frozen to bury them right away. That's where I've decided Garrett will go for now. Once it warms up a little, he'll be nothing more than a memory to Springfield. "You guys wanna come with?"

Killian answers before I do. "Sorry, but I promised Jas I'd be home as soon as I finish up here. Maybe next time."

Killian and Jasmine got married about a year ago now. For the first few months, the other guys gave him a gentle ribbing over how devoted he is to her, but when Twig— fucking Twig who didn't learn to shut his mouth all the way up until Link blew his cock off—went too far one time, and Killian knocked him out with a well-aimed punch, the other guys decided his wife was off-limits.

As she fucking should be.

Marco nods, wisely not saying a word to Killian before he jerks his chin my way. "What about you, Rolls?"

Good question.

Up until the beginning of November, that would've been a no-brainer. If Link didn't have a job for me special, and none of the Sinners needed me to step in between them and our boss, my backup gig was running the Devil's Playground. Officially, I manage the place. Unofficially, Jessie Byers does, and I sit in my assigned booth off the dance floor, keeping my eyes on things when Link can't.

The other Sinners like me being approachable. Compared to Link, I definitely am, and part of that means giving them access to me. The Playground isn't just our money-maker. It's our headquarters, with a club and a brothel and a casino out front, and the rest of our operation filling the buildings attached to it. We own the entire block the Playground sits on—and a good chunk of the surrounding streets, too, one way or another—and anything a good business needs, we have.

Me? I prefer the limelight. I don't mind everyone in the club knowing who I am, and even if they don't jump when I enter the way they do when Link does, I'm respected there—and welcomed.

But then, in November... well, I still spend a lot of my time at the Playground, but that's only because I have a reason to be there now. When I don't?

There's somewhere else I'd rather be.

"I don't know, Marco. Let's see. How 'bout... heads, I take a rain-check. Tails, I join you."

Pulling a quarter from my pocket, I give it a practiced flip. It goes about a foot high before arcing, landing in my palm. I slap it against the back of my other hand, snorting to myself when I see George Washington's profile peering up at me.

I tilt it so that Marco can see what it landed on, then palm it. "Looks like I'm gonna have to pass this time. But you have fun without me. Tell Jessie I said you get two rounds on the house to get the chill out of your bones, yeah?"

Case hoots. "'Atta boy, Rolls."

A muffled voice comes from the back of the van. "Since you're wimpin' out early, does that mean one of us can have your rounds?"

"Sure," I say with a shrug. I can just imagine All-

Thumbs' greedy expression in the back, and how quickly it'll slide off his bearded face when I add, "One for Marco. One for Case. None for the big mouth who thinks I can't handle the cold when he's the one who asked to be on bag duty."

Dickhead. He spent half the clean-up in the van, and he wants to yank my chain? I'm not Link. I won't retaliate by swinging my fist or pulling out my piece. But if depriving one of my guys of some free booze reminds him where his place is in our hierarchy?

Yeah. I'll do that, too.

Killian drives off first. Marco rolls up his window, more to drown out All-Thumbs' groaning that I'm being an ass than because Case is still complaining that it's cold out.

Once they get gone, I open up my curled fingers, glancing down at the quarter nestled against my palm. There's ol' George Washington again. With a grin, I flip it, nodding to myself when I see him on the other side. Maybe it's not fair, rigging my pockets with a double-headed quarter in the right one, and a double-tailed one in the left, but life's not fair, is it?

Besides, I never leave anything up to chance.

WHEN I STARTED CHECKING HER SCHEDULE, SEEING WHAT shifts Jessie put her on, I should have known it was more than just making sure the new waitress I hired for the Playground was settling in well.

At first, I told myself that she was new to the job *and*

the life. It isn't often we take on waitresses who don't have the sort of experience our girls need, but when Officer Burns suggested Nicolette Williams for an opening, I did the interview as a favor for one of Link's cops. If I didn't think she would be a good fit for us, I'd say I tried, then send her on her way.

Well. That was the plan.

Then I met her. I got my first glimpse into those haunted brown eyes of hers. I looked at her wavy, golden blonde hair—a few shades darker than my own—and imagined it spilling across my pillow. The tiny diamond stud in her nostril winked up at me, tempting me in a way I couldn't understand at the time. And when I asked her why she wanted the job, the frank way she said, "Because I desperately need money," resonated with me.

She had been working at an Italian restaurant in downtown Springfield already so she had server experience. When I probed her more on how much she was looking for, she had another honest answer: "More than I'm getting at Mamma Maria's, but not as much as I'd get if I sold myself alongside some whiskey."

I respected that. Anyone who's in Springfield long enough to learn about what the Sinners Syndicate sells discovers that we do the three g's: girls, gambling, and guns. For a cut of the profits and promised protection, we have rooms on the floor above the Playground where 'wallets'—our customers—can buy a night with one of our girls.

Nicolette didn't want to become one of them. She just wanted to sling drinks and earn tips, and with Burns's recommendation in my ear, I took her on—and that's fucking bullshit. Link's the one who deals with the crooked cop. I didn't hire her for Burns.

I hired her for *me*.

It's hard to explain. From the moment she walked into my office for the interview, I was snagged. She caught my attention, and I kept waiting for her to lose it. Due to my own twisted code of ethics, as soon as I gave her the job, she became untouchable to me.

Three months later, and I'm regretting that.

I don't fuck my employees. It's a thin line, but one I don't cross. And I would have had to have been a bigger asshole than I am to refuse her a well-paying job just because something about her made me want her at first glance.

So I gave her the job, put Jessie in charge of her, and tried to keep my distance.

Tried.

Definitely failed.

The spark was there during the interview. No denying that. Nicolette caught my eye, and whenever we were at the Playground at the same time, I unerringly found her. She seemed to fit in easily with some of the other waitresses, making friends with a couple of the downstairs girls. Then I heard through the grapevine that, despite how clear she made it she was in it for the cash, she gave one of the other girls half her paycheck so Tina could buy Christmas presents for her kids.

I arrange bonuses for the Playground employees every Christmas. Following Nicolette's lead, I doubled it for the front staff out of my own pocket so that anyone working for the Sinners had a merry Christmas. When I realized that I did that because I wanted *her* to have one... well, I didn't play favorites.

I *want* to play favorites.

She's so fucking cute. I *can't* explain it. I've gone for all kinds of women before. Knock-outs, plain Janes, women who are more adorable than attractive. I'm a 'personality' guy, first and foremost, and the little hints of who she is behind her apron and her serving tray intrigue me. More than that, though, she's *cute*. Only a couple of years younger than I am, the twenty-seven-year-old waitress has a perpetual smile on her face, and whenever she's not being drowned out by the thumping bass coming from the club's dance floor, she prances around the kitchen, humming songs under her breath.

I recognized one. Some Disney shit, about a spoonful of sugar. It's an infectious melody that got stuck in my head for days, to the point that I fired up my TV, found the film, and watched *Mary Poppins* for the first time in my life to see what she liked about it.

That's not all I did, either.

It's Link's fault. When I couldn't get her deceptively innocent face out of my head, I started watching her as she made her way around the club, taking orders and serving drinks. The tiny uniforms our waitresses wear might be good for business—and excellent for tips—but when I couldn't go a single night without stopping by my personal office and rubbing one out... I knew I was in big trouble.

Then, when I stopped chasing other women because none of them compared to *her*... I accepted that I was fucked, and obviously not in the good way.

So, pulling a page out of Link's book, I started to watch her. No. Let me be clear. It became stalking, and I knew I had crossed a different line the first time I looked up her schedule, saw she was off, tapped into the HR files, got her address, and went by. I just wanted to see if she was there, and when she *was*? I didn't leave.

Just like I caught Link doing three years ago, I sat in my car, and watched Nicolette's windows for any glimpse of her I could get.

I spied the cameras the first time I drove over to her house. They're not like the regular doorbell ones that some homeowners get. She has that, yeah, but two pairs of obvious surveillance cameras. One on each side of her house so that there aren't any dead spots, plus another couple posted on the back to guard the fenced-in yard.

The last thing I needed was it getting back to the Playground that the club's boss was stalking one of its waitresses. I stay away from them, but the amount of cameras —coupled with a few things I've picked up on since watching over Nicolette—has me sure that she's not just being diligent. She's looking out for something... and that gives me the perfect excuse to do the same.

That's how I justify it. I'm watching her. I'm keeping her safe.

From what? I have no clue. From the outside, nothing. She goes to work, she goes to the house that's in her mother's name, and she lives alone while her mother is currently visiting family in Florida; I overheard her mentioning that to another one of our servers and turned that into further justification for keeping my eye on her. Taking as many shifts as she can to get the money that she needs, she's at the Playground almost as much as I used to be, and when she isn't?

She's here.

And, *fuck*, I think to myself as I park my car in its usual spot down the street from her house, so am I.

Roll 'em...

TWO
THE DEVIL'S PLAYGROUND

NICOLETTE

Someone is stalking me.

I hate that I know the signs. I hate that I've lived a life that I don't even need actual evidence to know that I'm right. When my gut goes off, the shivers running down my spine, and I hear that bastard's whisper in my ear even though it's been nearly three years since I saw him last... more than anything, I hate that he can still affect me after all this time.

I don't know if it's Kieran. That's the worst part. Whoever it is is being very careful. In spite of the *five* separate cameras I have watching my home, I haven't been able to catch anything out of the ordinary.

Of course, that just tells me that—from the outside— whoever is watching me is acting very ordinary. It'll be someone passing by my street, covering their face so I don't get a glimpse of it. Or... or parking their car just out of the range of my cameras.

Do I know that I sound fucking paranoid? I do. I can't help it, though. Having spent eight years in an abusive relationship with a controlling partner who swore before I left that he'd never let me get away from him, believing he could be out there, watching, waiting... I *need* to be paranoid to stay safe.

But that level of high alert, of watching my cameras on my laptop, of checking my phone obsessively every time the doorbell camera goes off, is keeping me safe. I'm vigilant and wary, and because of that, I've found a way to make it through day-to-day life.

I have to. Because if I didn't?

I'd go fucking insane.

I won't let him beat me down again. I absolutely refuse to let this faceless stalker turn me into the shell of Nicolette I was by the time I finally had enough and escaped Springfield the first time.

I thought it was for good. I should have known better. With my mother and her most recent husband—before their divorce early last summer—still living in Springfield, I think I always knew I'd be dragged back here. I lived my first twenty-four years in this city, trading it for a small town six hours away where no one could find me, but when Mom got into her accident in August?

I never planned on coming back. Then again, my mother probably didn't plan on getting hit by a car, either.

It was a freak accident. A hit and run. She lives on a slow street in the quieter downtown area of the city. No one ever pays attention to the posted speed limit signs, and some idiot clipped her when she was bringing her groceries in one morning. Seems like he took a turn too fast, sent her flying, and my mom ended up with a broken hip.

At least, that's how she explained what happened. She barely even saw the car before impact, none of her neighbors were around to witness it, and—at the time— she didn't have cameras on her house.

I moved back in September, as soon as she got out of the hospital. The plan was to help her with everything she needed while she recuperated and recovered from surgery, then I could disappear to Willowbrook again. If I was smart and kept my head down, Kieran never needed to know I came home.

But because I've never forgotten what kind of man Kieran Alfieri is, I put cameras up my first weekend back.

I had no choice. Everything that happened when I was a kid... maybe she missed the signs, but that's because I willfully hid them. I couldn't blame her for mistakes I made, and, these days, she doesn't have anyone but me. Lance booked it to Europe once the no-contest divorce was signed. My Aunt Therese lives in Florida with her kids, and she couldn't fly up to help Mom recover.

That left me.

I planned on being gone by October. But then Mom had a setback, I was running out of cash, and I got a job. After a month, I traded that job for another, and maybe Mom thought that I was settling in because, at the beginning of the year, she announced that she was feeling up to visiting my aunt in Florida for an extended stay.

She left the first week of January after begging me to house-sit. I'd watch over her house in Springfield, wouldn't have to pay rent, and could leave again when winter was over and Mom returned.

I already sensed that someone was watching me. Here... at the Playground... I couldn't really explain it and sound sane, but I couldn't shake the feeling, either. Part of me knew I should tell Mom to forget it. I couldn't do it.

But, damn it, she's my mom. And not having to pay rent for a few months—after ending the lease I had in Willowbrook—might be a blessing in disguise for me. So I agreed, and it's been a month and a half since she left me alone in her house, and as I pull my curtain back, peering out onto the empty street in front of me, I wonder how much longer I can stand it.

If Kieran finds me...

No. I shove the black-out curtain back into place.

It can't be Kieran. Whoever I sense out there... they're careful. When it comes to me, Kieran's always proved that he's the opposite of careful. If he found me, if he figured out that I'm not only back in Springfield, but that I work for the Sinners Syndicate? He wouldn't be watching me from a distance.

He doesn't have the patience. He doesn't have the self-control, either.

He'd walk right up to my door, expect me to let him in, and in no uncertain terms, remind me that I've always belonged to him. He might laugh. He might smirk.

He might backhand me across the face and, when I'm down, start kissing me before it leads to more... but he sure as fuck wouldn't be a silent spectator that watched over me without making a move.

And that makes the sinking feeling in the pit of my stomach so much worse.

Because if that's not *Kieran* out there?

Who the hell is it?

———

THE WORST PART IS THAT, EVEN WHEN I GO TO WORK, I can't escape the eyes.

At least at the Devil's Playground, though, I know to expect it. The uniforms the serving girls wear are designed to catch attention. From the low cut, tight black shirt with the Playground's name splashed in teal across the front of it, to the teeny tiny shorts we wear, and the smile slathered on our faces no matter what, our customers expect an experience here—and they tip well to get it.

I need money. That's the truth of it, and like so many of the girls who work at this nightclub, I teeter on one side of the line between slinging drinks and slinging pussy to make ends meet.

Literally, considering this club is owned by the local mafia—the Sinners Syndicate—and the entire top floor is dedicated to giving clients the full experience.

Not me. When I first interviewed, the suave yet aloof manager who talked to me explained that, for a small cut of the profits, I could rent a bed upstairs to entertain 'wallets' with the Sinners' protection. It wasn't necessary to get the waitressing job, but the option was there. I politely declined, and since November, I have still made triple what I did serving at Mamma Maria's.

That doesn't stop some of the Playground's customers from trying, though. I consider it a good night when I only get propositioned once or twice instead of a dozen times. Luckily, since this is a Sinners' property, the wallets take rejection very well. If a girl says no, the answer's no, and if they try to push?

The Devil of Springfield steps in.

Technically, my boss is the same manicured, gorgeous blond who interviewed me. Royce McIntyre—who everyone knows as 'Rolls' because of his prowess at gambling—runs the Devil's Playground. My immediate manager is a tall, leggy redhead named Jessie, but when it comes to who rules the West Side of Springfield?

That's Lincoln 'Devil' Crewes, and if I never have to confront that scary SOB, I'll be happy.

But while nearly everyone in Springfield is afraid of him and what he's capable of, that doesn't mean that some of the customers here don't try to... *convince* us with a little more emphasis than necessary.

I have a handful of my own. I'm one of the more recent waitresses to sign on, so it could just be that I'm new meat. I have to prove myself, stand firm, and tell them to back off.

Most of them get that, but I do have one in particular who thinks that, for the right price, he can change my mind—which is why, when Britney snags me on my way to refill a scotch on the rocks and a gin and tonic for a cute couple on a first date, I'm not surprised with her message.

"Hey, Nic. Real quick, babe. Miles Haines was asking after you again."

Ugh. Miles Haines. A thirty-something, toothy bastard who flashes his cash like that means his shit don't stink. I went under his radar for my first few months here, but lately? It's like he's parked at the poker tables, roulette wheel, or slots during every shift I have, and he just won't stop with the come-ons and the heavy-handed persuasion.

It's not bad enough that I've thought about going to Jessie yet. I definitely won't go to Rolls. He might be my boss, but the gambler doesn't just run the Playground because—apart from the brothel upstairs and the dance floor that makes up most of the nightclub—it's the biggest casino in Springfield.

Nope. He runs the Playground because he's a high-ranking member of the Sinners Syndicate, second only to Devil himself.

Besides, the other night, I'm pretty sure I finally found a way to get Miles to understand that I'm not interested.

He thinks I have a price. I gave him one.

"Unless he has ten grand, cash in hand, I don't know why he's wasting his time," I tell her.

Britney giggles. She thinks I'm kidding.

And I am... but only sort of.

"You know," she says, "you could just tell him no instead of throwing out numbers like that. At the Playground, guys understand the word no if you're direct with them."

Maybe. But Kieran spent ten years training the word out of me, and it's a hard habit to break. I find it easier to just make ridiculous demands and hope like hell I'll be left alone.

"And if you don't want to say no and can get that bag?" Britney bumps her hip against mine. "It's not as bad as you'd think."

She's talking about fucking the clients for money. Her sly expression tells me that, despite her comment, she's absolutely sure that I would never take one of the wallets up on their offer, though she does when the mood strikes.

Britney's wrong. Not about selling herself the same time as she sells whiskey, but because I *do* know sex work's not as bad as people make it out to be. Why?

Because I've done it myself.

Unlike a certain sect of Bohemians from the '90s, I don't have the luxury of not paying rent. Sometimes, when it comes between having no roof over my head and no food in my belly or accepting a hundred bucks for fifteen minutes' work... you say yes and hope like hell they get it over quickly.

But that was when I was starting out in Willowbrook, and I was desperate to survive. Anything was better than returning to Kieran. Those days are over, though. If some cocky asshole wants in my shorts, ten grand is my price.

Hey. It's not like the wallets here can't afford it.

When I don't say anything to her comment, Britney shrugs her shoulders, her impressive tits bouncing with the motion. I think she's going to continue on her way back to the floor, but I should've known better. An overly friendly brunette with a tendency to gossip, she's not going to let me get away now that she had a reason to stop me.

Her hand lands on my upper arm, and if she notices the way I stiffen under her touch, she pretends she doesn't. My impression of Britney is sweet yet ditzy, so she probably has no idea that she's causing me to grit my teeth behind my smile.

"I almost forgot! Did you hear who's in tonight?"

I shake my head.

Her dark brown eyes brighten. "The Devil himself."

My stomach tightens.

Look. I know bad men. Being Kieran's property for so many years... I've met my fair share, and all of them pale in comparison to the rumors I've heard about the leader of the Sinners Syndicate.

Six feet tall and built like a damn linebacker, with dark eyes, dark hair, and a dark scowl, I've only ever caught glimpses of the man when he was sitting in a private booth, usually with Rolls McIntyre. And, okay, maybe I was sneaking peeks of the golden-haired, blue-eyed Adonis sitting with him more than the powerful mafia leader, but something about the way he sat in the shadows, lording over the whole club from his corner, made me think of the Phantom from *The Phantom of the Opera*.

I must have made a face because Britney nods in agreement. "I know, right? He's one hell of a scary bastard. I mean, I know he signs our paychecks, but, yeesh. Thank fucking god he got married. Can you imagine if he decided he wanted one of the girls here to belong to him like some of the other Sinners?"

Not really, though I wouldn't mind if one of them decided to make me theirs...

No. Bad Nic. The last thing you need is to get involved with one of Kieran's rivals just to piss him off. Because eventually he'll find me—if he hasn't already—and... yeah. As much as I have eyes for one of the Sinners in particular, I need to keep that to myself.

Especially since Rolls McIntyre hasn't shown any interest in me since he concluded my interview and offered me the job here...

Don't think about Rolls. Britney is bringing up Devil—

Lowering my voice, I tell her, "I heard, when he was just starting out with the Sinners, he ripped a guy's head right off his neck."

That's one of the horror stories that Kieran told me to get me to stay away from the West Side of Springfield. In my early twenties and beginning to lash out at the control he had over me, I thought about running away, hoping that the Sinners might take me in... and then he would remind me what the Devil of Springfield was capable of.

I wait to see if Britney will tell me I'm being ridiculous.

She doesn't. Instead, she bows her head in case she thinks one of our co-workers is listening in over the *thump-thump-thump* of the bass, the clanking of the silverware, ice, and drinks, the roar of the crowd when one of the gamblers hits it big.

And then, with a confiding smile, she says, "I know. I believe it, too. Last summer, when I was working the floor, someone bumped into the girl he was with... the one he ended up marrying... I swear, he beat the shit out of him for just *touching* her. Blood everywhere. It was *crazy.*"

You know what? I should be disturbed by that. I

should... but when I spent nearly half my life as the property of a gangster who equated violence with love, and
who kills for the head of the Libellula crime family on
the East End of Springfield?

Maybe... maybe it wouldn't be so bad to have a man
love you so much he'd go after anyone who hurt you.

It couldn't be worse than the one who claims to love
you being the one who actually *does*.

Roll 'em...

THREE
JAKE

ROYCE

I tried to stay away.

I really did. It hit me last week, when I was sitting in my car, watching Nicolette's house from just down the street, hoping for a sliver of her to appear in the dark windows... it hit me that I can't keep doing this.

I'm obsessed with a woman I can't have. It's as simple as that. I think about her constantly. I fantasize over her more than that, and it's fucking sick. Since I offered her the waitressing job at the Playground, I haven't said more than two words to her. For fuck's sake, she's off-limits as one of my employees.

Three months now, I've convinced myself that I was only watching over her because I sensed she needed it. That she was in trouble. But what if *I*'m the trouble that she can't escape?

No. I told myself that I needed to stop. If she really *is*

in danger, she's affiliated with the Sinners now. Even if I'm not the one to protect her, we have at least a hundred soldiers in Springfield who are loyal to the organization. That's not counting the inner circle, either. Nicolette might not have Link's mark on her—only full-fledged members of the syndicate get the devil horns and tail— but by working at our club, she's one of ours.

Untouchable to anyone in town who might want to hurt her, definitely, but even more off-limits to *me*.

I know better. Considering how much trouble a McIntyre has gotten into for obsessing over the wrong woman... I *know* better. And, sure, it took me a few months to accept that I needed to give up on torturing myself by watching her, getting close enough that I can catch a whiff of her perfume before slipping past her as she waits tables. Spending hours at a time in my car, imagining what she could be doing in that house of hers alone... because, damn it, she better be alone... plus the undeniable jealousy that kept washing over me whenever I thought about another man touching her... yeah. That's the nail in the coffin for me.

I had to back off. Before I fucked up and did something I'd regret, I needed to leave her alone.

That lasted six days. Six damn days of blue balls, of snapping at All-Thumbs and Banks when I needed to mediate some stupid argument the soldiers were having, of going home alone because it was too damn tempting to pick up a date—and the one time I tried, my stomach twisted so tightly *because she wasn't Nicolette fucking Williams* that I thought I was going to hurl.

The nausea only disappeared when I slipped into my

apartment, stripped off my clothes, pulled up a candid shot I took of Nicolette smiling at some no-name wallet, and jerked my cock until I was shooting my load down the drain. With one hand braced against the glass shower stall, the other gripping my erection tightly, I knew I was in even more trouble when I admitted to myself that some innocent blonde—who existed so far out of my reach—isn't just the reason I've been able to get hard at all these last three months.

Fuck. She's the reason I come. The reason I got any release, any pleasure, any relief at all from the constant weight on my shoulders. Not that I mind the pressure. Being the underboss is my job, it's my *life*, and that was the only thing that mattered to me... until *her*.

I still don't know why I fixated on this one woman. Honestly? I don't want to know why. The logical side of my brain says it has to do with seeing Link and Ava together. Deep down, I want a love like that. A love that defies reason and rationality, that can survive a fifteen-year separation and still have the two of them utterly devoted to each other now.

My whole life, I've equated success with money and power. I still do. But now? I want what Link has. I want a woman who will put up with all the bullshit that comes with being in *the* life, know exactly what kind of man I am, and still willingly sleep next to me after I spent the hours before cleaning up a murder scene.

Is that Nicolette Williams? I don't know. But so long as she's my employee, I'm not going to find out.

So I decided to go cold turkey. And, like I said, that

lasted about six whole days—and when I *do* see her again, it's not even my fault.

It's Link's.

Well, no—it's more complicated than that, but because I don't want to think about the real reason why until I'm sitting across from my boss and I'm forced to, I blame Link.

And I do it with a crooked smile.

It isn't usual that I get a summons to the Playground. Considering how often I spend my evenings at our club —and, if not our club, then the Sinners property attached to it—he doesn't have to call me over. I'm usually here. It's Link who only comes to make an appearance, to keep his men, customers, and girls in line.

Since his marriage to Ava Monroe, Link has better things to do than sip his drink while casting a dark eye over his domain. Of course. If I had a wife like that... I wouldn't be wasting my time here, either. There are still a thousand other things that take up his twenty-four hours —as the mafia leader, he's even busier than I am—but when he has the option of going home to Ava or sitting down and having a drink with me?

I'm his trusted second. His closest friend. Still, no fucking way he wants to sit in the booth that's considered 'his', looking at my mug if he doesn't have to.

I wish I could pretend I didn't know what this was about. Unfortunately, I'm as on top of what goes on on our turf as Link is; more, really, since it's my job to bring any issues to him. So when I got the call earlier that he wanted to talk to me about something personal, I had a clue what was going on. And though I knew that Nicolette was working at the Playground tonight, so my odds of going seven days without seeing her in the flesh aren't ones I'd play, I find myself maneuvering through the throng of customers toward Link's shadowed corner as I'm supposed to.

He's already seated on one side, an untouched shot in front of him. When he sees me, he nods, and I notice he has another one waiting in front of my usual spot.

Oh. So it's one of *those* kinds of talks, huh?

I slide into my seat. Like Link, I don't bother with my drink.

Not yet, at least.

"Hey, boss. How are ya? How's Ava?"

Link leans back in his seat, arm stretched out over the top of the booth. A self-satisfied smile tugs on his lips as he says, "Fucking glowing. Carrying my kid looks good on my wife."

He's not wrong. Ava is pretty in that 'girl next door' way, but though she'll complain about her swollen ankles and the way her belly is sticking out now that she's firmly in her second trimester, she wears her pregnancy well.

Plus, with her knocked up, Link is in an infinitely better mood these days. Part of that has something to do with the ring on her finger—and his name tattooed around her knuckle beneath the wedding band—but, more than that, the Devil of Springfield just needed to get laid regularly to put a self-satisfied smirk on his face.

Hey. I tried to get him to fuck off some of his aggression. He never took a mistress, though not for a lack of trying on my part, and now that I see him with Ava, I finally understand why.

For Link, it wasn't about getting off. It wasn't about chasing a quick nut, or finding release in a willing woman's body for the night. It was that connection he had with his childhood sweetheart, and if he couldn't have her, he didn't want anyone else.

I didn't get that. It wasn't like I was suggesting he marry them or anything. It was just sex, right? Close your eyes and a pussy is a pussy... and my dumb ass believed that until Nicolette.

Link called himself a sap once. For mooning over Ava when she was in a relationship with another man... but he still wanted her. He held out hope he'd get his second chance with her. And while I'm sure he'd prefer she didn't have to go through what she did for him to have it, he's happy with how everything turned out.

Me? I don't know what will come of my obsession with the gorgeous waitress, but I can finally say I get what Link meant. Because I haven't even been able to be with any other woman since the moment I met Nicolette, and I've never even *had* her. At least Link had memories of his Ava to keep him going on the lonely nights. I just have my hand, my wry attitude, and a couple of photos kept hidden on my phone.

I shake my head, trying to knock out just how fucking pathetic I am. Then, knowing this is unavoidable, I give Link my trademark winning grin. "Okay. You wanted me to stop by to see you. What's up?"

"Right. Got something to talk to you about."

"I'm listening."

Link clinks the bottom of his shot glass against the tabletop, the liquor sloshing slightly. "Jake."

Shit.

I knew it.

Keeping my tone light, I ask, "What did my cousin do now?"

What *won't* Jake McIntyre do?

"Did you know he was back in town?" Link asks.

I can't lie to him. For one, he'll know and get pissed. For another, I respect him too much to even try.

"He called me a couple of weeks ago. Mentioned that he met another girl—"

Link throws back his head, groaning loudly. There's a reason he chose this booth to claim for his infrequent trips to the Playground. Not only is it shadowed, giving us privacy, but the acoustics here are amazing. Despite how loud the crowded club is tonight, I can't pretend I didn't hear Link's groan—or his obvious annoyance in the sound.

I hold up my hand. "I know. I *know*—"

"I know you haven't forgotten what shit he pulled the last time he 'met a girl'."

A lump lodges in my throat. I swallow it roughly. "No. I haven't."

"If it wasn't for Jake... look. I know what happened with that other girl was a mess. A fucking disaster. But if Jake had listened to what you told him, it wouldn't have been our problem. You understand?"

"Yeah, Link. Of course. What? You think I like cleaning up after him and his messes?"

"Why not? Since that girl got killed, you've been cleaning up all of ours."

Ouch.

47

It stings double that he's not wrong. A guilty conscience is a bitch, and I've spent the last six years trying to find a way to smooth mine over. When Heather died... Jake took off. I gave my aunt and uncle some money to send him to a college on the other side of the country so that the fallout from her death didn't touch him. He was just a kid—barely twenty—and he had no idea that falling for the wrong girl would end up with the Dragonflies and the Sinners on the brink of World War Three.

Link smoothed it over without any other bloodshed; at least, not more than could be expected when a Dragonfly's sister dies in the arms of one of his enemies. Knowing that Jake was out of Springfield helped, and I figured he'd want a fresh start in California.

And then, at Christmas, he visited home and told me all about Simone Burke, the most recent woman that caught his eye—*in Springfield*.

You think I'm obsessed? That's nothing compared to Jake... and maybe that's another reason why I finally decided to give up on Nicolette. When my cousin tells me the lengths he goes to catch Simone's attention... at least I just followed her in my car.

Jake? He'll sprawl out on the backseat of his target's...

"I'll take care of him."

"We can't fuck up this truce, Royce."

As if I need a reminder of that. "We won't, boss. I promise. Don't worry about Jake. I got it."

"I know you do." Link takes his first sip of whiskey, a sure sign that the hard part is over. I grab my shot, scooting it toward me as he pointedly changes the subject. "Okay. Now, about that DB you guys cleaned up last week…"

I'm completely aware that Link's doing that on purpose. He got a full report on Garrett Fink's unfortunate demise. Agreeing with me that it looks drug-related —and not important enough to mention it to Damien— he clapped me on the shoulder for a job well done and that was all. But because I'm not the only one who gets tense when anyone brings up Heather Valiant, Link starts asking if I think that the two ODs I had to clean up on Monday have anything to do with Breeze.

Since Breeze is a party drug and those lowlifes had obvious track marks, I tell Link no, and move on. After all, drugs are Damien's domain. Us Sinners have our own focus, and while I purposely steer the conversation away from girls, and Link hates to hear me ramble on about gambling, we settle on guns.

For the next half an hour, we talk about a meet Link had with Falco, a new up-and-coming gun runner on the East Coast. He wants to worm his way into Springfield, and Link's thinking about it. As his second, though, he wants my input before he makes any final decisions, and we talk about the pros and cons until Link's private phone rings.

I finally learned why he keeps a second phone on him. With the cheapie device programmed so that only one person could get through, whenever it rings, I know that his wife needs him.

It doesn't matter *why* she's calling. I've seen him hold up a finger to some of the other powerful players in town, telling them to shut the fuck up all so he can talk to Ava, make sure she's okay.

The further she progresses in her pregnancy, the antsier Link gets. No one but me would even notice, and I'm for sure not going to point it out. When Link is antsy, his Sig Sauer gets drawn, and he's not so hasty about whether he pulls the trigger or not.

As Link answers his phone, I run my finger around the rim of my glass, gaze being drawn to the dance floor.

Damn it.

I tried. I really did. I wasn't even looking for her—but there she is. Standing by the bar, talking to Dennis—the bartender on duty—as he loads up her tray, there's Nicolette and, groaning under my breath, I drop my free hand to my dick. One glimpse. One glimpse of her sticking out her ass as she bends over the bar top, and I'm fucking *sprung*.

So distracted by her long legs, the way her golden hair hangs in seductive waves just past her shoulders, and how easily she carries the tray away once it's loaded, I barely notice that Link's done with his conversation until he raps his knuckles on the table.

My head shoots his way. "Yeah, boss?"

"That was Ava." Obviously. "She was wondering when I was coming home." A small smile tugs on his lips. "I'm telling you, Royce. She can't get enough of me these days. And when my wife needs me, you better fucking know I'm on my way."

Lucky bastard. "Have fun."

His smirk tells me he will. "What about you? Heading out?"

"Nah. I thought I'd stick around, watch the floor tonight."

Link gives me a knowing look. "Just the floor?"

He's my boss, the head of the syndicate, and one of the only friends I have. Even if I tried to hide my irrational affection for a woman I'm dying for, Link would see right through me.

Instead, I shrug.

Links shakes his head. "I don't know why you're torturing yourself. Shit. If you want her, go for it."

If only it was that easy.

"She works at the Playground," I mutter. "That means she's under syndicate protection, right? Even from me."

He huffs out a breath. "If you had a hard-on for the blondie so bad, why did you hire her? You could've bumped into her after turning her down, then done your charming 'Rolls' bullshit and there you go. She's yours."

I arch an eyebrow. "What do you mean, charming 'Rolls' bullshit?"

Link tilts back the last of his second whiskey. The bottom of the empty shot glass *clinks* against the table top as he sets it down. "You know what I mean. You tried it with my Ava."

"I didn't know she was yours."

"And like I said that night, the wedding dress gave it away."

Whatever. "Enjoy your bride. Leave me to my misery."

"Suit yourself. Just know that, if you change your mind, I won't say 'I told you so'."

And Link thinks that *I'm* the smart ass? I flip him my

middle finger as he laughs, moving his big body out of our booth.

Once he's gone, I pull out my phone. If Link wanted to talk to me about Jake, that makes me think my cousin got up to something in the days since I've talked to him last. As a favor to him—and my own stunted conscience —I took down the information he gave me about this Simone and had Tanner run her. The fact that Simone is married should've been a red flag to anyone, but Jake swore she was separated from the guy.

Maybe Link knows better. God knows that, even if she was taken, that wouldn't stop my cousin...

Just before I dial him, I glance out into the crowd. It's the underboss in me; I know better than to be caught off-guard. A quick survey around the club to make sure that everything is okay, then I'll call Jake, check in with my cousin that he won't be giving me any more grief than he already has.

One quick look and—

Hang on—

What's going on by the bar?

Nicolette is back—but she isn't alone. A man a head taller than her is blocking her path. She has her empty serving tray tilted up, shielding her in an obvious display of discomfort as he's talking down at her.

The wallet is too close. Too *familiar*. Completely taking over her personal space as he leans in, tapping the case he's holding in his other hand. Her eyes are darting to the side, looking for help, though no one else at the Playground seems to notice she's in trouble.

No one but *me*.

I look at my phone. Pocket it inside of my suit jacket, then slip out of the booth.

Know what?

Jake can wait.

Nicolette obviously needs my help—and I was a fucking moron to think I could really stay away from her.

Roll 'em...

FOUR
TEN GRAND

NICOLETTE

Sometimes I'm amazed that Officer Burns suggested I apply for this job.

That was back around Halloween. I'd only been working at Mamma Maria's for about six weeks then, but I met the steely-eyed cop and his young wife during one of my first shifts. Considering all of my prior work experience—that I was willing to put on a resume, at least—came from doing various serving jobs in Willowbrook, I settled in quickly at the cozy Italian restaurant near my mother's house in downtown Springfield.

It was fine. Set in a seedier part of the city, the customers tipped as well as they could. I was still grateful to have found a job anyway, but when one of my regulars mentioned that I might be a good fit for the local night-club, I was curious.

Then I discovered he meant the Devil's Playground, and I almost couldn't believe it.

I thought it was so odd. A *cop* of all people having an in with one of the local mafias... but who am I kidding?

Two years in Willowbrook didn't make me forget about the corruption in Springfield. I know from experience that the cops in this city are either in Devil's pocket or Damien Libellula's. The ones on the East End would never help me survive. They'd simply hand me right back over to Kieran if they knew the truth of who I was.

But Officer Burns? I think he saw in me a victim— fuck that, a *survivor*—and, regardless of whose payroll he's on, I'll always appreciate how he not only told me to apply, but he gave me a glowing recommendation to the man who interviewed me.

It was a formality. Rolls mentioned that Burns said I was his favorite server at Mamma Maria's, and while he and his wife, Angela, would miss me there, there was money to be made serving at the Playground.

And, like I told Rolls, I needed money. I've never shied away from the fact that I'm an independent woman who needs to survive on my own. Money makes that possible.

Did that mean I was for sale?

Men like Miles Haines obviously think so.

I don't know why I'm so against just taking a second gig upstairs. With my mom in Florida, it's not like I have anything else to do when I'm not working. Too worried about being seen, I go to the Playground and back, and that's really about it. I stay home. I watch television. I read books.

Why shouldn't I kill a couple of hours with some company, get paid well for it, and forget for a moment that I'm super fucked up when it comes to intimacy?

I want to say it's being here in Springfield. That the specter of Kieran Alfieri has me holding back, but if I'm being honest, it's more than that.

It's *him*.

I know I'm being silly. Ridiculous. Like a schoolgirl with a crush, I keep sneaking peeks at my gorgeous boss —not Jessie, but the man who hired me—whenever he's at the Playground. Maybe if he hadn't been the one to so matter-of-factly explain that I could stay downstairs and sell drinks, or I could go upstairs and sell myself, I might have thought about it.

But because it *was* Rolls who gave me the option, I found myself hesitant to do so. Almost like he would judge me or something.

I don't know. Add that to how the girls upstairs make me think of the 'lovely ladies' from Les Mis, and I just... it would take a lot for me to agree. I'm not as desperate as I was when I first left Springfield, and while I told Haines that the price for my pussy was ten grand, that's only because I knew he would never pay it.

Yup. I was wrong about that one.

It's closing in on the end of my shift. My feet are barking, my shorts gave me a wedgie an hour ago that I've been too busy to pick, I've had 'Memory' from *Cats* in my head for the last fifteen minutes, and I had just gotten over one of the more handsier wallets tweaking my tit for a twenty when someone taps me on my shoulder from behind.

Smile, Nic. Always keep that smile on your face.

Though, yeah, it kinda wavers a bit when I find Miles Haines standing behind me.

He's wearing an ill-fitting suit, dark hair in disarray from where he ran his fingers through it at some point tonight, dark brown eyes drawn irrevocably to my cleavage. One hand flutters anxiously at his side. The other? It's holding a plain brown briefcase about the size of a tablet holder.

"I got your message from Brit," he says to me.

I have no clue what he's talking about.

"Message? What message?"

He pats the small case he's holding. "Ten grand. Cash in hand. Isn't that what you said?"

What?

I laugh a little, keeping my good humor. "You're joking."

He has to be.

He's *not*.

Miles flips open the lid on the small case. I'm not sure what ten grand looks like bundled up in twenties, but, uh... that's a lot of money in there.

"You gave me your word. If I handed you ten thousand dollars to walk out of here with me one night at the end of your shift, you'd let me have the rest of it. Remember? From midnight to eight in the morning, I get you to do whatever I want with. You promised, right? And, well, I've delivered."

Holy. Shit.

"That's really ten grand in there?" I ask, stunned.

He nods, not even bothering to hide his slight smirk

or his lust-filled gaze. "I'm sure you'll want to count it. When I'm getting my room ready for you, you can do that, but once you see there's the full ten grand like I promised, I'll expect you'll do what *you* promised. What do you say, Nicolette? Do we have a deal?"

I can't believe this. For the last two weeks or so, every shift I've had at the Playground, Miles would ask me what it would take for a night. Not even just a quick fuck. He wanted a full night, with the only caveat being that I could get him to wrap up his dick. Other than that, nothing else was off the table.

And the only reason I agreed with something absolutely ridiculous so was because I never, ever in a million years thought *he* would agree with any of my stipulations. Maybe the condom, yeah, but the cash?

No way.

What do I say? Shit. I don't know *what* to say. I'm having a hard time tearing my gaze away from all that green, but can I really go home with this guy for eight hours? I... *shit*—

"What's going on here?"

My head snaps up. While I was staring at the money, someone else joined us.

Goddamn it. What would it take for an empty pit to open up beneath my feet right now that would conveniently swallow me whole? Because that? That would be great.

Honestly? Anything would be preferable to me standing here, discussing my price with a potential customer, when Rolls McIntyre suddenly appears.

His suit, I notice, is not ill-fitting. The white button-down fits him just right, and the black suit jacket—an exact match in shade to his perfectly creased pants—is tailored to his body. Up close, he seems deceptively slender, though I'd put money I don't have yet down that he's got a sculpted, muscular body hidden beneath the fancy clothes.

Miles smirk goes flat as he glances over at Rolls. "Nothing much. Just making arrangements with one of your girls."

Rolls looks at me, a pleasantly curious expression on his handsome face. "Is that so?"

What can I say? Technically, that *is* what's going on. "Yes."

And I know from the reactions of both men that that one word means that I've agreed. Because, well... I *have*. For that much money, I can't afford to refuse.

Rolls's blue eyes rove over the cash still on display. "I hope you brought more than that with you, Haines."

"Yeah? Why's that?"

He shrugs. "I'm hosting a private poker game in ten minutes. Big rollers only. I was hoping to invite you to it. There's a chance to make a lot of money... but you know the drill."

Miles's greedy dark eyes dart down to the briefcase. "'Cash in hand'," he repeats. That's how the Playground runs when it comes to the gambling in the back—and the girls selling themselves upstairs—and everyone who frequents the club knows it. "Alright. Yeah. No, this is just a little chunk of change I brought to make sure Nicolette is free tonight. I got more."

Rolls nods, his attention back on me. "Are you?"

"Am I what?"

"Free tonight."

Again, he sounds vaguely interested and more than a little chilly and aloof, but I can't help but wonder why he asked me that at all. Because I work here? Or is there something more to it?

"I guess," I tell him, shrugging slightly. When Miles's lecherous eyes lock on my tits again, I lift my serving tray higher to block him. "My shift is over at midnight—"

"And at 12:01, she's coming home with me," brags the sleazy wallet.

Rolls raises his eyebrows. "You're not taking her upstairs? That's not how we do things at the Playground."

I know why, too. It isn't just that the Sinners expect a cut of their girls' profits for renting the rooms upstairs. They—*we*—aren't paying for the space. It's the level of protection we're assured, where if any of the wallets try to take more than they paid for, someone will be there to make sure they don't.

"I know," Miles agrees easily, though there's a dare in the way he juts out his chin. "But for ten grand, I'd prefer to spend the rest of the night somewhere I'm comfortable."

"I see. Well, if you're interested in the game, come on by."

"I will."

He waits a moment to see if Rolls is going to walk away first. When my boss doesn't, he mouths something to me—I pretend not to see—then shuffles away.

As soon as he's gone, Rolls leans in so that I can hear him over the loud music. He obviously doesn't want

61

anyone else to listen in as he murmurs, "If you don't want to go with him, you don't have to."

I know that. But if I don't? I won't get that money, either. "Thanks for looking out for me, Rolls. I appreciate it. But if he's willing to pay..." I feel a little embarrassed admitting that, but what can I do? "You said, if I changed my mind about what I sell here..."

Rolls nods as my voice trails off. "I get it. Okay. It's my job to make sure to check in with you, but you're right. It's up to you if you want to go with him. But if you're looking for some extra trips tonight, tell Jessie I said to put you onto the casino tables instead of the floor until your shift's over. It's only another half an hour or so, but every little bit helps, yeah?"

I nod. "Yeah. Thanks."

His pretty blue eyes gleam warmly down at me. "Don't mention it."

It's the first hint I see of the ice around him beginning to thaw, and I just wish that had happened before tonight.

Roll 'em...

FIVE
BET

ROYCE

Nicolette isn't going anywhere with Miles Haines.

I didn't talk her out of it. I didn't expect to. From everything I've learned about this woman, once she makes up her mind about something, that's it. If she gives her word, she'll go through with it.

If I can't figure out how to keep that wallet from walking out of here with her tonight, she'll fuck him for all the money I saw in that case.

I don't know where he got that cash from. It doesn't matter. I know Haines. I know his reputation, both at the poker table and with the girls upstairs. He's got some money, plenty of disposable cash he throws around to seem like a big shot, but the most I've heard him paying the girls for their time is a grand, tops. For ten? Something's not right.

Add that to how sure he is that he has to take her out

of the Playground? I've never been able to pin him down on our turf, but I've heard rumors about the sick and twisted shit Haines does when he gets a woman alone. No foreplay. Rough sex that includes blood play, with or without consent. Forced anal with the excuse of 'it slipped'. That shit doesn't fly with our girls upstairs, but if he leaves and someone goes with him?

Unless they come to us to fix the problem, what can we do? If I went to Devil and asked to eliminate anyone with questionable kinks, he'd point out that he'd be one of the first in line to go. Especially when Haines could just say that she wanted it, and for the kind of paydays he provides, his victims often agree with him.

I'd need proof to off one of the big spenders here. Link might let it pass if I pushed it, but with all of this truce bullshit happening lately... Haines doesn't just frequent the Playground. He's a regular on Dragonfly turf, too.

So I can't pull rank and stop her; not as her boss, and not as a Sinner. But I'd be a shit fixer if I didn't have a plan within the next five minutes of how I was going to accomplish that.

Considering I pulled the idea of a big-stakes poker game out of my ass, I'm an even better one than I thought.

Haines has no idea, but he's already snared in my trap the second he joins me at the poker table at eleven-thirty. That Nicolette is milling around the quiet casino area to watch me pull this off?

That just makes this all the sweeter.

I'm keeping a close eye on the time. I have half an

hour to knock the other three players in the game out of it, then focus all my attention on Haines. Since two of the three are plants—prospective soldiers who want to be full-fledged Sinners—that's easy enough. The third is a well-known gambler in Springfield, but I've played against him enough to know his tells.

He's out even before one of the plants folds.

At ten to twelve, it's just me and Haines. I lost a couple of hands deliberately in order to build up his confidence and add to the chips growing in front of him, but when the clock winds down and I have him right where I want him, I get ready to make my move.

The betting for the latest hand started out low. A couple of hundred before the ante went up to a thousand. We both buy in. Haines takes two cards. I take three.

I nod.

Haines smirks. High on the thought he's walking out of here with Nicolette in a few moments, he's probably looking to get some cash back from the amount he promised her.

Why else would he say, "Two grand," as confidently as that?

Sucker.

Now, I could draw this out. Honestly? I'd rather see him squirm.

"I raise you." A tiny crooked smile. "Ten grand all."

Haines's eyes immediately drop to the floor. I know he's looking at the case he has by his ankles. He waits a moment, then slowly fans out his cards again.

He blows a breath out through his long nose. "I'm in."

"Put up the cash."

"You know I'm good for it."

I shake my head, swallowing my smile. This fucker's making it too easy, but I don't want to tip him off before I play my hand. "That's not how it works. Put up or shut up."

Haines works his jaw. "What about you?"

"What about me? I'm a Sinner."

"So?" he demands.

Just like I thought he would. "You want to see my ten k? Is that it? You don't think a Sinner's word is good enough?"

"I didn't say that—"

Yeah, he did, but I don't care. I make a display of looking around the faces gathered. I skip over Julio, landing on Killian. He's purposely standing off to the side, but closer to me so that Haines can't claim I'm doing something funny. I snap my finger at Kill, and he moseys on over to the table.

"Yeah, Rolls?"

"Go get me ten stacks."

"You got it."

Killian doesn't hesitate. A good man who knows better than to question orders, I'm proud to have him on my crew. Having been filled in minutes before I set my plan into motion, he doesn't take too long, either; I need this game done *at* midnight, not before, not after.

At eleven-fifty-eight, Killian lays out ten grand on the table, then nods at me before taking up his spot behind my seat.

"Your turn," I call.

"Come on, Rolls," Haines says, whining a bit now that

I've called his bluff. "You know that money's spoken for."

I do. Why does he think I've gone to all of this trouble?

"I know," I say simply before raising my voice. "You bought a night with one of our girls. Play me for it."

When I hear the gasp, I know instinctively it belongs to Nicolette. I slide my gaze over, finding her by the table, holding onto her empty serving tray. I'm not surprised she's there. I told her to have Jessie put her in the casino on purpose, just so she could witness this game.

Witness it, and refuse to be the prize if that's what she wanted.

I wait. I wait for Haines to change his mind, or for Nicolette to say that she's changed *hers*. When neither of them do, I cock my head at my opponent.

"Here's how it goes. I win this hand, I get the night with Nicolette. You win, you do—and this stack of cash. Deal? Or you can fold and game's over. It's almost midnight. You call?"

Haines looks at his cards. He must really think he has something because, after only a moment's hesitation, he retrieves the case from under the table, tossing it haphazardly, knocking over the stacks of Sinners' cash Killian lined up for me.

"I'm in."

"Show 'em."

Haines does. Not bad. He has a pair of aces, ten high after that.

My turn.

I reveal four of my cards. "I have a king, a queen, two sixes—"

69

Haines's hand shoots out, aiming for the nearest stack in the middle of the table, greed making him a little too hasty.

"Hang on a second." I flip my last card, pausing for dramatic effect. "Six of clubs. Three of a kind, Haines. Looks like I beat your pair of aces."

I nod at Julio. He moves away from his position, signaling behind me to Killian before settling near Haines's seat. Killian grabs Matt from the nearby onlookers, the larger soldier coming between Killian and Haines so that they can gather the stacks of cash back up before the wallet can try.

Haines is sputtering. Something about that last hand not counting, that I cheated, that the money is *his*. That he needs it, that he's taking the girl with him anyway—

Blah. Blah. Blah.

I won, and I have an entire crowd to back me up on that.

Ignoring the blustering wallet, I rise up from my seat. Leaning over the table, I wipe aside the cards, then grab the small briefcase he placed when he made his bet.

Out of the corner of my eye, I see him lunge for me. He still hasn't noticed Julio lurking behind him, so when he moves, my enforcer tackles him to the table.

I grin.

Nicolette is watching the entire scene with the most adorable look on her face. If I found her and she looked terrified at the prospect of spending a night with me, I would have dropped it. Given her the case, told her not to worry about any agreement she made with that asshole —or the bet I most definitely just manipulated her into—

and walked away while Julio and the other fellas handled Haines.

But then our eyes meet. She swallows, and I watch the motion down the slender column of her throat without any shield to the heat in my expression.

The heights of her tanned cheeks turn pink, and I know in that moment that my life will never be the same.

Approaching Nicolette, I gingerly remove the empty serving tray from her grasp. Once I toss that to the poker table behind me, I heft up the case, offering it to her.

"Go on. Take it."

She doesn't. Instead, she moves a small step away from me. "What? Why are you giving me this?"

I'd honestly second-guess what I was about to do if I really thought she wanted to put space between us. If I really believed that she would agree to a night with Miles Haines, then flinch at the idea of joining me in my bed.

But when she recovers her footing, leaning in toward me as though part of her recognizes that she belongs in my arms? That it isn't me she's unsure of, but the ten grand in my hand?

I make the biggest bet of my life: that Nicolette will be *mine*.

"Weren't you watching? I won the hand."

"I know—"

"And that means I get my prize." I press the handle of the case against her palm, waiting for her fingers to curve over it before letting go. "He promised you ten grand for a night with you. Here's the money. But that night? It belongs to me now."

And, eventually, so will she.

Roll 'em...

SIX

ROYCE

NICOLETTE

Holy shit. My boss just won me in a bet.

This can't be happening. It can't—but it *is*.

Just like Miles said before, once midnight hit, my shift is over and I'm going home with someone. Only, instead of that someone being the dark-haired wannabe, I'm leaving with the underboss of the Sinners Syndicate.

Who is also *my* boss...

It's all happening to so fast. By the time I realize what's going on, I have Rolls McIntyre's suit jacket over my shoulders, his hand pressed against the small of my back, his body shielding me from the crowd around us as he guides me out of the Playground. One of the other Sinners retrieved my purse for me so I have my wallet and my phone, but I guess no one knew which coat was mine so now I'm wearing *his*.

Rolls nods at the pair of bouncers guarding the doors,

and if they seem surprised that he's leaving with me, that's nothing compared to how *I* feel.

I'm moving under his power for a few more feet before I stop short. As though the wintry breeze outside has slappes some sense into me, the sudden shock at my situation fades, and I turn to look up at him.

He grins. "Not having cold feet, are you?"

Am I?

I don't think so. I mean, it's crazy. That, two minutes ago, I was watching a pair of men turn the idea of my body into a prize for one of them. But now that *this* is the man who actually won? I'm feeling a lot better than if I was heading out with Miles Haines, that's for sure.

But... why? I just don't understand *why*?

I don't ask Rolls, either. I'm afraid of what his answer could be, so I simply refuse to ask. Instead, I try to hand him the case of money back.

Rolls raises his eyebrows. "What are you giving me that for? I just told you. It's yours."

I wish.

Now, I want it. I want it desperately. Ten grand wouldn't just make up for the money I lost moving to Springfield. It would give me a nice nest egg and a getaway fund if the worst comes to pass and I have to get the hell out of here and *fast*.

But I can't keep it. It's one thing to tell Miles that I'd sleep with him for ten thousand bucks. Rolls didn't have anything to do with that. I went to work this morning without that money, and since I don't have to lay there as that sleazy wallet bounces on top of me, I can go home without it.

Even if I'd really, really rather I got to keep the cash.

But since—if I'm being honest with myself—I'd take Rolls McIntyre home with me for nothing but the promise of working some of my ridiculous crush out of my system... I really should give this money back to him.

"No. This is *yours*. I can't take it—"

He shakes his head. "Don't even think about it. You made a verbal agreement, yeah? A night with that fucking idiot? Well, I won. It's mine now. And I know just how I want to spend it."

I swallow nervously. "You do?"

His hand is still on my back. "I'm hungry. What about you?"

"Um. I guess?"

"Good. There's this little place a block away that I sneak off to when I get tired of what we have at the Playground. Come on." He gives me a gentle push, guiding me in the right direction. "I think you'll love it."

And that's exactly how I find myself having dinner with the second in command of the Sinners Syndicate.

———

I'M GRATEFUL WE'RE STILL IN THE HEART OF SINNERS territory. Kieran rarely leaves the East End unless he has to, and as paranoid as I am, I can't imagine why he would show up at a small diner on the West Side. Even if he did, this is my boss. I'm sitting with my boss, eating a bowl of chicken noodle soup that's all the butterflies in my stomach will let me get down, while he smiles charmingly at me—no more sign of his formerly icy nature—as he leads the conversation.

If I was a different girl, he was a different man, and this was a whole other type of situation... I'd say this was a first date. That's the kind of discussion he leads me into having; or, at least, it's the kind I'd imagine people have who got to *have* a first date instead of being someone's dirty, little secret.

He asks me if I want to be called Nicolette or if Nic's okay. Considering Kieran *insisted* on Nicolette—when I wasn't his darlin'—I jump at the chance to be Rolls's Nic. Then, feeling a little emboldened, I ask him if I should call him Rolls.

His smile widens, flashing me blinding white teeth. "Royce, if you don't mind."

My own smile is hesitant, but I do manage to muster one. "Okay. Royce."

He asks me about my likes. My interests. My hobbies. He seems amused when I admit I love Broadway musicals, but then tosses out that he'd love to take me to see one with him sometime. I know he's just trying to put me at ease so that I'm comfortable with him when it comes to spending the rest of the night together, and I keep that in mind throughout the entire meal.

When it's over, he pays—of course—before bringing me to his car. I'm surprised that it's this basic black sedan, though I regret being judgy in my next breath. If he can afford to throw ten grand away on a card game, he's not hurting. The car is discreet because, in Springfield, the big players don't need to be flashy.

It's just... I keep forgetting that Royce is one of them.

He's so... so *nice*, and I force myself to remember that Kieran was nice, too, when I first met him... and that all he wanted was for me to fuck him. Royce won me in a bet. He won me for sex. In a dangerous world like the one I spent way too long in, that's not unusual. Now I'm back in it again, involved with syndicates and mobsters and men who think a woman will do anything for a dollar—and I will, won't I?

It's just sex, I tell myself. When Royce asks me for my address, then drives me to my place, I've just about convinced myself of that. He's a man with needs, I'm an available woman who already sold herself once, and *it's just sex.*

Pulling up in front of my house, I'd be lying if I said I wasn't looking forward to what was going to happen next. I've been attracted to Royce McIntyre since he interviewed me, but I knew better than to ever think I had a chance with him. Especially when I came to Springfield, fully aware that I was tempting fate that Kieran might find me again... I didn't want a relationship with anyone, but I thought... who knows? Maybe I could have made an exception for Royce. I definitely thought there was a spark during that interview.

But then he was cool and aloof after he offered me the job, treating me like every other employee, and I had to admit I must've imagined that spark. A romance with Royce wasn't in the cards for me—until a fateful game of cards meant that it might be.

No. I was right the first time. There's no romance brewing between us. There's not even sex because, after a whirlwind night filled with questions about myself—and hard answers to swallow about why Royce refused to let Miles Haines win that card game or take me out of the Playground with him—I understand that placing that bet was never about a night of meaningless sex for my boss.

And he proves that by pressing a gentle kiss to my cheek before getting out of the car, then opening my door for me. After helping me out, he walks me to my house, waits for me to head inside on my own before heading back to his car, and I spend the rest of my night wondering what the fuck just happened.

I DON'T HAVE WORK THE NEXT NIGHT, AND CONSIDERING MY head is still spinning at what happened the last time I was at the Playground, that was a good thing.

At Rolls—*Royce*'s insistence, I go to the bank that morning and deposit the case of cash I 'earned'. I hesitated for a moment since I can't deny I only got the money because I agreed to a night with Miles Haines and that, by 'night', he meant sex. It wasn't the act of agreeing to exchange money for my pussy that had me feeling guilty. Oh, no. It was that I had a small case full of money and, though I would have willingly gone to bed with Royce McIntyre if that's what *he* wanted, that's obviously *not* what he was looking for from one of his waitresses.

He was rescuing me from Miles Haines. He admitted as much over dinner. I might have willfully ignored the warning signs—that Haines insisted that I fuck him off of Sinners property, that he was willing to pay *ten grand* to do so—but Rolls laid it out very clearly for me.

Miles hurts people. For his own pleasure, he would've hurt me and not even thought twice about it. He wanted rough sex, and I was the perky blonde Barbie doll he thought he could take it from... for the right price.

Until Rolls saved me. By wagering his ten grand against the night that I agreed to spend with Miles, when he flipped that six of clubs, I ended up with the money *and* a night with 'Rolls' Royce McIntyre.

I should've known better than to think he did it because he wanted to fuck me instead. Not only is he my boss, but I'm pretty sure I'm not his type. Besides, getting involved with a Sinner is a bad, *bad* idea. I should just be grateful for the cash and being let out of my agreement to sleep with someone for it.

That's how I justify depositing the money into my account. I need it, and I would have earned it if I had to. Way I see it, I technically *did* spend the night with Royce. So we went to dinner instead of upstairs to the Playground's private rooms. I upheld my end of the bargain. That was the end of it, right?

Yeah... not even close.

I'm friendly with a couple of the girls at the Playground. I wouldn't say that any of them are my actual *friends*—Kieran never let me have any, and my introverted nature stems from that, I guess—but we chat. Gossip. Talk between tables.

I'm only an hour into my first shift back at the Playground when it becomes obvious that the topic of conversation among the staff is Royce and me. They all want to know what went down after the poker game ended and the Sinners' underboss whisked me away.

I explain to three different waitresses that we had dinner before I stop trying. They all give me a knowing look—coupled with jealous eyes—that tell me they think I'm lying.

I wish I was.

It's Britney who finally believes me when I tell her that the most I got was a respectful peck on the cheek from the gorgeous mafia man. Her reason, of course, is simple—and cuts me to the quick.

"Oh, sweetie, I knew that that would be it. Not for nothing, but you wouldn't be the first girl who thought she might catch Rolls's eye. But he's not like that. If we work at the Playground, he won't bother us. No matter how much we wish he would."

That makes sense. He was so careful with me the other night. "I guess he's picky when it comes to his bed partners."

Britney giggles. "Oh, honey, *no*. Where did I give you that idea? Since I've been working at the Playground, I've never seen a man more run-through. It's just us girls he won't hook up with. But the women who pay his bills? He's more than happy to take them upstairs."

Oof. I... I kinda wish I didn't know that.

The worst part is that Britney isn't even exaggerating. Though I've only been working here for three months, I'd be lying if I wasn't curious about the man in charge of my job. Set aside the fact that he's gorgeous and offered me the chance to make more money. It was easy to develop a crush, especially when I knew he was a safe target to have a crush on. There was no chance of anything happening between us, but a girl can dream, right?

But then the other night happened. He rescued me, and maybe it's the teenage girl deep inside of me who needed to be and *wasn't,* but something shifted during dinner. I thought... I thought that maybe he noticed me. That he *saw* me.

And, true, while I'd heard rumors about his reputation before, I just believed they were exaggerated. Kind of like how everyone has heard a different reason behind Devil's nickname. I haven't seen Rolls with another woman since I met him, and as pathetic as it is to admit it, I've been paying more attention than I had any right to.

Well. As if that simple kiss he gave me didn't make it clear that he would never be interested, Britney's comment definitely did.

I will say, though, that my fellow server is pretty perceptive. That, or living in Willowbrook meant I lost all my skills to hide what I was thinking from Kieran. She takes one look at me and pats me on my shoulder.

"Ah, don't worry about it. On the bright side, Miles Haines hasn't been back since Rolls humiliated him. And who knows? Maybe I'm wrong. Rolls didn't come back to the Playground when you were out last night, but I just heard from Lulu that he's sitting in his usual booth." She waits a beat. "Alone. Kelly has that section. For a cut of the tips, I'm sure she'd switch."

"Thanks, Brit. I appreciate the heads up."

Especially since I have no intention of going over there to serve him.

Roll 'em..

SEVEN
ON A BREAK

NICOLETTE

Does Rolls know that I'm avoiding him?

The Playground is fucking huge. I could easily keep to one side of the club and conveniently stay away from him—except for when I need to stop by the bar to pick up drinks.

I purposely refuse to look in the corner where I know Rolls's usual table is. If I don't see him, I can try to ignore the pit in my stomach. A mixture of undeniable attraction and embarrassment that I honestly thought he might want *me* has me skittish, but also determined. As far as I'm concerned, he had his night. I got paid. That's all there is to it.

And I believe that until halfway through my shift when, all of a sudden, he's *there*.

Shit. *Shit*. He's standing right in front of me, baby blues narrowed down in an expression that has hints of the charm from the other night—and a little bit of outright frustration.

"How much longer did you expect me to sit in my booth alone, Nic?"

I lick my lips, nervous—and, damn it, *attracted*. What is it about me that, the moment a guy shows a hint of danger, I'm already creaming my fucking panties?

Nic... just the way he growled the shortened version of my name like that has me fantasizing about dropping to my knees in front of this man. And, hell, I knew I was easy, but my undeniable arousal is such a shame when he isn't interested.

But I know that look... that's not the look of a man who *isn't* interested.

What is going on here?

"I'm sorry, Rolls—"

"Royce."

"Royce." I guess I'm not going to be able to distance myself by going back to his nickname. "Sorry. But Kelly's your server. If you need another drink—"

"Believe me, baby, I'm not drinking tonight. I want to be stone-cold sober for this discussion." His lips quirk up in a daring grin. "You hiding from me?"

Yes. "What? No. I have tables—"

Royce's gaze darts around. When he sees Jessie—easy due to the pound of fire-engine red hair she has piled on top of her hair—he flags her down.

"You need me, boss?"

Boss, I remind myself. This man is my *boss*.

"Cover for Nicolette. She's going on a break."

"I am?" I ask, confused.

He grits his teeth. "You are."

Oh. I guess I am.

Jessie looks between me and Royce, a small smile tugging on her bright red lips. "Okay. Sure thing. Just let me know when your break's over, okay, Nic?"

Royce takes my hand in his. "Don't worry. She will."

It's like the other night all over again. Instead of his hand on my back, guiding me where he wants me to go, he cuts through the crowd, leading me out of the hustle and the bustle of the club. It takes me a second to recognize that he's leading me out of the customer section, near the back, but when he stops in front of a closed door, my forehead wrinkles.

"The supply room?"

It's more like a closet, really. About the size of my bathroom in my mother's house, it has shelving surrounding the four walls. It's where we keep napkins, glasses, condiments... everything for the actual restaurant part of the Playground.

"It's as private as we're going to get here. I could bring you to my office, but that's a five-minute walk. This is faster."

Faster? For what? And... "Private? What do we need privacy for?"

"This."

Before I know what's going on, Royce has shuffled me into the closet, pulling the door closed behind him. The automatic light comes on, a dim orange that highlights the look of hunger on Royce's face before he drops one hand to my ass, holding me in place as he lowers his mouth to mine.

It takes me a split second to understand that he's kissing me. The tongue forcing its way into my mouth as he strokes mine, teases it, caresses it is one hell of a clue, as well as the muffled groan he lets out against my lips as he tilts my head back, kissing me deeper.

In the aftermath of that split second, I have to make a decision: do I want to shove my boss away, or do I want to let him kiss me?

I think we all know the answer to that.

Going up on my tiptoes in case this is the only chance I ever get to kiss Royce McIntyre, I give back as good as I get, only realizing what just happened when we break for air.

If he didn't have his hand on my ass, I would've stumbled all the way back against the rack of glasses behind me. That's how shocked I am.

Lifting my hand to my mouth, I demand, "What was that?"

"A kiss," Royce answers, panting softly as his eyes twinkle in the dim light. "And I'm going to give you another one."

Yes.

No.

"*Wait.*"

He pauses, lips inches away from mine. "Yes?"

"That kiss... that wasn't like the one you gave me the other night."

"Oh, I know. And if I wasn't so sure that I'd have sent

you running in the opposite direction, I would've." He lowers his head again.

I stop him with my hand against his chest.

"Yes?" he says, a hint of impatience in his tone. He obviously paused because I wanted him to, not because *he* did.

I didn't want him to, though. I *need* him to.

I need to *understand*.

"I don't get it. If you wanted to kiss me, why did you..."

I can't even say it. The rejection I felt when he left me behind at my place still stings more than I want to admit.

"I know, baby. So, let me make this perfectly clear. I didn't just want to kiss you. I wanted to touch you. To make you come, and to fuck you so thoroughly, you forget that you promised yourself to another man first."

Another man?

Kieran— no. Miles. Not Kieran. Miles Haines.

"But that," he says, oblivious to my minor freak-out, "is why I didn't. When I fuck you, Nic, it won't be because you're getting ten grand out of it. That's not my style. It'll be because you want me as much as I want you. I thought you did... I thought we had something. But tonight... you ignored me."

"I didn't mean to—"

"You're such an adorable liar. Yes, you did. I don't think you expected me to lose my fucking mind like this, but do you know how hard it was for me to let you go the other night?"

"I... no?"

"Hard," he says firmly. "And then to watch you walk

around in those shorts... you don't know what you do to me, Nic."

He's right. I had no clue.

"Royce—"

"Devil told me to go for it. If I thought you were down, make a move. What could it hurt?" He laughs ruefully, squeezing my ass, holding me close as his obvious hard-on digs into my lower belly. "Well, tell that to my aching cock. Because I'm fucking fiending for you, and the most I can hope for is a stolen kiss in a supply closet like I'm back in school."

Bowing his head, forehead pressed against mine, he whispers, "What were you like in school? The goody-goody, huh? I bet you never let a guy be touchy-feely with you in a closet before."

He's not wrong about that. When I was back in high school, I wasn't making out with a gorgeous classmate in a janitor's closet. Oh, no. I was waiting for my twenty-one-year-old boyfriend to sneak out of his room and into my bed so he could fuck me.

The very same man that refused to ever leave it— until I found the guts to leave *him*.

No.

No.

No more thinking about Kieran. It's crazy and it's reckless, but I'm in this supply closet with Royce McIntyre—and though I'll probably regret this later, I have the taste of his mouth in mine, and the sudden desire to pretend I'm that goody-goody with a kinky side he seems to hope I am.

"I don't know," I tell him. "Why don't you touch me now, and I'll see if it rings any bells?"

Royce sucks in a breath.

I nod encouragingly at him. From his expression, it's clear he never expected me to agree so easily, but I don't care. He's the one who wants to fool around in a supply closet?

Sure. Why not?

Taking his hand, I move it in front of my lycra shorts; in the Playground, the heat's on blast so that we can all forget that it's fucking freezing outside. It doesn't take much effort at all to slip his fingers an inch past the material.

He doesn't have to do any more than that. I called his bluff. He was annoyed I ignored him after dinner with him, and while I desperately want to believe that the only reason he didn't make a move the other night was because of the money and the bet, I'm not sure I do.

Your move, Royce.

And, oh, does he *move*.

It happens in a flash. One second, I'm sure he's going to remind us both that he's my boss and that we've gone far enough—and then he has his fingers sliding through my soaking wet slit, finding my entrance, filling me up with his thick middle finger.

"Ah, that's my girl," he murmurs. "I just knew you'd be able to take me so easily."

He's not even talking about his dick. He's talking about his finger, but from this angle? It could be the same goddamn thing.

"Okay. Not gonna lie, I didn't think you were actually

attracted to me like that," I gasp, going up on my tiptoes so that Royce can finger me deeper.

Maybe he's not. Maybe I'm just an obvious target, easy prey, and he decided to have a little fun tonight.

Honestly? I don't care, so long as he keeps doing what he's doing.

Royce takes my bottom lip between his teeth, nibbling it gently while never slowing in his pace. His middle finger goes in and out leisurely, his thumb circling my clit, sending jolts of pleasure through me.

"Then you weren't paying attention, baby. I stayed away. I was trying to behave. Fuck that. If you think I didn't want a night with you, you're wrong."

"But we already had one—"

"We did. And I decided one will never be enough. So if you want to doubt just how attracted I am to you, put your hand on my cock. Touch me the same way I'm touching you. Because, fuck me, Nic... you feel this?" He flicks my engorged clit with his thumb. "You want me. I want you. Attraction is definitely not our problem."

No. It's not.

But we have plenty, don't we?

Know what? I don't care. It's been so long since someone's touched me like this, like I'm precious, and that's assuming anyone has. This is definitely a new experience for me. Instead of demanding that I pleasure him, he followed my lead, taking over while still focusing entirely on me.

Royce isn't touching me like I'm his possession. Like I'm his *property*. This is the caress of a man who is sure of

THE DEVIL'S PLAYGROUND

his welcome, but still wants the woman in his arms to enjoy his embrace.

The man I've known of—that I've seen lurking in the shadows, eyes sliding away from me on the occasion that ours meet—has always seemed so aloof, yet charming in his way. Like he's completely aware of his effect on the world around him, and while he doesn't use it to his advantage, he's not going to say sorry for it, either.

Just like he's not going to apologize for the quick work he makes of my body.

"Come for me," he whispers, sucking my earlobe into his mouth. "Show me what I can expect when you give this pretty pussy to me."

I don't know what does it. The heat of his mouth, his dirty words, or the way he's fingerfucking me to completion, but I dig my nails into his arm as I gasp out my release.

"Yes," he hisses. He has two fingers stretching me out, giving my pussy something to clench around as my climax hits. "I fucking knew it. From the moment I saw you... you'd be such a good girl for me."

Good girl.

I don't know how he knows it, but I've always had a thing for praise kink. I guess it was inevitable. When I would piss Kieran off and he took his temper out on me, he would punctuate any slaps, any bites, and any rough thrusts by telling me I deserved it for being such a bad girl.

To keep him happy—when I still cared about that asshole being happy—I would do anything to be his good girl. The damage is done now, and all it takes is a man telling me to shut up and take his cock like a good girl, and I'm ready to do just that.

Not gonna lie, I'm definitely ready to take Royce's *now*.

My hand drops to the front of his slacks like he invited me to before. Running my fingers over the bulge I find there, I know that Royce is, too. Half out of my head with lust, the idea of yanking down my shorts, bending over, and letting him fuck me in the storage room has a certain appeal.

And I might have suggested it... if it wasn't for the sudden buzz vibrating in the small space, killing the mood and bringing me back to reality.

I stiffen in his arms, though Royce doesn't react as quickly as I do to the reminder that there's a world that exists outside of this closet. Instead, his eyes on mine, he slowly withdraws his two fingers from my pussy, slipping the slick digits between his lips. He licks them clean with relish as he uses his other hand to pull his phone out.

It's all over in an instant. The second he sees the number on his screen, his fingers come free from his lips with a *pop*-ping sound as he curses under his breath.

"Fuck. I have to take this." Turning away from me, running those same wet fingers through his slicked-back blond hair, he jabs his phone with his other thumb, then lifts it to his ear. "Hello? Ava? What's wrong?"

Ava.

Who the fuck is Ava?

I don't know. And since Royce simply says, "Of course. You need me. I'll be right there," I'm pretty sure I don't want to know, either.

Oof.

He's not yours, Nic, a little voice in the back of my head says. It kinda sounds like Britney. *He can never be, and you know it.*

We had our night. I got a kiss. So he fingerfucked me. That was probably a huge mistake, especially when I have Britney's comments about Royce's other women running through my brain.

Anything after that... he's my boss. He asked me if I was single during dinner the other night, and I was so relieved to tell him I *was*—but I realize now that I forgot to turn the question around on him.

Looks like I might've just gotten my answer.

Feeling silly and super exposed, I hurriedly adjust my panties and my shorts as Royce wraps up his phone call.

"Sorry about that," he says, pocketing his phone. "But when duty calls—"

"It's okay," I tell him, cutting him off. It's probably for the best if I don't hear the rest of that. "Speaking of duty, I should be getting back to work."

Royce frowns. "Is everything okay? I didn't... we're good, right?"

If he's asking whether or not I was an enthusiastic participant in being fingerbanged in the supply closet? "Yeah. We're good."

Relief flashes across his face. "Just checking. Look. This shouldn't take long. What time is your shift over?"

I shouldn't answer.

I shouldn't—

"Ten."

Reaching out, running his thumb along my upper arm, he says, "I'll try to make it back."

I guess I wasn't the only one hoping for a quickie tonight. But there's a difference. Now that I know he has another woman he's running home to, it doesn't matter how attracted we are to each other.

This can't happen again—and not just because Kieran would kill me if he ever found out.

"Sounds good," I lie.

Roll 'em...

EIGHT
FRYING PAN

NICOLETTE

Being back in Springfield is hell on my nerves.

That was the best thing about living in Willowbrook the last couple of years. I had to leave my city because I knew that Kieran never would, but now that I'm back, I expect to see him everywhere.

It's such a shame that that rendezvous with Royce in the closet is as far as we're going to go. Not only was he a pleasant distraction to take my mind off my past for a while, but he's a Sinner. I'd be lying if I said that I hadn't hoped that maybe one of them would take pity on me and protect me while I'm in town.

That's part of why I went along with it when Officer Burns suggested I go for the job at the Playground. Even if I couldn't catch the attention of one of the mafia men, just working at their establishment gave me some level of protection.

And I must have somehow convinced myself of that

fact over these last three months because tonight, when I returned home from the end of my shift *alone*, I was actually shocked when I realized that my biggest fear had finally come true.

Kieran found me.

I think I was too quick to dismiss my gut feeling that I was being stalked. Or to assume that he didn't change over the last three years. I mean, I did, didn't I? I'm nothing like the Nicolette I was. Even my mom picked up on it, though that shouldn't be surprising. It's been a long time since she's known the real me. First, because I moved out when I was nineteen; then, because *I* didn't know me. I had no idea who Nicolette was when she wasn't Kieran's Nicolette, if that makes sense.

I don't know. Maybe it doesn't. I'm not really thinking straight.

And all because of a tiny dragonfly figurine.

On my mother's coffee table, I have my laptop open. Next to it, the tiny trinket I found waiting for me in my mother's mailbox—and the reason why I have my laptop out.

It's maybe three inches tall. Sculpted out of ceramic, painted with shades of purple and blue—the same as the full dragonfly tattoo that Kieran has on his back—there's no denying what it is: a *warning*.

I almost dropped the damn thing earlier. I'd scooped that, along with Mom's mail, from the mailbox, but it's dark out; the white clouds that promise another obnoxious snowstorm is on its way were blocking out the moon, making it seem darker. I'd hurried inside, locking the door behind me, and that's when I saw it.

Tucked between some credit card bill and a circular I'd never look at before tossing, I found a dragonfly.

Only one person in the world would put it there. Just like only one person would see it and not be like, "Huh. That's weird. A small dragonfly statue."

My mom would... if she was here. She's not. And, okay, I think I knew there was a better than good chance that Kieran might eventually drive by her old house—*our* old house—for shits and giggles, but even if I wanted to pretend this isn't for me, I *can't*.

The videos saved to my laptop prove it.

While I was being fingered by Royce, Kieran Alfieri— wearing a black hooded sweatshirt, black jeans, and that old, familiar smirk—appeared on one of my cameras. He knew it, too. There's no sound on these, so I don't know if he called me 'darlin' out loud or not, but the exaggerated mouth motions he made in front of the camera are obvious.

Hi, darlin'.

Fuck.

I was already locked up tight in the house when I checked the camera footage. A quick tour through the downstairs, then the upstairs to make sure he didn't find my hideaway key—thank fucking god he didn't—before I sat down on the couch, turning the cameras from past footage to live.

After he placed the dragonfly into the mailbox, he disappeared. I know that. He crossed through three other cameras, brazen as hell, then walked away as though he didn't just shake up my whole life by revealing he knows I'm here. I didn't see him outside when I came in, blissfully unaware he'd been by, so that's good.

Right?

Maybe.

And I'm fooling myself if I believe that he won't come back now that he guesses I'm here.

The illusion of safety is such a fragile thing. Barely an hour ago, I knew that Kieran would come after me if I gave him a reason to. I just... I thought, if I *didn't*, he would go on, living his life on the other side of town, completely unaware I was back in Springfield. Now that I have irrefutable proof that he at least assumes I'm hiding out in the city again, that illusion has shattered into a thousand different shards.

It's like, now that I've seen him on my camera footage, I have to keep staring at the live feed to prove to myself he *hasn't* come back.

Two hours. It's a good thing I changed out of my work uniform—throwing on an oversized sweater and a pair of sweatpants before I left the Playground at ten—because, otherwise, I'd be sitting on the edge of my couch in the same short shorts I'd had on when I willingly allowed Royce to touch me.

I don't regret it. In a way, I feel empowered by what happened in that closet. He might have been the one to initiate it, but I didn't want to stop. Hell, if *Ava* hadn't called him, I don't know if I would have.

I was so jealous. When he dropped a quick kiss on my mouth, frowning only a little when I jerked my head and his kiss landed on the corner, all I could think about was how much I was attracted to him—and how much I wished I was the woman he'd drop everything to run to.

He never came back. To be fair, I didn't really think he would. I'd *hoped* he would, though, and tried not to take it personally when ten o'clock came and went, and there was no sign of Royce in sight.

Now? Maybe it was a good thing that I didn't invite him home with me. I don't even want to think about how Kieran would react to *that*...

It's after midnight. I keep telling myself that I should just shut the laptop, try to get some sleep, and figure out what I'm going to do tomorrow. Nothing's really changed. I promised Mom that I'd house-sit until she came back from Florida, so it's not like I can up and leave. How would I explain myself to her if I did?

Especially since she thinks I should get back together with Kieran. Of course, that's because I've kept every bad thing he's ever done to me *from* her, but still. I can't tell her the truth.

It's not like he'll hurt me, either; at least, not purposely. He uses violence for control, but he knows better than to come out swinging with me. Oh, no. To get me to do what he wants, he needs to be that manipulative bastard I fell for once upon a time. The warning—the *gift* —will only be the beginning, but he won't, like, kidnap me or anything.

I hope.

No. Picking up the dragonfly statue, I shove it in my pants pocket; I don't want to look at it anymore. I place my hand on the edge of the laptop. I need to shut it. I need to go to bed. I need to—

Wait.

What the hell is that?

I was watching. I swear I was watching. I never saw a car coming down our quiet street except for two that belonged to my neighbors, and that was closer to eleven. And, yet, someone is crossing my yard.

Black hoodie, hood pulled up over their head. Black pants. Unlike how Kieran flaunted his face in front of the camera before, this person—man, I think, taking in their size and their walk, it's a *man*—he's careful to keep his hidden. From the wind? It hasn't started to snow just yet, but the temperature's dropped.

Or maybe, I think, watching as they cross my yard and move to stand in front of my front window, they don't want to be caught on my camera.

I stop breathing.

The man is on the other side of my front window— and he's not moving, either.

"Go away," I mutter under my breath, panic welling up inside of me. "There's nothing to see here. Go away."

It's true. Besides, I remembered to draw the black-out curtains earlier. I don't always—and I better start—but unless he's trying to peek in through the tiny sliver that exists between the curtain and the window, he needs to leave again.

He's *not*.

Damn it!

Is it Kieran? It has to be. I can't imagine who else could be out there, and honestly? I could give a shit. It's after midnight, a man in black is peeking into my window, and I'm so wound up from finding the dragonfly that I fucking *snap*.

The only thing I can think about is protecting myself. In Willowbrook, I had a baseball bat that I slept with under my bed. I didn't bring one to Springfield, though I'm sorely regretting that now.

Weapon. I need a weapon.

Kitchen!

My mom has a huge knife block on her kitchen counter. Grabbing the handle of the biggest one, trying to avoid how my hand is shaking, I look down at the thick blade.

"'He ran into my knife'," I whisper, half-hysterical, quoting 'Cell Block Tango' as I twist the butcher knife, catching the kitchen light on the large blade. "'He ran into my knife ten times.'"

Could I kill Kieran? I couldn't before. No matter what he did to me, that was never an option. Leaving was the most rebellious I could be... but I've had a taste of freedom. I'm not so sure that there isn't anything I wouldn't do to keep it.

But murder?

No.

I shake my head, dropping the knife back into its place in the block.

Okay. Knife's out.

What else?

I know! Dropping down, I fling open one of the lower cabinets, grabbing the first heavy frying pan I can find.

Perfect.

If it's Kieran, I won't need the pan to protect myself. I

have neighbors and a camera, and he's not stupid enough to do anything where he might be implicated. A few sharp spoken barbs and he'll back off, wounded, like my defiance physically hurts him.

Of course, once he gets me alone, I'll pay for it—but I don't plan on ever being alone with Kieran Alfieri again if I can help it.

But if it's someone else... my mom's house isn't in the best part of Springfield. She got it after her second marriage imploded, and joked through my early teens that it was the only good thing that came out of her three-year stint as Mrs. O'Donnell.

Lucky her. She got a house.

When she married Dave Alfieri the next summer, I got Kieran.

Talk about running on adrenaline. Instead of turning off the lights, hiding upstairs, and pretending to be asleep, I'm creeping around the side of my mother's house, holding a frying pan, trying to sneak up on the psycho peering into my front window.

Part of me hopes that I'm being fucking ridiculous. That it was some would-be robber who got curious and went on his merry way. Even if it's Kieran fucking with me, I'm praying he's gone, and that when I tiptoe around the corner, there won't be any man in black standing near the house.

At this point, I'd be a-okay if I imagined everything I saw on the screen...

I didn't. I know I didn't, and my bigger fear right now is that it *is* some burglar and I'm sneaking around in my sweatpants, with a frying pan in my hand, against someone who might have a gun.

Good going, Nic. What a time to think about that...

It's been a few minutes. I'm hoping that that was enough time that they're gone—and that they're not sneaking around the back while I'm going around the front—but when I peek around the corner, I see a shadowy black figure still standing there, almost like he's frozen in place.

And, yeah... I panic.

I totally panic.

Before he can turn around, I rush across the yard, cold grass biting into my bare feet because dumbass Nicolette forgot to grab shoes in her hysteria, and I *swing*.

Thwack.

"What the fuck!"

I don't hit him again. I got the guy in his arm, hitting him flush with the back of the frying pan to get his attention. If I wanted to kill him, I would've gone for the head, but I didn't—and, whoa, am I glad when I recognize that growl of a voice.

I'm so used to it sounding cultured and professional that the sudden—and completely rational—anger catches me off-guard before I can even swing again.

And then he spins on me at the same time as he lowers his hood. Even in the dark of night, he seems *golden*.

Royce.

Roll 'em...

NINE
CONTROL

NICOLETTE

"**W**hat are you doing here?"

"What am I doing here?" he shoots back, glaring at the frying pan that I assaulted him with. "I couldn't make it back to the Playground before you were done, so I thought I'd see if you were home—I didn't think you'd try to brain me with a frying pan!"

"I'm so sorry! I... I didn't recognize you." I take in the sweatshirt that, up close, is actually pretty different than the one Kieran had on. "You usually wear a suit!"

"That's when I'm on duty. I'm off, and it's fucking cold out here. Forgive me for throwing on a hoodie."

I ignore that.

"If you wanted to come over, why didn't you call me first?" I ask, conveniently forgetting that I didn't give him my number.

But I guess I didn't have to because he crosses his arms over the front of his hooded sweatshirt and says, "I did. You didn't answer. I got worried and drove over." He waves behind him, showing that the reason I didn't see his car was because he parked it just out of my camera's range—and I realize that I hadn't looked at my phone once since I've been home. "I could've sworn I saw something flashing over here. I was checking it out when you hit me."

Unfolding his arms, he shows me something in his hand, and my stomach sinks.

It's a tiny camera. Wireless, with suction cups that would keep it on my window so that it could peek inside.

"Oh, that's—"

"I know what it is. I just don't know why it's out here. Usually, surveillance cameras are pointing out, not in, unless someone's spying on you."

Yeah. I know.

He sees it. He sees the lack of a reaction on my face and knows there's something darker at play here. Especially when it doesn't even occur to me to accuse Royce of being the one to put the camera up.

I watched my footage earlier. I saw Kieran standing in that same spot before, though I couldn't quite see what he was doing.

Now I know—and so does Royce.

He lowers his voice. "Nic... why did you come out here with a frying pan?"

I don't answer him. I can't. Maybe I could have before, but after that night we had over dinner? My latest impression of Royce McIntyre is that he has a savior thing going on. If he finds out I have a stalker, he'll want to save me the same way he did from Miles Haines.

Instead, I latch onto the excuse he unwittingly gave me by grabbing the sleeve of his sweatshirt. "I really didn't mean to swing at you. I was just scared"—for obvious reasons, yeah—"and panicked when I saw you. Let me make it up to you."

Royce gives me a curious look. On the one hand, I doubt he'll let me get away with avoiding explaining myself and the extra camera. On the other?

He's still a man who got cut short in that supply closet. "How do you plan on doing that?"

I roll my eyes, then lead him around back. When he seems even more curious, I explain that the front door's locked, but I left the back open when I saw someone on the camera.

Once we're inside, I put the frying pan away in the kitchen, drop the dragonfly statuette from my pocket into the trash sneakily, then lead Royce to the living room. A quick tap on my laptop's lid to close it, then I gesture at his arm.

"Okay. Let me see how much damage I did to you."

He shakes it. "It's fine."

Somehow, I knew he would say that. "Shirt off, please."

A crooked grin that erases some of his annoyance from before as he says, "Well, when you put it that way... how can I resist?"

He takes off his hooded sweatshirt. As soon as he

does, he looks like the Royce I know: black trousers, white button-down, expensive shoes.

The white button-down covers his upper arm. I expect he's going to unbutton the sleeve and roll it up. He doesn't. Instead, reminding me I told him to take off his shirt, he makes quick work of the buttons.

He doesn't have an undershirt on. I get my first glimpse of his muscular chest before I give my head a clearing shake, then shove the right side of his shirt down enough to see.

It's red. Duh. Not broken, I don't think, but it's definitely a big red mark on his upper arm.

I lay my fingers lightly along his skin. "I'm so sorry."

"It's okay. Like you said, you were scared and I was acting shady. You seem to be expecting someone. From the way you reacted, though, I'm not so sure it's a friend." He pauses, eyeing me closely. "You are single, aren't you?"

I nod. "And you're not."

That catches his attention. "What? Of course I am."

"What about Ava?"

"Ava?" His nose scrunches, and he laughs. A full-throated laugh that has his shirt falling back, revealing his entire chest. "Do me a favor, Nic? Don't ever say that in front of Devil. If he thinks I'm gunning for his wife, I'm a dead man."

Wait—

"*Devil*'s wife?"

He nods. "He had syndicate biz, and she needed help at the penthouse. She has my number and knows that I can be there in no time if I'm at the Playground."

"Oh."

His blue eyes seem to twinkle. "Were you jealous of Ava?"

I open my mouth, think about how I want to answer that, then totally change the subject when I notice the design etched into the left side of his chest. It's about twelve inches long, an elaborate design of... is that a devil?

"You have ink?" I murmur.

"Just the one. You?"

I don't answer him. Instead, I push off the other side of his shirt so that I can get a good look at it.

It is a devil.

About twelve inches long, inked from hist left pec to the height of his pubic bone, the devil has horns, a swarthy grin, a curved tail that reminds me of the mini-malist design I've seen the other Sinners branded with, plus a pair of dice showing off ones; snake eyes, I think. In an old-fashioned font, he also has two words tattooed on him as part of the design: *roll 'em*. From his nickname, I bet, and a very impressive way of showing just how important this man is in the syndicate.

So important, in fact, that he doesn't even need to have his devil—a way of showing off a Sinners loyalty to the Devil of Springfield—visible to the rest of the city. It's hidden under his obviously expensive shirt, and I feel a flutter low in my belly as I realize that he's preening a bit under my curious gaze.

My fingers ghost over his skin, eager to touch him but not quite sure I should. "Wow. That's really nice."

He starts to shrug off his shirt. "You want to get a better look? I can show you."

I would like that. But at his invitation, I know there's someting else I'd rather do with a half-naked Royce. And maybe I *shouldn't*... but I'm gonna anyway.

"In a second," I tell him, my voice a breathless whisper as my hand finally lands on his hard chest.

Later, I won't really understand why I made the move I did. Whether it's because that camera Royce found pissed me off, or I really did want to send a massive fuck you to Kieran if he was out there somewhere, or even if the sudden relief I felt to hear that Ava is *Devil*'s wife makes me wish we were back in the supply closet at the club again... it doesn't matter.

Earlier tonight, Royce kissed me.

Know what? It's my turn now.

And I kiss *him*.

It just seemed like a good idea at the time. Royce was asking questions I didn't want to answer, and I thought: if he's kissing me, he can't ask inconvenient questions, right?

One hand on his chest, the other cupping his jaw, I go up on my tiptoes and kiss him.

When I'm done, Royce is panting, I'm just about ready to climb him like a fucking tree, and he *knows* it.

"Yeah." Guttural. Husky. *Hot.* "Okay. Later."

Or now.

Now sounds good.

I grab Royce by the front of his shirt. I don't know if he thought I was going to take a peek at his ink, but I suddenly have a much better idea. Tugging on him, I drag him so that he's standing by the living room couch. I push him down on it, completely aware that I'm only able to do this because he's letting me.

I reward him with a grin as I shimmy my sweatpants down past my ass. I kick them off, then yank off my panties. By the time I'm climbing onto his lap, Royce has caught on to what exactly I want to do.

He could reject me. He could say no. He could remind me again that he only wanted to fuck me when I wanted to fuck him.

Well, guess what? This is me showing him that, at this very moment, there isn't anything I want to do more in the world.

I straddle him, putting one of my legs on each side of him. My left hand is on his chest again, supporting my weight as I reach down between our bodies with my right.

Royce goes for the bottom of my sweater.

No.

I stop him. With a gentle shove at his hands, I shake my head when he looks up at me.

"You can take your pants off," I whisper in as throaty a voice as I can, "but my shirt stays on."

It's my one boundary. I'll fuck him. I really, really want to fuck him. But if me keeping my shirt on is a deal-breaker right now? Then it's better we get that out of the way before I go past the point of no return. I won't sleep with him if he does, and I hope he gets that.

He does. Burying his face against my chest, he muffles, "As long as I can touch them over the shirt, I'm okay with that."

I think I can handle that much.

But when I try to help him take off his pants, he gives me the most lascivious grin a man can manage as he says, "You keep your shirt on. Don't worry about the pants. If I don't get inside of you now, I'm gonna fucking blow. Just take me out."

Sounds good to me.

Flicking the button on his trousers, unzipping him as quickly as I can, I find his erection already tenting his boxers and feed him through the hole in the front.

I hesitate for a moment. He's hot and heavy in my hand, and though I haven't gotten a good look at his dick, it feels like a good size as I grip it with my hand.

"Condoms—"

"I'll use 'em if you want, but I don't have any."

Neither do I.

Shit.

You know fucking what? I think I already passed the point of no return.

"I'm on birth control to regulate my period," I murmur. "We'll be fine."

And then, because I don't want anyone talking me out of this—not me, not Royce, not my missing common sense—I lift my ass up, grabbing his cock so that our bodies are lined up right where they need to be before letting gravity take control.

It might as well. As I gasp out at the intrusion of his cock inside of me, and Royce digs his heels into the floor so that he doesn't start thrusting while I'm getting used to him, it seems like the both of us are on the verge of losing it.

I haven't gotten laid since I've been back in Springfield for so many different reasons. I'm so glad that Royce fingerfucked me earlier because the ache would've been so much worse now if he hadn't. Since he did, though, all I feel is a sense of delicious fullness as he grabs the back of my head, tugging me toward him so that he can take another kiss.

Once he has, he starts moving. I throw my head back as his rocking motion starts out slow. Arching my back, giving him access to my tits, I encourage him to give them a squeeze.

"Do you know how much I fantasized over this?" he asks, finding my nipple through the fabric and tweaking it just enough to have me moaning. "Not just tonight. For so fucking long... Nic. Ah, *yes*. That's my girl."

Hey. He's squeezing. Turnabout's fair play as I contract my inner walls, strangling his cock.

His thrusts are shallow, but I don't mind. I'm on top for a reason.

I want to ride.

And that's exactly what I do. Laying my hands on his shoulders to steady myself, I start off slow, getting used to his size. It feels like a perfect fit, rubbing along all the right nerves as I push myself up, settle back on his lap, and start a rocking motion.

It's about connection. Our groins touch, his taut chest tempting me as he leans back into the couch, watching me move with a lusty expression. His lips are tugged in a crooked half-smile as he murmurs my name softly.

I can barely hear his whispers over the sound of our slick bodies coming together—and my not-so-subtle groans as Royce lowers his hands from my boobs. One clutches my side desperately, as though he's trying to bury himself even deeper inside of me; the other dips between us, flicking my clit to give me stimulation at the same time as I lazily ride him.

I don't want this to be over so soon. I was eager to fuck this man, and I thought it would be a two-minute quickie before my sanity returned. By then, what was done was done, and I could worry about how much of a bad idea it was to fuck my boss in my living room, no condom, no protection except my birth control, especially when he showed me proof that someone—*Kieran*—tried posting a camera to see into my house.

Can you imagine if he could see me now? Riding one of his rivals...

Fuck. The idea that he *could* has me edging closer to coming already, and from the way Royce's chest is rising and falling, matching his heavy breath while his jaw goes tight, holding back his own orgasm... he's right there with me.

When our eyes meet, I dip my head to kiss him, part of me surprised when he matches my rhythm, increasing it even as he grabs hold of me by the back of my neck so that he can take control of our kiss.

It's messy. Our teeth clash, lips getting caught between them as I groan into his mouth. He swallows it, answering it with a muffled moan of his own, lifting his hand from my clit to trace the edge of my jaw with his sticky thumb.

Drawing back from our kiss just enough to press the corner of his mouth to my cheek, Royce's breath is hot on my skin as he mutters, "I knew it. I fucking knew that you would be worth the wait."

My fingers are threading through his previously styled blond hair. I keep him close as I giggle. "Wait? It's only been two days."

Royce nips my bottom lip. It's not enough to hurt, but the slight jolt of pain is like a rush of lightning going from his mouth straight to my pussy. I arch my back again, my reaction having him hitting me at an entirely new angle. So overwhelmed by that onslaught of pleasure, I hardly notice it when he says, "That's what you think."

"Royce? What—"

"Hold on, baby," he says, shifting our position so suddenly, I forget what I was going to say. "It's my turn."

Before I can ask what he means, he lays me out on the couch, rising up on his knee so that he can increase his pace. His turn... ah. He goes from a leisurely stroke to a rhythm that is so quick, once he's back in me again, he refuses to leave.

And I *love* it.

He holds his body over mine, gripping the arm of the couch to give more power to his thrusts. I'm moving beneath him from the force of it, but when he bends his head down, forehead pressed to mine, he pins me in place so that all I know is Royce's baby blue eyes, plus the ache of his cock claiming me as deeply as he can.

Just when I start to gasp that I'm getting close, Royce shifts our position again. It's not enough to break me from my growing pleasure. Sitting on his lap once more, his fingers go right back to my clit, helping me along.

The second I start to climax, almost squealing with

how fucking amazing it feels as something low in my gut explodes, causing my legs to shake and my pussy to contract around him, he grunts.

And then—

"Kiss me, Nicolette." His voice is ragged. Hoarse. His eyes are heavy-lidded with desire, chest slicked with sweat as I come first, but all he wants is a kiss—badly enough to say, "*Please*."

How can I resist?

This is the last moment I want to think about my ex, but as I throw my arms around Royce's throat, hanging on for dear life as he chases his orgasm, it's almost impossible not to compare. There's something in the way that Royce is overpowering me, offering me unexpected affection, a ton of pleasure, and both giving and taking complete control in between one thrust and the next...

Kieran was my first lover. I've had more than I want to think about since I left him. Some, because I wanted to fuck the memory of his touch off of my skin and out of my head; others, because they were willing to pay and I was desperate. So many bodies. So many nights I've blocked out... but I already know that, whatever happens tomorrow, this won't be one of them.

Kieran didn't say 'please'. He demanded, and he expected obedience.

Something tells me that, if I told this powerful male under me to get on his knees and beg for my kiss, he *would*... and I have no idea why.

But he said 'please', and I've spent so many lonely nights wondering what it would be like to kiss this man... so many nights feeling guilty for crushing on my boss, no matter his affiliation... but he's here, he wants my kiss— he wants *me*—and, if only for tonight, I'm going to pretend I can keep him.

So I kiss him, and the moment our tongues touch, Royce's body tightens beneath me as he empties himself inside of me at last.

Roll 'em...

TEN
ABOUT FUCKING TIME

ROYCE

Sex is awesome. I mean, the act of fucking is great. It feels good, it's a great tension reliever, and it's a fantastic way to get some cardio in.

But sex with someone you actually care about? That you have a connection with?

Fuck, it's *addicting*.

I already knew I was in trouble when I pulled a Link and started watching over Nicolette from the shadows back when all she thought was that I was the manager of the Devil's Playground. I took the first opportunity to get close to her that I could, and while I patted myself on the back for not forcing her to sleep with me the way that twisted wallet would, I'd be lying if I said that I haven't been dying to get this woman in bed with me.

I know my rep. From the way Nicolette regarded me in the beginning, I'm sure she did, too. I want to prove to her that, despite playing for that night with her, it wasn't only about sex for me.

Sometimes I wish it was. If I just needed to nut and thought she'd be down, I could have turned her away for the waitress position, then been a class-A asshole and taken her out for an apologetic drink. With the right words, I could've landed her. I'm pretty sure of it.

But I didn't want this woman to just be another one that I fucked, then moved on from. Do I know why? No. Do I *care* why? Not even a little. When some part of me told me that she was special, that she was the *one*, I listened... and fucking regretted it when I had to follow through with my self-proclaimed creed that I wouldn't mess around with our employees.

Ah, well. There's an exception to every rule, isn't there? Looks like I've found mine, and her name is Nicolette Williams.

As the Sinners' underboss, it's my job to help Link enforce the rules for all of our members. I've never broken any—not even during the whole shit show with Jake and Heather—and, hell, it's about time I did. Especially since it's not a crew rule, but one that I made up for myself for no other reason than I'm the king of self-sabotage.

Besides, my rule says that I don't go after Playground staff. I didn't.

Nicolette initiated with me. Can I help it that, once she gave the signal that she was open to sex, I ran with it?

Now that it's over, though, I'm waiting to see her reaction. Will the skittish waitress who seemed surprised I paid ten grand for a kiss return? Or will it be the determined, sexy vixen who climbed on top of my lap and fucked me on her couch?

I don't give her the chance to be either. As she comes down from her orgasm, dripping with the evidence of mine, I try not to think about how long it's been since I've fucked anyone without a condom. Since I was a dumb twenty-year-old, maybe? The more wealth and power I accumulate, the more careful I am to wrap it up, just in case. I've heard too many horror stories of some of my fellow gangsters getting baby-trapped by someone who liked the idea of having a Sinner to support them.

Not me. I've never been big on the idea of having kids, and though I'm looking forward to being Uncle Rolls to Link and Ava's, I don't need a bunch of little McIntyres running around. Condoms are a must, but when Nicolette had my dick in her soft hand, assuring me she's on birth control...

I know she's clean. I didn't ask—just like I didn't offer my own status—but it's another one of Link's paranoid quirks. When he says he scans anyone affiliated with the Sinners, he means he has Tanner run a full detail. Our tech whiz can tell things about a vial of blood that I don't even want to know about, but that didn't stop me from checking Nic's file like the obsessed man that I am.

She's clean. I'm clean. She says she's on birth control, and if she's not? Well, I *do* want to keep her. I'd rather not have to knock her up to do so—I'd prefer she give herself to me because I'm amazing, not because she doesn't want to be a single mom—but, hey, a man's got to do what a man's got to do.

And right now? This man has to take care of his woman.

She's still sprawled out on my lap. I dip my head, taking a quick kiss before lifting her lightly, settling her next to me.

The afterglow of fucking me lasts just as long as it takes for her to realize that my load is leaking out of her... and onto the couch she's sitting on.

"Oh, shit." She drops her hand, cupping her pussy. "My mom's couch!"

I drop another kiss to the top of her head. "Don't worry about it. I got it." Standing up, my shirt is open, my cock is out, and I preen as Nicolette's gaze travels from my chest to my dick. Her hungry expression has it already starting to stir again. Give me another ten minutes, and I'll take her again.

But first—

"Where's the kitchen, Nic?"

She gives me a strange look, probably because we came in through the back door and she already led me through it, then points at a connecting hall.

I figured, but it didn't hurt to ask. "Be right back."

I tuck myself into my pants as I head in the direction of her point; I don't bother zipping up since I'm being an optimist tonight, hoping she'll accept me again once we both recover. In the kitchen, I grab a plain white towel hanging on the oven door, wet it in the sink, then bring it back to the living room.

Dropping to my knees, I push aside her hand, using the damp towel to wipe her pussy for her. Once I have, I fold the towel, flip it around, then scrub a little at the damp spots our fucking left on her mother's couch.

"There. All clean."

"Remind me I need to bleach my mom's kitchen towel before she comes back from Florida," she murmurs, tanned cheeks turning pink.

I grin, shoving the edge of the towel into the back of my pants for later. Then, taking her fingers so that I can help her stand, I say, "I remember where your kitchen is now. So where's your bedroom?"

For a split second, I'm sure she's going to shake her head and refuse to tell me. I'm perfectly aware that I'm pushing kinda hard, prepared to take this thing brewing between us from casual to not-so-casual. Did she think it was just sex? I don't know, but it wasn't. Not to me.

And I won't let it be for her, either.

I nuzzle her neck, squeezing her ass as I pull her so that she's flush against the bare chest peeking through my open shirt. "Tell me, baby. 'Cause I can stumble around and find it, or you can invite me up, and we can get comfortable."

Her tits push against my skin. "You don't have to stay."

Like hell I don't.

I was already trying to figure out how I could earn a way into her bed. Add that to how fucking frightened she was earlier and, sorry, Nic, but I'm not leaving any time soon. She admitted after I found the camera that she's worried someone's been watching her house. Not just for tonight, either, but for a while.

Now, I didn't put that camera there. I really did get curious when I saw the soft green light flashing, and this makes me even more determined to keep her safe because if I didn't do it, someone else did. As for sensing a presence just outside her house these last couple of months...I know that's me.

She doesn't.

Is it sneaky and underhanded to use her fear against her? I know it is. I should be ashamed of myself, and I am. That's not going to stop me, though.

"I told you that I'd stay and make sure no one bothers you. I'm gonna do it. You won't make me sleep on the couch, will you? In the wet spot?"

Nicolette laughs. It's a soft laugh, almost like she made the sound and didn't mean to, but I heard it. It makes my chest puff out with pride, too.

I like her laugh. I like being the one to cause it.

Almost as much as I like being the one to make her cry out as she comes.

I drop my hand, laying it possessively on her naked ass. "Nic? Bedroom?"

"It's this way," she says, pressing a quick kiss between my pecs—and I know that she just needed a little push after all. "Upstairs. Come on. I'll show you."

I let Nicolette lead me nearly the entire way. Once she shows me to a smaller room on the upper floor, I verify that it's hers, then swoop her up into my arms. She squeals, arms immediately going around my neck, though she doesn't demand for me to put her down.

Good. It's a small sign of trust from her, and I'll take it.

And that's not all I want...

Moving across the room, I lay her out on the bed. It's smaller than what I'm used to—it's maybe a double, while the bed at my place is a king—but if I could manage to fuck her on her mother's couch, I'll have more than enough room for *this*.

I start to bend over her, annoyed when my pants limit my range of motion. Add that to the open shirt getting in my way and, well, they have to go, don't they?

The shirt is easy to get rid of. I kicked my shoes off downstairs, and I drop down to the edge of Nicolette's bed to yank off my trouser socks. After that, I make quick work of my pants, all while she's watching me curiously.

Completely naked now, my dick—semi-hard before her perusal—twitches, then grows bigger as Nicolette's lips part, her eyes suddenly glazed over with desire.

I'm a vain bastard. When half the time I'm reduced down to my appearance more than anything, it would take a man a shit ton stronger than I am not to let it go to my head.

Giving my cock a leisurely stroke, I stalk back toward the bed.

"Scoot back, baby. Sit up against the pillows, grab the headboard, and hold on."

It takes her two seconds to understand what my intentions are. When she does? She does the last thing I expect after what just happened downstairs.

Nicolette closes her legs, clamping her thighs together.

"What's the matter, Nic?"

She mumbles something.

Frowning, I say, "I didn't hear that."

"I said, I haven't trimmed lately, okay? You don't want your face down there, trust me."

Is that what's going on here?

"Oh, Nic... I'm dying to find out how you taste straight from the source. You think a little hair is going to stop me?"

She shrugs, hugging herself.

This is happening. I just need her to be comfortable with it before I dive in...

"What's the deal? We both know I didn't have a problem with it before."

"Well, yeah. I mean, in my experience, guys don't care if there's bush when they stick their dick in. It's a little different when that's where your face goes."

My plan was to ease her into this. To make her absolutely addicted to me so I can justify just how addicted I am to *her*.

Until she says that. Suddenly, it feels like the ice from outside has settled in my gut.

Guys...

'Guys' implies plural, and when she says 'in my experience', she's talking about the other men she's been with.

Fuck, *no*.

I'm no saint; not just because I'm a Sinner, either. Since Heather, I've lost track of my one-night stands and the women I spent a week or two with before I moved on. Even before her, I had a couple of girlfriends. While each one was important to me once—and I have good thoughts and fond memories of most of them—I keep them where they belong: in my past.

The Nicolette I've seen tonight is obviously no doe-eyed virgin. I never thought she'd be. It's one of the things that drew me to her in the first place, the haunted look in her soft brown eyes that warned she's seen some shit, and how she found a way to smile past it. There is still a touch of naiveté about her—or desperation—that I saw when she agreed to spend a night with Miles, and I almost pity the poor bastard for losing out after she climbed into my lap before.

Ten grand? The way she arched her back, completely naked below the waist while insisting she keep her top on... it was so fucking erotic, I don't know how I didn't nut right away.

Even now I'm humming in place, the musk of our sex clinging to our skin, her tempting pussy only inches away from my watering mouth having me on the edge of losing complete control...

I need this, and she's going to give it to me.

"Hey. Why don't you let me show you what I can handle. Yeah?"

"I don't—"

"Open your legs, Nicolette." It's an order, and I don't care if that's how she takes it. I'm her boss at the Playground. If I have to, I'll be her boss in bed, too. "You gave me your pussy already. Way I see it, it's mine tonight." It's gonna be mine *forever*. "That means your orgasms are, too. You haven't let me use my tongue to give you one. That's not fair."

Her brow furrows. "Fair?"

I inch closer to her on the bed. "That's right. You want to be fair, don't you? Of course you do. Now go on. Show me my pussy."

She sucks in a breath—and then she does just that.

I barely notice the blonde curls covering her pussy.

All I see when she splits her legs are the pretty pink pussy lips, the dark hole stretched out because of *my* cock, and the glistening moisture that tells me she wants me to do this almost as much as I do.

Almost.

I don't give Nicolette a chance to change her mind. Once she opens herself up to me, I wedge my shoulders in between her thighs, making it impossible for her to close up again.

Then, using my thumbs and forefingers to spread her labia, I begin to feast.

One taste. Just like I thought. It takes one fucking taste of her cream hitting my tongue, and I know that I'll never find anything this amazing again. Because this is Nicolette. This is her giving herself to me, trusting me, and it couldn't be any better.

I only rise up long enough to rumble, "Goddamn it. You tried to keep this from me? Oh, but you're a good girl, aren't you? Letting me feast on this pussy. It's fucking delicious."

I curl my tongue, traveling all the way up her slit before sucking her clit into my mouth. When she gasps, I grin. She's relaxing around me, and as I take her hand, guiding her to grab my hair so that she's got something to hold onto, I go to town on her.

So, yeah, I'm no saint, but I might just be a fucking hypocrite because I still can't handle the thought of Nic with any other cock stretching her out but *mine*.

I'd only planned on worshiping her, showing her how good we could be together after she gave me pleasure downstairs. But now...

Just as her legs start to quiver her release, I grip her thighs tight, throwing her legs over my shoulders. In this position, I can bury my face against her pussy so that she has no choice but to ride out her orgasm on my face.

Nicolette digs her heels into the meat of my upper back. Her fingers are tugging on my hair, almost like she's using it like fucking reins, steering me exactly where she wants me to go. Her back arching up off of the bed, she cries out before dropping down on it again.

I'm sprawled on my belly, face in her snatch. My nose is nestled in her curls, my tongue plunged up inside of her, gathering all of her moisture as she shudders in place.

"That was," she says, her voice suddenly strained. "That was..."

I squeeze her thighs one last time, then sit up, lowering her legs back to the bed. She probably expects that I'm going to grab that towel from before to wipe off my face.

Not a chance. Not only do I like smelling Nic's cunt on my face like this, but now that I have her loose and limber and wanting... I take one leg and, with a show of strength she wasn't expecting, I flip her easily from her back to her front. She gasps in surprise, but stays where I put her as I sandwich her legs with mine, bracing her as I climb on top of her back.

I grip her hip with one hand, lifting her up just enough that I can grab my cock and slide it into her pussy from behind. Between fucking her downstairs, then fucking her with my tongue just now, there's not as much resistance as before. The angle is different enough to squeeze my cock in a whole new way, though, and when I tighten my thighs, making her legs do the same... my eyes almost roll back in my head, it feels so fucking good.

She hisses out a breath, fingers digging into the sheets. Once she gets used to the unexpected intrusion, she looks over her shoulder at me, sweat dotting her brow.

She wants to move. I can see it in the way the chords on her neck stand out, and it's obvious in how she's rocking just enough beneath my weight. But I'm keeping her pinned on my cock, in complete control this time, and her pretty face turns pleading.

"I told you, baby," I say, answering her unasked question. "Your orgasms are mine. And I'm pretty sure you've got one more in you."

"*Rolls—*"

I bite her back through the material of her sweater. Not enough to hurt her, but to catch her attention. "It's Royce to you, Nic. I told you that, too."

She nods into the sheets, then throws her head back, moaning as I buck up into her.

"Yes. God, *yes*."

"That feel good?"

Again, she nods.

I trail my hands down her back. "You want more?"

"I want *everything*."

I grin to myself as I pull out, slamming back home again. "Good. Because that's exactly what I'm going to give you."

I MAKE NICOLETTE GIVE ME *TWO* MORE ORGASMS BEFORE I finally let her get some rest. I find a new washcloth in her attached bathroom after encouraging her to pee, then give us both a quick clean-up before joining her in bed.

Forever a gentleman, I end up sleeping in the wet spot anyway. Considering it's only there because I got to fuck her twice, I don't complain. Instead, I lay down with her, inviting her to snuggle up next to me.

When she does, I've never felt more victorious.

Just before I nod off myself, I remember that—for all intents and purposes—it probably seems like I disappeared off the face of the planet tonight. Here's hoping that none of the guys needed me, but now that I have that thought, I go rooting along the edge of Nic's bed for my pants.

I had my phone in the back pocket. I refuse to let go of her, so retrieving my phone takes a bit of gymnastics as half of me stays on the bed, the other half nearly falling off, but finally I have it and—

Shit.

Twelve missed calls. Thirty-five texts.

Rolling my eyes, I go right to Link's name. Anyone else can wait, but the boss?

They call him 'Devil', not 'patient'—and his to-the-point texts back that up.

> I called you five times.

> You dead?

> You better be dead, Royce.

Ah. That's Link for you. He has a history of disappearing on the syndicate, and when he's with Ava, the goddamn Playground better be burning down before we interrupt his time with his wife, but the second I ignore my phone for more than a couple of hours, he assumes the worst—and *then* he threatens me.

No, boss. I'm not dead. In fact, after spending the night with Nicolette, I realize just how much I've been sleepwalking the last six years. Blaming myself for some cocky Dragonfly taking a shot at me and accidentally killing a woman I barely was acquainted with. That's the life, and I knew it, but I let it affect *my* life.

Not anymore.

In response to Link's latest text, I snap a pic. My phone's angled so that all you get is her blonde hair sprawled out on my chest, the top of my devil tattoo peeking out from between the tousled waves. Smirking to myself, I send it to Link and wait.

It takes two minutes.

About fucking time.

I know, Link.
I know.

Roll 'em..

ELEVEN
BREAKFAST

NICOLETTE

Something's burning.

I'm pulled out of a deep, dreamless sleep when my nose wrinkles at the acrid, smokey smell. The smoke alarm itself isn't going off, so I'm pretty sure my mom's house isn't on fire, but when you're half-asleep and wondering if the house you're in is about to go up in flames, 'pretty sure' just isn't good enough.

Sitting up, I squint as I look around the room. For a moment, I'm confused when I see the men's button-down strewn on my floor since it's not anything I would wear—until realization slaps me upside my head, and last night comes rushing back.

That's Royce McIntyre's shirt.

After I initiated sex with him on the couch down-stairs, he carried me upstairs and got naked before joining me in bed and giving me the best head I've ever had in my life. Glancing down quickly, I'm relieved to see that—while he passed out in my bed without a stitch of clothing on his amazing body—I still have my bra and sweater on. No bottoms, though my legs are twisted up in the sheets.

The *empty* sheets.

Royce is gone. His shirt is here, though, and now that I'm *awake* awake, I'm beginning to realize that my house shouldn't be smokey for no reason.

What is he doing?

I scurry out of my bed, pausing only to throw on a pair of sweatpants to cover up as I try to tame my bedhead before heading downstairs.

He kicked off his expensive-looking shoes by the front door. They're still here now, and when I hear the sound of metal clanging together coming from the kitchen, I figure that's where he went. Since it's also obviously the source of the smoke, I jog across the living room, heading right for the attached kitchen.

The first thing I notice is that he's standing at the stove, head bowed over a pan of burning bacon. The second thing? Is a sculpted back on display that has my tongue darting out, dabbing at the corner of my mouth.

Royce must have heard my footsteps coming; that, or he can feel the heat of my stare against his gorgeous back. After giving the pan another shake, he turns around.

His smile is *breathtaking*. "Morning, baby. Hungry? I was just about to wake you up." He gestures at a plate piled high with fluffy yellow eggs he has sitting on the counter. "I made some scrambled eggs since I didn't know how you take yours. The bacon's almost done, too."

Honestly? The eggs look alright, but that bacon was probably done five minutes ago.

I don't tell him that, though. Why would I? Not only am I stunned that Royce just gave me a pet name—he called me 'baby' so casually, like it was the most normal thing in the world for him to do—but he actually got up, rifled through my kitchen, and decided to make us breakfast while I slept.

"Um, yeah. Thanks. I am a little hungry."

Royce winks over at me. "Thought you might. I can say that I definitely worked up an appetite last night. Go on. Sit down. I'll serve you when it's done."

Something about his easy-going tone still has enough of an edge to it that says he's used to being obeyed. Whether it's because he runs the Playground or is high up in the Sinners Syndicate, I'm not sure, but I don't even think about refusing.

Instead, plopping down in one of the two kitchen chairs by the corner table, I watch him move around my space.

He's got on the same slacks as last night. No socks. No shoes. No shirt, either, and I'd worry about the fat spitting up from the too-hot pan if it wasn't for the fact that Royce obviously thought ahead.

My mother is a big woman. She has a few inches on me, with a busty chest and a nice round belly. Her house has a state-of-the-art kitchen going to waste because cooking is her passion, but it sure the hell isn't mine. She used to joke that the reason she snagged four of her five husbands was because of her pot roast and her apple pie; the first—my dad—liked her cooking, but loved her ass.

When I try to make a meal, it looks like a bomb went off in the kitchen which is why I can't judge Royce for trying. He's probably doing better than I would with breakfast.

There's no denying that 'cooking' is my mother's thing, the same way as 'musicals' are mine. That's why, for as long as I can remember, all of the gifts I would buy for her are cooking-themed, including a joke apron I bought her the Christmas before I moved to Willowbrook.

It's a shocking neon pink, oversized so that it could cover her tits, wide enough to wrap around her comfortably. On the front, in a bright white print, it says: *Today's Menu: eat it or starve*, with a drawing of a knife beneath it. The face she made when she unwrapped it was worth the thirty bucks I paid for it, and I knew that she would keep it, but never, ever wear it.

I left later that spring. Between Christmas and May that year, then when I spent some time with her before she went to Florida this year, she certainly didn't. To be honest, I'd completely forgotten all about the eyesore of an apron... until I walked into my mother's kitchen and found Royce McIntyre *wearing* it.

My laugh catches in my throat. Any nerves I might have had about the morning after—or the fact that he's my *boss*—evaporate when I see him in neon pink like that.

He raises his eyebrows at me.

I gesture at him. "Love the apron."

Royce grins. A spatula in one hand, he plucks at the front of the apron with the other. "I hope you don't mind me borrowing this."

THE DEVIL'S PLAYGROUND

Oh, god. He thinks that thing belongs to *me*.

"No, no, no. That, uh, that's not mine. It's my mom's. But it's okay. I'm sure she wouldn't care that you're using it."

Of course not. Mom would be way more concerned with the fact that I assaulted this man with a frying pan, felt so guilty that I invited him into her house, and somehow ended up sleeping with him. And if that wasn't bad enough, once the deed was done, I didn't help him gather up his clothes and boot him out the door like I've done with the handful of lovers I actually chose to have since escaping Kieran. Oh, no. Breaking every rule Mom had when I was living under her roof as a teen, I allowed a guy to spend the night.

Poor Mom. After the stigma she dealt with all her life, she did everything she could to keep me from becoming a teen mother myself. She had no idea at the time that by forbidding me from dating, she was leaving me ripe for the pickings for her stepson. Kieran lived in this house until Mom and Dave called it quits. Kinda hard to hold up the 'no guys sleeping over' rule when the one I was fucking under her nose lived here.

For her own sanity, I let her think that my relationship with Kieran didn't start until after he and Dave moved out. I was nineteen at that point—not the sixteen-year-old he groomed into taking her virginity the first time, or the fourteen-year-old prey he set his eyes on when he first moved in—and she had to admit that it made sense. We hadn't grown up together, and since Kieran is five years older than me, it never would have

141

occurred to her that he had eyes for her teenage daughter.

It took me a long time to admit that I was groomed into being everything he wanted. Some part of me still believes it was my fault. I could have said 'no'. At the time, I thought he was the man of my dreams... only to discover that he really was the reason for my nightmares. Mom would blame herself if she knew—which is why I've made sure she never, ever found out.

Royce is different. I might have initiated sex last night as one more 'fuck you' to Kieran, but when we were finished, I didn't *want* him to leave. In the heat of the moment, I could forget that this whole thing started because of a bet, because he has this 'white knight' thing going on, that he thinks I need saving... and because I did, didn't I?

But that was last night. Now? Watching him poke at the smoking bacon with his spatula, jumping back when a sizzle of the fat finds skin beneath the apron built for a body-type way different than his, I'm torn between being amazed at this other side of the formerly aloof gangster —and remembering again with a swift kick in the ass that this man is my *boss*.

The nerves were gone, but as he turns to fiddle with the bacon, my stomach sinks as they return.

Oh, boy. Did I really allow my attraction to Royce— and my dysfunctional relationship with Kieran—to over-rule my brain? Sleeping with another guy to prove to myself that Kieran no longer has any hold on me is one thing. But complicating my employment after what happened with that fateful poker game?

What was I thinking?

Well. That's easy enough to admit: I *wasn't*, was I?

Shit.

What am I going to do?

What is *Royce* going to do?

My boss is currently occupied in the kitchen, leaving me to watch—and worry.

"Goddamn it," he mutters, the metal spatula scraping against the pan. It's non-stick, and even I know you shouldn't use a metal tool when you're cooking with a non-stick pan, but that's the least of his worries. Somehow, while he was flexing and I was staring—at him, at the apron, at *him*—the bacon got so burnt, it's stuck to the pan. He grunts, knocking the black hunks of shriveled meat around before realizing it's no use.

Shutting off the burner, he glances over his shoulder at me again. "I hope you like your bacon extra crispy." He frowns, seeing something in my face I wasn't quick enough to hide. "Hey. Nic. You okay?"

No.

"I'm fine. Just hungry." Though there's no way I'm going to try that bacon. I appreciate the effort, but... "Thanks. I wasn't expecting breakfast. No one's ever done that for me before."

"Then your previous lovers were all assholes," Royce says. "And, for the sake of me keeping my appetite, we won't talk about any of them. I'm your lover now. Get used to breakfast."

He sets the plate of eggs on the kitchen table. In his other hand, he's holding the pan of burnt bacon. With

143

another frown, he shrugs, then places the whole pan on top of the wooden tabletop.

Royce's hands are free now. Turning toward me, he brushes his thumb along my cheek. He's already lowering his head, prepared to take a morning kiss as his thanks.

I jump up, avoiding him. "Plates," I blurt out. "We need plates."

"Nic—"

"Two secs. I'll be right back."

Roll 'em...

TWELVE
HIS

NICOLETTE

As I hurry into the kitchen to retrieve plates, utensils, and napkins, my head is spinning from what he said. *I'm your lover now*... does that mean this wasn't a one-night stand? He's obviously jealous over the other guys I've been with before... but why?

More importantly, what happens now?

I don't know, and instead of asking, I purposely steer the conversation in a different direction.

"How's your arm?"

Royce glances down at it. He bends his elbow, showing off the swell of his bicep as he gives it a once-over. Is the flexing on purpose? I can't imagine why it would be. After last night, he has to know that I find him attractive. If Britney can be believed, I'm not the only one, either.

He's jealous over my previous lovers. Me? I want to

shut down when I think about Royce's. Maybe he's right. Maybe it's better for both of us if we keep what's happening between us *between us* until we figure it out.

He's still standing by the table, moving aside so I can place the plates, forks, knives, and napkins down.

"Arm's fine," he says. "You got a good swing on you, but I'll be alright. And now that I know you're worried about someone sneaking around your house, I'll make sure to ring the doorbell next time I stay over."

I fiddle with the hem of my sweater. Like Royce, I haven't taken a seat yet. "So... that means there will be a next time?"

Royce's jaw tightens, his easy humor taking a back seat as he looks me up and down. "Yes. There will." His blue eyes flash, daring me to tell him he's wrong. When I don't, he says, "You started something with me last night, Nicolette. I'm not about to walk away from it."

"If this is about that stupid bet—"

"The bet only made it so that you'd get used to me. It was never about one night. I need you to understand that, yeah? Sinners play to win. If you ask me, I got my prize last night all right, but it wasn't you inviting me to stay over. It was you finally figuring out that you're mine."

What? "I... I am?"

"You are. You have been. I was just waiting for you to realize that."

"Royce, I—"

"Breakfast's getting cold."

Breakfast can wait. "We need to talk about this. If you honestly think that we can turn last night into a... a relationship or something, then... we have to talk."

Royce crosses his arms over his chest. He'd look a little more intimidating with that pose if it wasn't for the apron, and I wonder if that was another reason he put it on. Kinda hard to be afraid of a mafia man in neon pink.

A half-smile tugs on his lips. "I've said what I wanted to say. I've considered you mine since the moment you walked into the Playground. I kept my distance since I didn't think it would be appropriate to use my position of power to convince you to be with me, but I'll remind you, Nic... you came on to me last night. As far as I'm concerned, I didn't make you do anything. And if you decided to fuck me because I run the Playground? I'm good with being used. Think nothing of it."

"It's not that," I begin.

"You sure? You're not trying to take back last night because I'm your boss?"

Okay. Maybe it *is* that.

He's got one thing wrong, though. "Last night... I didn't go after you because of what you are. My boss, I mean."

That was actually one of the reasons I stayed away. Like Royce, I was sure that it would be inappropriate if I went after him, especially when all of the other staff at the Playground made it clear that he never mixed business with pleasure.

Then there was the fact that he's second-in-command to the leader of the Sinners Syndicate. After all those years with Kieran, I almost imagined each of the West Side gangsters to have literal devil horns and tails rather than just the brands on their skin. That's how evil the Dragonflies made their rivals out to be.

But while Royce might have a devil's tattoo on the side of his chest, the man I'm getting to know is nothing like what I expected—and more than I could ever hope to have.

Which is probably why I'm having such a hard time believing he could ever want *me*...

As though Royce has no idea how much I'm struggling right now—or maybe he *does*—he shows he has another one of my favorite personality traits: a good sense of humor.

Smiling down at me, he waggles his eyebrows. "Let me guess: you seduced me because of my good looks, but you just got super fucking lucky when you pulled out my amazing cock?"

I can't help myself. I laugh again. "Don't forget you're so very humble."

Royce snorts. "Fuck being humble. I know what I can offer a woman. When I decide to make one mine... trust me, you won't want any others. And you *are* mine. So I suggest you get over your hang-up about me being your boss since it doesn't matter, eat your breakfast, then let me have some."

The way his pretty blue eyes dart to the crotch of my sweatpants makes it obvious what he's referring to. And while sex was amazing last night—and I'd be lying if I said I'm not insanely attracted to Royce—I still can't get over the fact that he wants me for more than what we've already had.

When I stay quiet, he obviously thinks that I haven't gotten over that one particular hang-up about him being my boss after all.

Royce slips his hands into his pants pockets. Honestly, I'm immediately distracted by the way his chest moves, muscles in his forearms flexing as he digs deep, fingers moving around as though searching for something. In the morning light streaming in through the kitchen window, I can just make out a few blond hairs dusting the space between his nipples.

I kissed him there last night. Pressed my open mouth against his pale pink nipple and fell asleep with my cheek nestled against the front of his shoulder. He's wearing my mom's apron instead of searching for his shirt, and seeing him standing over a frying pan full of burnt bacon, I realize I'm suddenly very hungry after all —just not for food.

A lump lodges in my throat. I swallow it as Royce jerks his chin at me.

"Hey. Listen… if it makes you feel better, let's flip for it. Heads, I fire you. Tails, you stay at the Playground, and I couldn't give a fuck what anyone says. I won you, Nic, and I took. But, you know, we can leave it to chance and blame that." He lifts his eyebrows, humor—and a dare—written in his baby blues. "Unless you have a preference."

He's still too much of a gorgeous distraction. That look on his face makes it hard for me to think right now, and he said something about firing me, and now I'm inwardly panicking. He won me. For a night, at least, and I figured things would go back to normal after that… but I fucked my boss.

How in the world could they ever be normal again?

I don't know, but the most I can get out in answer is, "I like my job—"

Before I can finish, he pulls out his right hand. A shiny coin—quarter, I think—is clutched between two of his wicked fingers. A practiced flip, an arc about three feet into the air, and then—

"Tails."

Huh. I'm distracted, but that's pretty fucking convenient. "Can I see that?"

Royce winks, tossing the coin my way. I fumble the catch, recovering before it hits the kitchen tile. It is a quarter, and I'm looking at the eagle. Turning it over, I'm not even a little surprised to see another eagle.

I meet the amusement that replaced the dare in his expression. "You rigged the toss?"

He shrugs, making the apron bunch up around the midsection. "You like your job."

"Is that what you do? Cheat?" I mean for it to be a tease, but now I'm thinking about the other night at the Playground. "Is that how you beat Miles?"

"I don't need to cheat to beat a bogus gambler like that. Fucking moron has a tell he's too dumb to realize. But that doesn't mean I won't tip the odds in my favor from time to time."

"Oh. Okay." I reach out my hand, offering him his quarter. "Then you'll probably want this back."

He takes it, then quickly wraps his fingers around my wrist. "That's not all I want."

A gentle yet forceful tug and, suddenly, I'm pressed up against that silly apron as he drops his forehead down to mine.

Our mouths are barely an inch apart as he breathes out, "Don't think I didn't notice you trying to get out of kissing me good morning, Nic. I'll take that now if you don't mind."

My cheeks heat up. I didn't want him to notice that—or think I was rejecting him—but he's not wrong. I *did* try my best to avoid his kiss before.

Swallowing roughly, I admit, "I didn't brush my teeth yet."

"And?"

"You know. Morning breath."

Royce snorts. The rush of air is warm on my face as he drops his mouth to mine. Against my lips, he murmurs, "Oh, baby, didn't you get the hint last night? You're perfect to me. There isn't anything about you that doesn't turn me on."

Really?

Wrapping my arms around his lower back, mimicking the way he's done the same to me, I blow out a small puff of breath. "Even that?"

He chuckles. "Even that," he promises, and to prove it, he slants his mouth over mine, turning a simple good morning peck into a kiss so deep, I forget any of my nerves, my insecurities, and my fears because, when Royce McIntyre has me wrapped up in his embrace, I don't fucking have any.

Breakfast is icy-cold, definitely burnt, and a little rubbery by the time we eventually get to it—but believe me when I say I've never had a better meal.

Or better company.

Roll 'em...

THIRTEEN

THE PHANTOM OF THE OPERA

ROYCE

I t's been three weeks since I stood in Nicolette's kitchen, wearing the most ridiculous apron I found in her mother's collection, realizing that the idea of surprising her with breakfast seemed a lot easier in my head than in reality. Coming from a guy who eats out for every meal—or bums cooking from Mona on the rare occasion I don't—I haven't cooked more than microwaveable shit in almost a decade.

I did it to show my new lover that I was more than a pretty face and a gun. If I wanted her to think of me as a partner, I needed to show her what I can bring to the table that isn't just my money, my power, and my dick.

I mean, I plan on giving her all of that, too, but Nicolette... she's different than so many of the women I've met since being a Sinner. She's obviously been hurt by someone before, and I get the vibe it's someone like me.

I want to show her that I'm different than what I seem, too.

As a fixer, I have a skill. I can do anything, get anything, *arrange* anything. If it doesn't come easy, I focus. I plan. I learn. Right now, my goal is to make Nicolette Williams mine. Not for a night, and not because I was at the right place at the right time. You could even argue that I *wasn't*—I got a frying pan to the side because she thought I was trying to break into her house—and, yet, she still invited me inside where one thing led to another, and yeah... I got my night.

I want *more*.

Breakfast was my first step. To show her how thoughtful I can be while also setting the stage for step two: claiming Nic before she could even think of brushing that night off as a one-time thing. I was glad when she didn't try to tell me that fucking me was her way of calling us even. As far as I'm concerned, the ten grand I was out is a small price to pay to keep her out of Miles Haines's disturbed fantasies.

Once I got my first taste of her, though? I knew I was right. No matter why she caught my attention in the first place, she has it now—and every day that passes makes me fall deeper and deeper for this woman.

It started out as curiosity. By the time I was stalking her around Springfield, telling myself I was just keeping an eye out for her... it was obsession. But the more time I spend with her? Getting to know every facet of Nicolette? I'm beginning to wonder if this is what being in love is like.

I want to say it is. This feeling, like every fucking

breath I have is dedicated to her, that when she smiles, I smile, just because her happiness brightens my day. When I was in high school, I had a few girlfriends that made me feel this way. Silly puppy love where I'll do anything for her approval, and one kiss from her makes me feel like I *can* do anything.

I've never experienced this as an adult. In my early twenties, I was busy working alongside Link, building up the syndicate. Fuck knows that he wasn't interested in chicks back then—even if it took me a while to find out why—and without that being a focus for him, I wasn't really too concerned with getting into a relationship myself. I dated, sure, and I screwed around, but it was never anything serious.

And then I held a near-stranger as she died when I was twenty-four. She told me she loved me. I barely knew her... and she died in my arms.

After that, I never thought I'd love *anyone*—until Nic.

But there's a dark side to my overwhelming love for her, too. When I first stepped off the straight and narrow path when I was a kid, I realized that life isn't made up of blacks and whites. It's shades of grey, and just like how I went from being vice president of the student council when I was a senior in high school to falling in with organized crime shortly after I gradu-ated, the dangerous parts of life have always attracted me.

Is it because I have a dark side of my own? Probably. And the more time I spend with Nicolette, the more I find myself fighting against it.

It's times like these that I understand why Link

walked away from Ava, and why he did everything he could to keep her when he had his second chance.

The darkness hidden beneath my crooked smile and Ken doll looks is just begging to get out, to cocoon Nicolette, to love and keep her and eliminate anyone who would take her from me. I'm *obsessed* with her... and she acts like this is just a fling to keep her warm through the winter.

It's been three weeks, and while I got her to agree that we're exclusive—and, trust me, it was a blow to my ego that even getting that out of her was like pulling teeth—that's *all* I could get her to agree to. She has no idea that I'm playing the long game here. What we have... this is it for both of us. We're forever. Even if there's someone else I might ever feel the same way about, I don't care. She's mine... and I know her well enough that, if she believed that I truly meant it the first time I told her she was, she'd spook and run.

Nic is hiding something. That tiny spy camera I found was a huge clue, though she shuts down whenever I try to mention it. Still, there are times when she looks at me like I've hung the fucking stars for her, and others when our eyes meet, but I know she sees someone else. It's in the way she constantly looks over her shoulders. It's in the multiple surveillance cameras she has posted around her house. It's in the way she whispers my name wistfully as I fuck her in her childhood bed, in her mother's house, trying to make her mine any way I can while I know—I just *know*—that she's counting the moments until I walk away from her.

Because that's the thing. I get the feeling that Nicolette isn't going all in because she's not interested. It's because she *is,* and she doesn't believe that I could be.

Which makes it my responsibility to prove to her that I *am.*

As much as I want to, I can't pull a Devil; not unless I want to lose her completely. Link forced Ava into marrying him so that he could keep her, and though the idea of making Nicolette my wife has me rock-hard, I know better than to bring it up. As far as she knows, it's only been a few weeks since I paid her any attention. If she found out I've been watching over her since *November?*

Yup. That'll spook her. Worse, I'm absolutely convinced she'll take off. Just run, leaving me behind, and though I'd find her... I'd rather I didn't have to.

So, instead, I've devoted any free moment I have—when Link doesn't need me for Sinners biz, or I'm not checking in with Jake—to making Nicolette comfortable with the idea of forever with me.

She gets antsy when we go out to dinner? Since it becomes pretty clear that, of the two of us, I'm actually the *better* cook, we order in and eat together in the living room. When I realize that Nicolette's favorite thing to do is curl up and watch a musical? I force myself through the first few before admitting they're not so bad.

Plus, since most of the song-and-dance movies are like three hours long, she's more than happy to invite me to spend the night after they're done. Throw in the fact that she likes the more romantic ones, she's usually in the mood to fuck when they're over, and I'm happy to oblige.

I'm happy to give Nicolette everything she wants—and that includes *time*.

No one knows that we're together. No. Scratch that. No one in *Nic*'s life knows that we're together. Link was aware from the moment I sent the shot of her hair on my chest. Of course, that means that Ava also knows. Then, because I'm a high-ranking Sinner, I had to let the guys know that Nic isn't just a Playground employee. She's important to me, and it's their balls if anything happens to her.

With her mother sticking it out in Florida through the winter, she decides to hold off on introducing me until she's back in Springfield. She has no dad in the picture, and all of her friends are back in Willowbrook. Since she was so determined to keep her job at the Playground, we're keeping it hush-hush there so that none of the other staff accuse her of getting preferential treatment.

That was Nicolette's idea. I went along with it against my better judgment, telling myself it didn't matter. Anyone who counts is fully aware what role she has in my life, and as much as she wants to act like I'm her dirty little secret, that's kinda hard when I whisk her away at every chance to my personal office next door so that I can remind her just who she belongs to.

Because she's mine—and, sooner or later, everyone will admit that.

Including Nicolette.

I'VE FUCKING OUTDONE MYSELF.

Tonight marks one month since I've made it obvious to Nicolette that she's it for me. And though it's beginning to piss me off that I can't shake the feeling she has one foot out the door, I'm determined. I will make this impossible woman fall in love with me or die trying.

She likes flowers, and I spent enough at the florist shop where Burns's wife works to keep that place afloat the rest of the year. When her favored sweatpants got a hole in them after I was a little too eager to get them off of her, I bought her three pairs to replace them—then figured out how to use a needle and thread to sew it up myself because it was how well-worn they were that she liked.

Tonight, though? If she's holding onto any doubts that I'm in this for good—that this isn't just me playing around because that's what 'Rolls' Royce McIntyre does—it's my plan to erase all of them with one impeccably planned night out.

At first, Nicolette has no idea where I'm taking her. She seems surprised—and, admittedly, a touch suspicious—when I tell her that we're heading out of Springfield, though she relaxes once I add that we're heading into Riverside.

Riverside is a local city to Springfield, about a forty-minute drive away. It's not as populated, with about half as many residents, but it's full of museums, restaurants, and theaters.

Once I learned that Nicolette's big 'thing' was Broadway, I went into research mode. Luckily for me, there was a national tour of one of her favorites passing through our area. For about two weeks, the touring cast would be performing *The Phantom of the Opera* at the Riverside Performing Arts Center.

With one hell of a donation made by 'anonymous', I was able to get a pair of primo seats on the night of our anniversary.

Nicolette's already bouncing in place while I'm valeting the car. As soon as I said Riverside, I think her mind started whirling. Of course, I couldn't contain myself, giving her a few hints during the drive, and by the time we're walking into the large theater, she knows exactly why I've brought her here.

"I've always wanted to see this live! I mean, I've watched the movie a hundred times, and then there's the 25th anniversary concert, but an actual performance? This is amazing!"

I love her excitement. As a fixer, I get a jolt of pleasure whenever I pull off a seemingly impossible task. Some people get turned on by a flash of skin or a pair of tits. Me? I'll appreciate a nice rack as much as the next hetero guy, but I'm all about getting a job done right.

When she throws herself into my arms, kissing me in the middle of the crowd outside waiting to have their tickets scanned, my cock twitches down below. I was already hard—that's my usual state around this woman —but the sweet hug and honest affection she shows me? I want nothing more than to hoist her up, wrap her legs around my waist, and encourage her to show me how grateful she is.

Of course, I can't do that. But I do drop my mouth to hers, kissing her deeply while claiming her publicly. She's never allowed me to do that, and I love seeing this side of her. Of Nic not caring that there are others around as she goes up on her tiptoes, threading her fingers through my hair during our kiss.

Someone whistles nearby. Nicolette jerks, as though suddenly reminded that we're not alone. Her tanned cheeks turn red as she flushes, but I could give a fuck. This is the first time I'm able to show her off without her wondering what people will think about her sleeping with her boss.

I know that still bothers her. She tells me it doesn't, but I'm pretty good at figuring out when someone is lying to me.

I don't call her out on it. Not yet. Instead, I work on proving to her that it doesn't matter. She has her job, I do my best not to interfere too much, and we spend as much of our free time together as we can.

Like tonight.

Taking her fingers, I lead her past the growing line. A few theater-goers mutter about me cutting, but when I flash my ticket at the usher up front, he sees where I'm seated, knows that I must've paid a pretty penny for the location, and lets us go in.

Or maybe spending the last decade at Link's side means that some of his 'don't-fuck-with-me' attitude has rubbed off on me. Despite my crooked smile, no one stops us as we step inside. In fact, another usher beelines right toward us, ready to escort us to our seats.

I wave him off since I already got a tour last week when I came by to pick out our box, then tuck Nicolette against my side as I start across the lobby.

After a small stop, I find the stairs that will take us to

our seats. Only after we reach the heavy red curtain and I pull it aside before gesturing for her to go ahead of me do I explain: "I got us our own private box. Just me and you, baby."

She takes in the small enclosure with only two seats. It overhangs the left side of the stage, high enough that the other patrons might see our faces in the light, and that's about all. Once it's dark? They shouldn't see even *that*.

Her soft brown eyes light up as she takes it all in. When she finally turns to look at me again, I say, "It's not box five since they're not numbered like that, but I thought it worked for the occasion."

Nicolette blinks. "You know about *Phantom*?"

Roll 'em...

FOURTEEN

CONNECTION

ROYCE

I didn't.

Before Nicolette, I knew shit about anything musical theater-related. Like, I remember hearing there was a weird show that has humans playing cats that was famous before I was born. Bonnie and Clyde had a short-lived show about them that I only heard about because, when I was a teen, I was fucking obsessed with Clyde Barrow. Other than that, I wasn't interested.

But Nicolette is, and I made it my mission to learn.

"No," I admit, taking one of the seats. I wait for her to lower herself into the other. She's wearing a skintight, black cocktail dress that had me seconds away from calling the whole night off just so I could have the pleasure of peeling it off of her, and she moves carefully as she turns to look at me. I run my thumb along the edge of her jaw. "But you like this stuff. And if you like it? I'll look into it. I'll give it a try."

"Oh, Royce..."

I knew I outdid myself.

It's not that I picked a random musical that just so happened to be playing locally, either. It's that I took the time to research the show to make tonight as special as possible. I drew the line at putting a half mask over my face, though the beaming smile she shot my way when I stopped and bought a rose from a vendor in the lobby makes me wonder if I should have.

The private box earns me more brownie points. It's recessed on the side of the theater, with a curtain behind us to give us privacy. It doesn't have the *best* view of the stage, but I figure the trade-off is worth it. Despite being in a theater with a thousand other people, in this box, it can be just the two of us.

With my free hand, I take hers in mine, twining my fingers with hers. "I want to like the things you like."

I see it when she swallows roughly, a hitch in her voice as she asks, "What about the things you like?"

"Me? I like being a Sinner. I like gambling," I tell her honestly, "and I like *you*."

She sucks in a breath. Since the lights go off the moment after I tell her that, followed by a round of applause from the audience, I figure that's what caused her reaction.

I've never been so fucking happy to be wrong.

Leaning over the seat, she pushes past my outstretched hand, laying hers on my cheek. She gives me a quick kiss, telling me more with actions than she can with any words as the show begins.

I have never been to one of these things before, but

even I know there's a certain etiquette in regard to how to act.

Fuck that.

I shift in my seat, collaring her throat, keeping her where she is as she begins to back away. That one kiss just reminds me how much I hunger for her. She started the kiss, and as the thunderous chords to the overture echo around us, I take that kiss, turn it around on her, and devour her in the darkness.

She's panting softly when I finally break it. "Royce," she murmurs softly, "the show's started."

I know. But whether I was planning this or not when I got the idea to book one of these private boxes, it doesn't matter. As though I've got Link whispering in my ear, I'm reminded of a talk we had a few years ago over a couple of shots of whiskey.

I couldn't understand why he'd willingly give up all women when he couldn't have Ava. He couldn't understand why I'd hop from bed to bed, getting nothing out of it except a quick nut and a sense of self-loathing when I abandoned another conquest.

There was, however, one thing we agreed upon: the best sex happened when there was a connection.

Right now, as a huge ass fake elephant comes rolling onto the stage, behind a shrill redhead singing far more opera-y than I was hoping, I think I finally understand what my boss was getting at all those years ago.

And, suddenly, I *crave* it.

Letting go of Nicolette's neck, I pull on her hand. I'm still holding it, and I squeeze her fingers, wordlessly gesturing for her to come closer before releasing her hand.

She leans over the armrest, a curious look in her eyes. "What's up?"

No. I need her closer. I pat my lap.

Her eyes widen. She points at herself, then at my thigh.

I nod.

Nicolette chuckles. Her eyes go even wider at the sound, and she slaps her hand over her mouth. In the shadows of the private box, I can just about make out the amusement dancing in her eyes as she shakes her head.

I raise my eyebrows, pressing my palms together.

Like me, Nicolette leans more toward being agnostic. We had the discussion once while watching *Fiddler on the Roof*. While I was raised Catholic before leaving the church as an adult, Nic's mother bounced from religion to religion, depending on her husband du jour. She says she was baptized, was pretty sure she had a Confirmation— which makes me think she was Catholic once, too—but she hesitates about whether she believes there's a God or not. Though the gesture might look like I'm praying, it's more like I'm pleading.

She leans in. "You really want me to fuck you right now? The show just began."

Exactly. We have at least an hour before intermission —but that's not necessarily what I *do* want.

"No fucking," I tell her. Not yet, at least. "I just want you to sit on my lap." *For now.* "If you're worried anyone will see, don't be. They're watching the stage."

"We should be watching the stage, too," she whispers back.

I reach out, stroking the column of her neck with my fingertips. "You'll have a better view from my lap."

Nicolette throws her head back, preening at my gentle touch even as she mutters softly, "You don't know how to quit, do you?"

I don't—and it's about time she figures that out.

She had her chance to refuse. Pulling my hand back, smirking when her head snaps down again, mourning the loss of my caress, I rise up from my seat. Just like I thought, no one is paying any attention to us as I take Nicolette's fingers again, tugging on them until she's standing up on her high heels.

Another tug and, oops, I'm sitting down, and she's sprawled across my lap.

I give her a moment to adjust her position, satisfied when she doesn't even try to get up and scurry back to her own seat. Instead, giving in to my desires, she leans into me, resting her head against the shoulder of my suit jacket.

I leave her that way for the next few songs. If she notices the erection beneath her pert ass, she doesn't pay it any attention, and I'm so used to being hard around her that I can handle the temptation of her curves for a little while—until the Phantom starts singing a love song to the girl on stage and Nicolette sighs.

That does it for me.

I hike up her skirt. So engrossed in the scene, she doesn't seem to notice that I'm pulling on both sides of her dress, lifting it slowly until it's bunched up around her belly button.

I worried when I saw she wasn't wearing any hose earlier. It's March, and though it seems like we've said goodbye to inconvenient snowstorms, it's still fucking cold outside. Now I'm grateful for it since the only thing coming between me and her pussy is her thin panties.

I hook my finger beneath the fabric, shuddering out a breath when I find that they're soaked. Her panties are barely an inch wide where it counts, and it's easy to move them past her pussy lip, baring her to me.

Nicolette can't pretend not to notice that, though she gives it a good try. But when I slide my finger through her slick heat, gathering the moisture, bumping her clit with my pointer finger before dipping low, fingering her gently?

She squeezes my thigh as she moves just enough to take the first knuckle inside of her before shifting, searching for more.

Oh, baby... if she's feeling empty right now, I have something that will fill her up more completely than my finger.

Placing my palm beneath her ass cheek, I lift her up so that I can reach my zipper. I wait until the song finishes and the audience claps to tug it down, the applause drowning out the tell-tale sound. It's only a matter of maneuvering her just so to get my cock out, and that's what I do.

Pulling my finger out of Nic, I try to replace it with my aching erection. The head of my cock immediately finds her entrance. As wet as she is, it slips right past, but the nudging is enough to have Nicolette turn and look over her shoulder at me.

I take advantage of her distraction to grip my shaft, fumbling in the dark to angle it right before—*yes*—I'm lodged inside of her.

She sits up straight, arching her back the same time as her hands slap out to her sides, gripping the armrests of my seat.

"Royce," Nicolette hisses just as the actress on stage sees some creepy doll wearing a wedding dress. She drops, the Phantom catches her, then carries her to a bed while still crooning about the music of the night. "I thought you just wanted me to sit on your lap."

"That's what I said. That's what you're doing. I just want you to sit down and—" I shift my hips, feeding her another inch of my cock—"be comfortable."

"Comfortable? With your dick inside of me? In *public*?"

"No one can see you, remember? And think of it as just keeping me warm and cozy while the show goes on. That's all."

"Well... if that's *all*..." She takes a breath and, exhaling it softly, lowers herself down so that she's fully seated on me.

I have to grit my teeth to keep from groaning out loud.

Instead, I whisper, the heat of my breath—or maybe the way I'm stretching her out—causing her to shiver, her pussy contracting around the intrusion of my cock.

"Yes... that's it, baby. *Fuck*... do you know how good this feels?"

She backs up against me, forcing my cock to move as she does. "I might have an idea."

I hiss at the pleasure rushing through me.

My body wants to move with her, but I stay motionless. That felt fucking amazing, too, but I don't want her to think I was slowly tricking her into fucking me. When I want sex, she'll know it. When I want to sit here, this gorgeous creature on my lap, holding my stiff cock inside of her as if it was made for her perfect pussy alone... she'll know that, too.

I nuzzle her neck as my hands go to her waist. Digging my thumbs past the bunched-up material of her dress, I put enough pressure there to keep her from wiggling again. "Don't move," I breathe, pressing an open-mouth kiss to her skin. "Just sit right here, baby, and enjoy the show."

I know I definitely will.

Sex is great. Stealing Nic away from some lowlife at the Playground who thinks his two dollar tip is enough to keep me from my girl, then enjoying it when she drops to her knees, sucking me off eagerly on one of her "breaks" is more than a bastard like me deserves. Waking up with her blonde hair spilled across my chest, her hand splayed across the devil on my side, and her legs entangled with mine? I *love* it.

But having her trust me enough to lean back, her fingers moving from the armrests to settle on top of my thighs as I spread her wide open, my cock nestled inside of her heat while a love triangle plays out on the stage?

This... *this* is what I've been waiting for—and there isn't a single thing I won't do to keep it.

As the first act draws to a close, I start to thrust a little. She's comfortable now, but Nicolette isn't Ava Monroe; exhibitionism isn't her thing. She'll sit on my lap in the dark, but once the light goes back on? She'll scatter, leaving my dick wet and my balls ready to explode.

Good thing I have a solution for that problem. And when my slow thrusts pick up speed, Nicolette immediately matching my rhythm as she realizes that I *am* fucking her right now, I'm so close to coming that I have to edge myself before I blow my load, leaving her wanting.

If there's one thing I'm not, it's a selfish lover. So, while I guide Nicolette to ride me in the theater seat, I reach around her, using two fingers to rub her clit until she begins mewling softly.

She'll never forgive herself if someone hears her being fucked while the show's going on. That's why, right as the chandelier comes crashing down, I grip Nicolette by the chin, tugging her mouth down to mine. I swallow her cries as she begins to come around my cock, and just as the lights flicker on for the intermission break, I buck up inside of her, filling her completely as she goes boneless against my suit.

Once we're both finished, I press a kiss to the top of her hair as I run my sticky fingers along the side of her thigh.

Now *that*'s a connection worth writing home about.

FIFTEEN
KIERAN ALFIERI

ROYCE

It's amazing how carefree Nicolette is in Riverside.

The arrogant part of me wants to believe it's from our theater fucking. Could be. Once she got used to just sitting on top of me, keeping me warm and the both of us connected through the first act of the show, she lost most of the tension she had been carrying with her earlier. We both headed off to the bathroom during intermission to freshen up, and when the show re-started, she laid her head on my shoulder again after returning to my lap, snuggling close throughout all of act two.

There was no reason to interrupt her during the second act, and I actually found myself following the plot as I looped my arm around her middle, holding her close. I enjoyed it more than I thought I would, though I made it a point to tell Nic that the female lead—Christine— fucked up by not choosing the Phantom in the end.

"The Phantom?" Nicolette swats me in the jacket as

we file out of the theater. "Were you watching the same show as me? He was the bad guy."

Taking her elbow lightly, I help guide her past some of the passersby on the street. "He loved her."

"He *stalked* her."

"Because he loved her," I point out.

She wrinkles her nose, and I get it. Some women might not swoon to know that their love interest is so obsessed that they'd watch over them... and if she's one of them, it's probably for the best that I keep the last couple of months to myself.

"He took her captive, Royce. Forced her into a wedding dress and then tried to make her choose between marrying him or watching as he killed her lover. And if you say he did all of that because he loved her... I think he was just obsessed."

Is it bad that I'm still on the Phantom's side here? "He let her go in the end," I remind her. "That pussy—"

Nicolette snorts. "The viscount."

Whatever. The blond asshole was a pussy. "He didn't deserve her. What did he do to show that he cared? Nothing compared to the Phantom."

Nicolette's brow furrows for a moment. "He rescued her when the Phantom hung that guy."

I don't remember that part. "When was that?"

She bumps her hip into my thigh as we cross over onto the next street. We'd both decided it was too early to call it a night and, after the show, we *somehow* worked up an appetite. With a handful of restaurants surrounding the venue, she suggested we take advantage of the nice night to walk over instead of getting the car from the valet.

"When was that?" she repeats. "Somewhere around the time you started fucking me."

"Are you mad?" I ask.

"Mad that my gorgeous date couldn't keep his hands off of me?"

"Yes."

Pausing on the other side of the street, Nicolette turns into me, bracing her hands on my chest. She tilts her head up. "Mad that you want me so bad that you couldn't wait until after, that you just had to fuck me then?"

"When you put it like that, you better not be."

She pats my chest. "I'm not. Surprised, maybe, but not mad." Going up on her tiptoes, she strokes a lock of my hair. "You'd make an excellent Raoul."

I give her a questioning look.

"I don't know. The suit. The hair. The way you're loaded, and you whisk me away on these adventures even though I'm poor as fuck."

Her voice is light, but a muscle tics in my jaw as she adds that last part.

Money is a sore point between us. It's not just that I'm her boss; I have more money than she does, and that bothers Nic. She'll accept dates and dinner, and even a new diamond nose ring that I bought after she playfully confessed hers was cubic zirconia. She told me that she understood that my love language was spoiling her with gifts, and if she rejected them, it was the same as rejecting me.

I'll admit, I had no fucking idea what she was talking

about, but after I dropped her off at her place that night, I parked my car around the corner and Googled the shit out of it.

There are a bunch of different love languages. Nicolette's not wrong when she says that I show my affection by giving her everything I think she deserves. As for her, after doing my research, I decide that *her* love language is 'words of affirmation'.

She needs to hear me tell her how fucking amazing she is, and how much I'm into her. Once I started to do that, so much of her hesitation seemed to melt away over the last few weeks. Throw in her praise kink and how happy it makes her for me to watch some old musical with her, and it's almost like I unlocked the secret to making Nicolette Williams want to be with me.

Now Nic accepts my gifts, and I give her my cock while rumbling that she's my 'good girl', and we've settled in a rhythm that works. Which is why I don't say anything about what she just said... until she finishes her thought.

"If the Phantom's the bad guy in the story, Raoul's the good guy." Nicolette presses a kiss to the underside of my jaw. "You're the good guy to me."

Me?

I'm a killer. Doesn't matter that I never fired a gun—I've never *had* to. I've lost track of how many lives I've ended with a nod, or how many I disappeared after Link decided they were expendable, a threat, or just because he was in a shitty mood that day. For fuck's sake, I run guns, allow Breeze to be sold openly at the club, and enable a very well-run prostitution ring.

I've manipulated her into a relationship that I will

never, ever willingly end... I've stalked her and, though I pretend we don't have a power imbalance, I've done everything I can to keep her... and *I'm* the good guy?

I don't say anything to that. I can't. If there's one thing I *can* say, it's that I won't lie to Nicolette. I might not tell her the truth, either, but a flat-out falsehood? Nah. She'd never trust me if I did, and while I can justify a lot of shit I do, purposely deceiving her isn't one of them.

Letting her come to the wrong conclusions, though... I can't help that, can I?

I don't know. But because she's looking up at me with such adoration in her soft brown eyes, all I can do is say, "It's chilly out, and your legs must be freezing. Come on. Let's go see if any of these restaurants have a table."

WE NEVER MAKE IT THAT FAR.

Later, I'll blame myself for being distracted by Nicolette. Growing up in the seedy underbelly of Springfield, if you're not aware of what's going on around you at all times, you're dead. Just because we were in the suburban Riverside instead, that doesn't mean that danger doesn't lurk around every damn corner.

In this case, danger comes in the form of a dark-haired, pleasant-faced, hard-eyed bastard in a long duster, a pair of black jeans, and a smile that makes me think about slugging him when he calls out to Nicolette from behind us and, immediately, she tenses.

I'm not afraid of this fucker.

Nic is.

It happens so quickly. One second, we were discussing whether we wanted seafood or Italian. The next, a male voice is hailing *my* Nicolette, calling her by her full first name to catch her attention. She didn't turn around, though she did stop.

Me? I spun on my heel, getting my first look at him.

Whoever he is, he's not familiar. I've never seen his face before, but when our eyes lock? It doesn't matter that he's not someone I've ever met. Like knows like, and whoever he is, he's a dangerous bastard.

When she sees that I've turned around, Nicolette reluctantly does so. To my surprise, she also takes two pointed steps away from me.

"What are you doing here?" she asks.

I know her well enough to catch the slight tremble to her voice.

So does this asshole—and when he hears it? The smug smile on his face widens. "I haven't seen you in ages, and that's how you greet me? Shit, Nicolette. I couldn't believe that it was you when I came heading down this street. I just wanted to say 'hi' since we happened to bump into each other. You can't fault me for that, can you?"

She opens her mouth, but nothing comes out. After a moment, she closes it, and nods.

Okay. Something's going on here. I don't know what it is—and I don't like it.

"Nic, you gonna introduce me to your friend?" I ask.

He holds out his hand. I don't take it.

He shrugs. "Name's Kieran." Kieran smiles, then adds, "I'm her brother."

Nicolette avoids his smile—and my gaze. Her eyes dart over to the man, then drop to the sidewalk. "My step-brother," she murmurs. "*Ex*-stepbrother."

"Your mom might have given up on my dad before moving on, darlin', but I haven't given up on you. We're *family*."

I go still, my own empty grin freezing on my face. "Darlin'?"

What the fuck? He's got the same Springfield accent as I do—which means *no* accent—and, yet, he affects this Southern drawl shit as he calls *my* Nicolette 'darlin''.

"Yeah," he says daringly. "A little pet name for my sister. What about you? You got a name?"

Not one he needs to know.

"This is my boss, Kieran. So cool it, okay?" Nicolette is still refusing to look at me as she says, "Stop this overpro-tective BS. You know how much I hate it."

He says something in response to it, but I'm not listening.

Nah. I'm a little preoccupied by what she called me.

'Boss'. Not 'boyfriend', which I get because I'm thirty and not a boy. 'Guy I'm fucking' might be too much for her, but what about 'guy I'm seeing'? Hell, I'd even take 'partner'.

But '*boss*'?

Is that all I am to her?

And what about this guy? He seems a little placated now that she's told him who I am—though I do notice she also didn't give him my name—but I haven't forgotten the way he called her darlin' like that.

Know why? Because, as far as I'm aware, she doesn't *have* a brother.

Tanner ran Nicolette. Because Devil is a paranoid bastard who's only gotten worse since he knocked Ava up, he has our tech guy run anyone who might integrate with the syndicate.

The only family Nicolette Williams has is her mother. That's it. Her mother was recently divorced from some insurance adjuster in Springfield. No kids for him, so how the hell does she even have an ex-stepbrother?

I don't know, but I'm sure as hell going to find out.

Because this is obviously a conversation for the two of them, I stay quiet as Nicolette wraps it up as quickly as she can. She uses the excuse that we have dinner reservations, then hooks her arm in mine before waving the guy off.

He's obviously not ready to end it, but what can he do? Giving me one last assessing look, he nods before strolling back the way he came. Meanwhile, Nicolette is trembling—and something tells me it has absolutely nothing to do with the March chill.

I let her lead me to the first restaurant we see so that she can sell her reservation story. However, before we step inside, I unloop my arm from hers and, fisting my hands at my side, I demand, "Who was he?"

"I told you who he was," Nicolette mumbles, ducking her head in the light from the restaurant's open doorway. A curtain of pretty blonde hair covers her face. "He was my stepbrother. That's all."

Hell fucking no. She's hiding. Hiding her face, hiding the truth...

No. Not from me.

Lifting my hand, I tuck her hair behind her shoulder. Then, once her face is clear, I cradle her chin, forcing her to look at me. "Nic. Who was he?"

Her eyes are panicked. He's gone, and now that he is, I can see the fear she struggled to hide during their conversation.

"Who is he?" she asks, her voice cracking. "That's Kieran Alfieri."

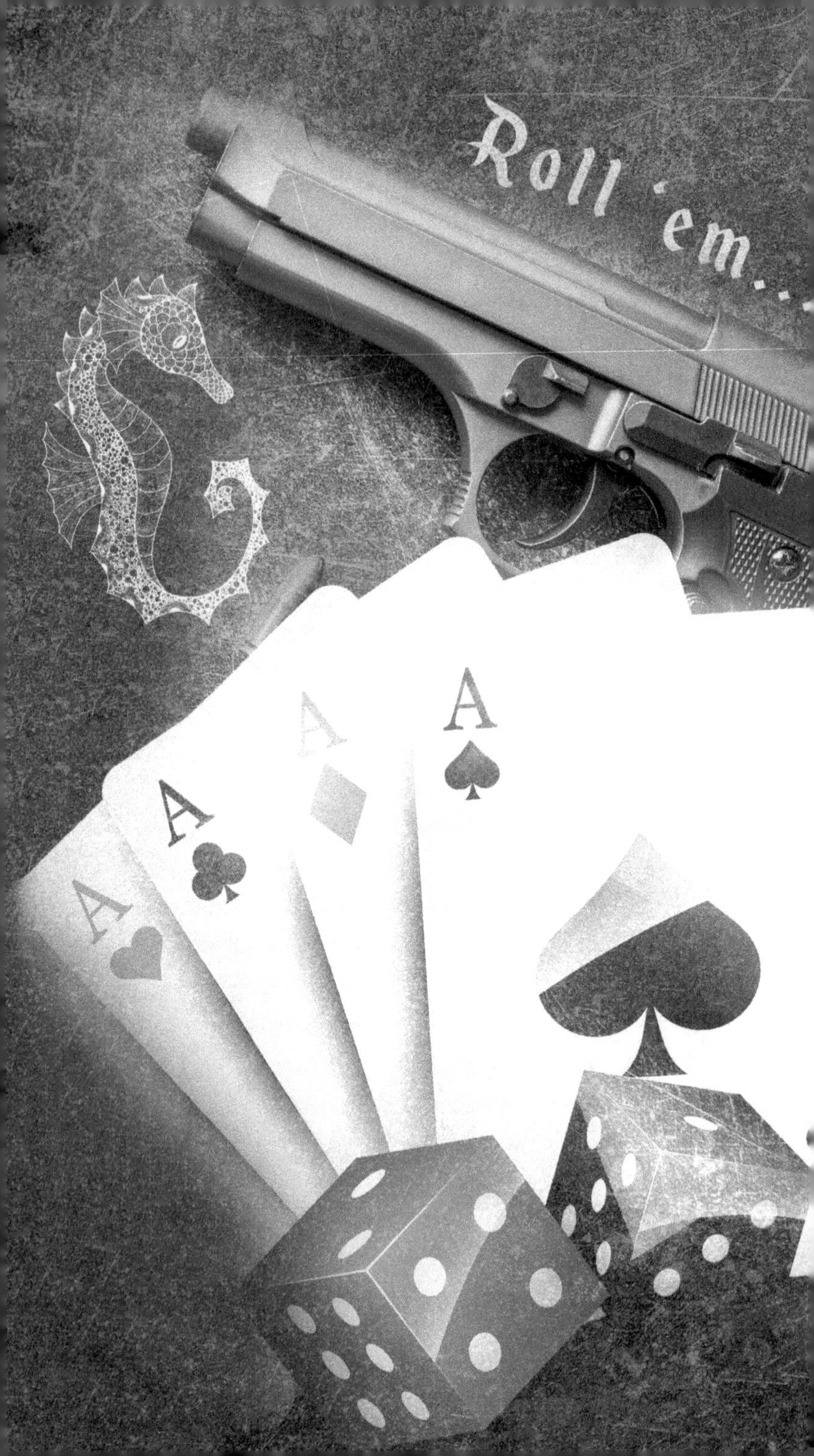
Roll 'em...

SIXTEEN
ADMISSION

NICOLETTE

I f I thought that Royce McIntyre was going to let me get away with just giving him a full name and that was it, then I haven't gotten to know him at all these last few weeks.

And since I *have*... yeah. I was able to get out of telling him just who I mistook him for the night I whacked him with a frying pan, though I always sensed him prying a little, trying to see if I'd slip up and confess things to him that I've spent years holding close to my chest.

I know that that's what I've been doing. It's not even because of him, either. For nearly half my life, Kieran's been my problem. My secret. First, because he was the cool, older stepbrother who flattered me with his attention. Then, once he convinced me to enter into a relationship with him, we couldn't let my friends know. My *mother* know. I was a mature sixteen-year-old, right? They wouldn't understand that I was grown enough to date a twenty-one-year-old—but he did.

And when we finally went public after I was 'legal' and my mom and Dave were no longer married... that's when secrets of a whole other sort began.

The things he did to me. The things he made me do to *him*.

Royce doesn't demand anything from me. He takes what I give, and gives me even more in return. Starting with the morning after when he made me breakfast, all the date nights we had in because he could sense I didn't want to go out until he pushed me past my limits tonight and brought me out of town to enjoy *Phantom*... he's been perfect.

And how do I repay him? By hiding Kieran until my ex just so happened to find us in Riverside.

Kieran doesn't leave Springfield. He certainly doesn't hang around musical theater venues... but he was here tonight, and he saw Royce—and, more importantly, Royce met *him*.

Damn it!

Dinner's out. Obviously. I don't have any appetite, and Royce's face tells me that sitting down to a meal is the last thing he wants to do at this moment. He doesn't say a word. He doesn't have to. He just places his arm over my coat—just about daring me to shake him off again—before guiding me back toward where his car is parked.

Talk about an awkward wait for the valet. Part of me is waiting for Kieran to pop out again, see Royce's arm slung over my shoulder, and question my 'he's my boss' lie. The other part wants to explain, to apologize, to justify, *some-*

thing, but when I try, Royce shakes his head, murmuring, "We'll talk in the car."

The wait is awkward, but it's not that long. The fifty he slipped the valet to cut the line probably helped, and if any of the other patrons bitched that we got helped first, they shut their traps when Royce's head shoots over his shoulders, glaring at any whisperers.

He nods at the valet, just about snatching the keys from the kid before striding toward the passenger's side of the car. As obviously pissed off as Royce is, he doesn't forget his manners. Holding the door open for me, he stands there and doesn't move until I take my seat.

I wince and, knowing this is unavoidable, do just that. Royce makes sure I'm tucked inside, shuts the door with more force than probably necessary, and stalks to his side.

I expect him to bombard me with questions about who Kieran is as soon as we drive off. Though I know he wants to do so, he plugs in an address to his phone— Paradise Suites, I notice, not my place—and starts down the road first.

Five minutes. I make it five minutes in the tense car before I blurt out, "It's not what you think."

Royce's jaw is tight. His eyes are straight ahead, locked on the road, as he says, "Funny that, since I have no fucking idea what I'm supposed to think. Tell me, Nic. That guy... I got his name, yeah, but you never really told me who he was. Is he really your brother? Sorry. *Step*brother? Or is he your stepbrother the same way I'm your boss?"

I knew from the expression on his face earlier that

calling him my boss bothered Royce. And while he *is*, we both know damn well he's more than that.

But that's the thing. I didn't want *Kieran* to know that.

"He is my stepbrother," I begin.

He snorts. "Darlin'."

I flinch.

Royce's eyes dart over to me. "He's more than just your stepbrother, isn't he?"

As if my reaction to Kieran's pet name for me didn't give it away. "Yes. But... I told you. It's not what you think."

"Okay." Royce pushes a button on the dash, engaging the hazards before coasting over to the side of the road. With the car idling, he shifts so he's looking at me. "Fine. Then tell me what it is so I know *what* to think."

A lump lodges in my throat. I shake my head. "You'll hate me."

Royce grips my chin between his fingers, forcing me to meet his baby blues. "Don't be fucking ridiculous, Nic. There isn't anything you can tell me that would ever make me hate you."

I want so badly to believe it. "Kieran is my ex."

"Ex-stepbrother."

"No. *Ex* ex. Like, ex-boyfriend."

He doesn't look surprised. "So you dated your stepbrother. Is that it? Why is that a problem? You're not blood-related, right?"

"No. I didn't even meet him until I was fourteen. That's when my mom married his dad. Dave. Dave Alfieri. They were together for five years before they divorced when I was nineteen."

Royce nods. "Okay. And what about the guy? You got together after your parents broke up?"

Not exactly. "I was with him for eight years. Not that I wanted to be, but because he refused to accept it whenever I tried to break up with him. He..." My voice trails off, but there must be something in my face that tells the true story because Royce's expression turns murderous.

"He hurt you?"

"Yeah." Simply put. Yeah. He hurt me in a lot of ways. Emotional. Physical. Sexual... he hurt me. "I was young. He's got five years on me, and he decided that I was his. And I was... until I left Springfield three years ago in May. I finally got away from him, and I hoped he hadn't realized I was back when I came to help my mom recover back in August... but, well, it looks like he has."

And I can only imagine how long he's been watching me...

Royce's eyes crease at the corners. I can just about see the gears whirring in his mind as he does the math. "Eight years... what? You hooked up when you were sixteen and he was—"

"Twenty-one, yup. But Kieran... he only called me his girlfriend once I hit sixteen. He called me his when he first moved into my house."

"When you were fourteen."

I nod.

"So he molested you."

Five years ago, I would've denied that's what he had done. Now?

"I thought he loved me," is all I say. "I know better now. I cut him out of my life. I haven't seen him face-to-

face since I left Springfield almost three years ago now...
until tonight."

"'I haven't given up on you...' That's what he said. He
thinks you still belong to him."

I have no other answer to that except for: "Yes."

He hesitates for a moment, thinking about everything
I said. "That camera... he put it up, didn't he? That's why
you hit me with the frying pan. You thought I was him."

I shudder out a breath. "I don't know for sure... he's so
goddamn careful, but... yes. I thought he was coming
after me again. He left me... this tiny statue thing in my
mother's mailbox that night. It couldn't have been anyone
else, but then he seemed to disappear and I wanted to
think I was wrong."

"But you weren't."

"I wasn't sure, though—not until I saw him tonight."

I haven't given up on you...

Royce gives his head a rough shake. "Fuck that. No. I
told you, Nic. You're not just my lover now. You're mine.
And if that pedo-asshole thinks he has a claim to you?
He'll have to get through me first."

I want to believe that. For so long, I hoped there was
someone out there who might protect me from Kieran,
but I learned that the only one I can rely on is myself. To
involve anyone else is to put them in the mafia enforcer's
path, and I know that's a dangerous place to be.

Royce doesn't.

I try to tell him. I try to confess that one of the reasons
Kieran had such complete control over me was because
of his status as a member of the Libellula Family.

I never get the chance.

As though Royce has heard everything he needs to, he nods to himself, turns off the hazards, and starts to drive again. And, well, I lose my nerve after that.

Because I saw him inputting his address into the GPS, I'm not surprised when he takes us back to the apartment complex where Royce and a few of the other Sinners live. I haven't gone inside of the Suites just yet, though I've been in the car when he stopped by to grab something from his place.

Tonight? It looks like I'm finally getting the chance to see where Royce lives... and I believe that until he uses a card from his wallet to engage the elevator, taking us all the way up to the penthouse floor.

Part of the reason I kept quiet for the last leg of the drive was because Royce was on his phone, furiously texting. I didn't have the nerve to point out that texting and driving was a shitty idea, and by the time he's knocking on the door, nodding at the dark-skinned man opening it up for us, I'm even more confused about what's going on—until the man at the door says, "Hey, Rolls. Devil's already headed out. He said he'll meet you at the Playground."

"Thanks, Case. You're gonna keep an eye on the girls?"

"That's what Devil told me to do."

Royce checks the watch on his wrist. "Is Ava sleeping?"

"No," comes a woman's voice. "Even if my husband wasn't whisked away by his second before I could take him to bed with me, this kid has decided that kicking me

193

and sending me off to pee every two seconds is their idea of fun."

"I told you," Case says as the mysterious Ava steps into the hallway. "That kid of yours is gonna be a football star someday."

"Football. Soccer. That's fine. I just can't handle it being my bladder. It's like I'm going to piss on myself— and, oh. I didn't realize Royce was bringing a guest. Is this Nicolette? I've been dying to meet your Nicolette."

His Nicolette, huh?

I look over at Royce. Then I look at Ava and, yup, a couple of different things fall into place for me. Because while the pretty brunette with the stunning green eyes has a petite build, that just means the large belly protruding from her middle is all the more obvious.

She's pregnant. Very pregnant.

And, somehow, she knows who I am.

"This is Nic," Royce says, introducing me needlessly. She'd guessed right. "Nic, this is Ava Crewes, Link's wife."

Oh.

Oh.

And there goes the last of the puzzle pieces.

Whoops. Looks like I wasn't just jealous of Devil's wife. It's his *pregnant* wife. Well, at least that explains why Royce had to go running to her side all those weeks ago since she's pretty far along now... even if I don't quite understand why he's brought me to meet her at nine o'clock at night *now*.

And then he kisses me on the forehead, and my attention is completely on him as he says, "Stay with Ava. I'll be back soon."

"Where are you going?"

"To make sure you're safe," is his response. He takes my hand in his, squeezing my fingers, then nods at Case. "I'll be back for her as soon as I'm done." Over Case's shoulder, he adds, "Take care of my girl, Ava."

"Take care of my husband, Royce, and I will."

He gives her a crooked grin, squeezes my fingers one last time, and then he's gone.

With one hand on her belly, Ava gestures at me to move further into the very expensive-looking hallway with the other. "Come on in, Nicolette. Case? We're going to sit in the living room."

"I'll watch the door. Don't worry. No one's getting past me."

She beams at the man, but as soon as she gestures for me to follow her into this massive living room with a chandelier attached to the ceiling, and couches I'm afraid I'll dirty by sitting on, she whispers to me, "Sorry about the bodyguard. That's all Link. We're never safer than in the Suites, but he insists, and I'm sure you'll agree: with these men, it's just easier to pick your battles."

I can't say she isn't right.

Ava picks a white loveseat to plop down awkwardly on. She pats the cushion next to her. "It's so nice to meet you. I've heard so much about you."

My back goes ramrod straight without even joining her on the couch. "You have?"

"Of course. It's a big thing when one of the Sinners in the inner circle get a serious girlfriend. Right now, there's only two wives, me and Jasmine... have you met Jas?"

I shake my head.

"Not surprised. Royce is so head over heels for you, he's keeping you to himself for now. That's okay. Once he realizes that the rest of us won't scare you away, I'm sure he'll bring you around more. Maybe not when I was getting ready to take my husband to bed... I'm telling you, these pregnancy hormones are no joke... but if you're half as amazing as Royce tells Link, I'd love a friend."

You know what? I would, too.

And because I'd like to start this budding friendship on the right foot, I say, "I'm sorry. I don't even know why Royce brought me here—"

"Really? He didn't tell you?"

I shake my head.

"Oh. It's because he's meeting my husband at the Playground so they can figure out how to get rid of the creep who thinks you're his."

I blink. "What?"

"I know, I know, you probably don't want me to know about that. I promise, it won't get past me and Link. Well, Case, too, but he's not listening. Right, Case?"

"Right, Ava," he calls back.

My legs are shaky. I'm already not the best in heels, this dress was a much better idea earlier this evening, and I think the shock of seeing Kieran has finally worn off. No surprise when I stumble, then drop down on the couch.

Ava pats my hand. "Don't worry. All of this organized crime stuff was rough for me to get used to in the beginning. But it gets better."

Yeah.

I wish I could believe *that*, too.

Roll 'em...

SEVENTEEN

HEATHER VALIANT

ROYCE

The building attached to the Devil's Playground is Sinners Syndicate property. From the outside, it looks like it could belong to an everyday, ordinary office. It has plenty of space, even a few cubicles we don't use, and a conference room we *do* use for our meets.

One of the largest offices we own belongs to Tanner Fielding, our resident tech whiz. With screens everywhere, more keyboards than any guy could need, and—because this is Tanner—a hammock hanging in one corner, it's his home away from home... and the spot where Link and I meet him.

I had to involve my boss. For one thing, I had to make sure that jumping to murder wasn't me being hasty—because that's what I want to do. After hearing Nicolette tell me who that bastard really was, I wanted to kill him.

But that takes me to the other thing.

Kieran Alfieri. The moment she gave me that name, it triggered something. It was familiar in a hazy sort of way, and I texted Link about it on my drive back to Springfield. He confirmed what I suspected: I'd heard that name before because Alfieri is a Dragonfly.

Abso-fucking-lutely *wonderful*.

That shouldn't stop me. I mean, we're all criminals here. But there's being a mobster, and being a goddamn pedophile. Nineteen-year-old guys shouldn't be molesting fourteen-year-olds, the same way as a twenty-one-year-old shouldn't have a sixteen-year-old girlfriend. It's as simple as that. Add that to the fact that Nicolette made it clear that he abused her in more ways than one, and I should just arrange his murder.

But he's a Dragonfly, we're in a fucking truce, and that makes things more difficult.

That's where Tanner comes in.

Before I hired Nicolette on at the Playground, Tanner ran her. At some level, anyone who hopes to work for the syndicate has to go through our version of a background check. We have to make sure that we know who we're letting into our organization. It didn't matter that she was slinging drinks at our club. If you work at one of our properties, you're an honorary Sinner.

It's a cursory search, though, checking for ties to other syndicates. The blood test checks for any diseases. That's imperative when our wallets expect a certain standard for the girls who entertain them upstairs, and while Nicolette assured me she wouldn't want to rent a bed to increase her pay, that, too, was standard.

Nothing flagged on her end, and Tanner explains why when I walk into his office to find him and Link waiting for me.

Because Nicolette told me during her interview that she used to live in Springfield, moved to Willowbrook for a handful of years, then came back, the search didn't dig too deep. Tanner only went as far back as her mother's most recent ex-husband—not the four others, including one David Alfieri, and his son, Kieran.

Now that we know what to look for, though, I pace around the room, listening as Tanner discovers what he's learned about Nicolette's smarmy ex.

Kieran Alfieri has been a part of the Libellula Family since he was twenty-two. He worked as a runner at first, then a soldier, and when I was beginning to hope that he was a bit player that Damien would sacrifice in favor of continuing our truce, Tanner runs his fingers through his shoulder-length straw-colored hair and drops the bomb:

"He's an enforcer now."

Shit.

"He has fourteen leaves."

Even better.

We have the name, but it's the Dragonflies who really act like sinners. I understand that, in this line of work, death is sometimes necessary; considering I'm here, trying to see if I can take Alfieri out without jeopardizing the truce, I get that. We have enforcers, too. Hell. I'm in charge of clean-up because I think of it as my own type of penance, so I see what our enforcers really can do.

I've also seen what a Dragonfly enforcer is capable of.

Sick fucking bastards.

To make it even worse, they don't accept death as a part of the job. Oh, no. They celebrate it, each of the enforcers tattooing a simple green leaf down the back of one of their biceps whenever they have a kill that benefits their Family.

And Alfieri has *fourteen*.

That's not just Alfieri being a Dragonfly. That's Alfieri being someone essential to Damien Libellula—and just about untouchable to me.

He hurt Nic. And, because of my position as the underboss of the Sinners, I can't retaliate unless I want to start up another war.

What happened with Heather... I never could have seen that coming. If I purposely go ahead with any plots of revenge against Alfieri, I'll be inviting a war that might end with even more blood being on my hands.

Fuck!

Link is standing with his back against the only bit of wall in this room that doesn't have a screen on it. His arms are crossed over his broad chest, a scowl tugging on his features as he watches me pace.

Then, as though he knows what I'm thinking—and I'm pretty sure he does—Link says, "Remember the truce, Royce."

"Fuck the truce."

I'm frustrated. I'm usually so much better at controlling myself, especially when Link and I are around other Sinners.

He knows it, too. Jerking his chin at Tanner, he says, "Take a walk."

Like me and the rest of the inner circle, Tanner's been here since the beginning. He knows when to test Link—and when to lower his head, grab one of his tablets, and get the fuck out.

Link waits until Tanner shuts the door behind him before he pushes off of the wall. "Listen to me, Royce. I get you're upset. I'm fucking pissed we missed this, too. Truce or no truce, we've got someone with Dragonfly ties slipping in right under our noses. But you and I both know that this... this isn't just about your waitress."

"The hell it isn't—"

"This is about you sleepwalking through life the last six years, blaming yourself for what happened to the Valiant girl. Now you're awake again. You have Nicolette, and you want to be the hero."

I know better than to curse out Lincoln Crewes, but I'm close. Closer than I've ever been—which is why I clamp my mouth shut.

He steps into me. He's got a couple of inches on me, and he uses them to his advantage as he looms. "You didn't pull the trigger, Royce. Her idiot brother was pissed, and a wannabe enforcer had shitty aim. She died. So did the enforcer. But it wasn't your fault. Shit... even standing up for your fucked-up cousin was a good thing."

I sputter out a laugh. "Jake is fucked-up."

Link claps his hand on my shoulder. "Yeah. At least we just kept an eye on our girls. What he does... I've heard the stories. He's your blood, but the sooner he's out of Springfield, the better."

I know what Link's doing. In his way, he's distracting

me from going after Alfieri by igniting my protective instincts for my cousin.

Joke's on the boss. I can be protective over Jake *and* Nicolette.

"Don't worry. I got eyes on him."

"I do, too, and he's been toeing the line so far. But I'm not worried about Jake right now. I'm worried about *you*."

He's not the only one.

I shake off his hand, then demand, "Do you trust me?"

"Royce—"

"Link. Do you trust me?"

"You know I fucking do."

"Then I got this." I give him my winning grin even though, behind my smile, my jaw is tight, my teeth grinding. I breathe in through my nose and pretend to relax. "You're right. I won't fuck with the truce. I'll leave Alfieri alone, keep my eye on Nic at the same time as I make sure Jake doesn't get into any more trouble."

"That's all I ask."

"But if he comes after her—"

I don't even have to finish my sentence. This is the man who watched Damien Libellula put a gun to Ava's head in order to get his damn truce. It made sense at the time, but I know Link. He probably wonders why he didn't put a bullet in Damien once Ava was safe.

I've never shot anyone before. But if I'm put in a situation like that?

I *will*.

THE FIRST THING I DO AFTER OUR MEET IS SPLIT OFF FROM Link, then head out to the club.

Jessie's off tonight, but Francesca is in charge of the floor. Considering she's as much Jessie's second as I am Link's, I have a quick conversation with her over the posted schedule. At the Playground, Jessie makes up three weeks in advance, letting the waitresses, the bartenders, the barbacks, and the bussers know when they're expected to work. If they can't, it's on them to find a replacement.

Tonight? I put Francesca in charge of covering about half of Nicolette's shifts. Taking her off the schedule completely might be too much. The last thing I want is to be as controlling as her asshole ex was, but if he could follow us to Riverside? If he's been leaving fucking *trinkets* in her mailbox, walking around in a hoodie on her camera? How much do I want to bet that he's been sneaking around the Playground?

I don't blame her for keeping him a secret. I wish she hadn't, if only because it makes my job protecting her that much harder when I didn't even *know* that she needed to be protected from some Dragonfly scum.

Know what else makes it hard? Link's goddamn truce.

My first instinct is to ban any of Damien's guys from our club. Since part of pretending like we don't hate the damn Dragonflies just for existing is letting them visit the Playground if they dare to, it would be going against the truce to block all of them from entering. Since I can't do that, I settle for showing a picture of Kieran Alfieri that Tanner sent me to the bouncers, warning them that it's their dicks if they let him in.

I can't ban all of the Dragonflies. I sure as fuck can ban this one.

Between cutting the amount of time Nicolette spends here and putting the fear of Devil into the staff to keep Alfieri out, my bases are covered for now. I head back to the Suites to retrieve Nic.

That's another issue. I want her to move in with me so that I'll know where she it at any given moment, but I know better than to push that right now. The most I can do is invite her to stay over tonight while she's shaky, then hope that she doesn't want to go back to her place tomorrow.

The hug she gives me when I walk into Link and Ava's penthouse tells me that she missed me while I was gone. It's late at this point, after one in the morning, so she doesn't argue at all when I bring her a couple of floors down to my apartment instead of bringing her back to her mother's house.

I do expect Nic to give me shit when I tell her that she needs to cut her shifts back while we figure out just how we want to handle the Alfieri situation. Is it a dick move to tell her when she's still shaky from seeing him? Probably. Should I have waited until morning when we were both rested and a little removed from what happened tonight? Oh, yeah.

Do I?

Nope.

I expect her to give me shit, though I'm hoping that she won't because I'm dropping this news on her before she gets some sleep. To my surprise, she doesn't.

Instead, she takes my hand in hers, tilting her head back so that she's meeting my gaze. "Okay."

We're standing in the foyer of my apartment. I flicked on the light after I invited her in, but she's not looking around at my bachelor pad. Her eyes are completely on me.

"Okay?"

"Yeah. If you think that's a good idea, I'm okay with it. Not for long... I can't give up all that cash... but I trust you."

Whoa.

I look down at her. Earlier tonight, we set out for a five o'clock showing of *The Phantom of the Opera*. Nicolette had her hair styled in tousled waves, make-up on point, the skin-tight black dress hugging every curve. Fucking stunning.

Now?

She's braided her hair loosely, tossing it over her shoulder. The make-up's been wiped clean, revealing purple circles beneath her soft brown eyes. The dress is gone, and while I mourn that, she's wearing a pair of low-slung sweatpants and a white t-shirt that shows off her black bra. It's some of Ava's pre-pregnancy clothes, an outfit that Link's wife let Nicolette borrow so that she'd be comfy while I was gone.

You know what? She's still fucking stunning.

And I don't deserve her at all.

I trust you...

Heather trusted me once, too. I barely knew the girl. Because I was being her 'hero' by standing between her and Jake, she thought she was in love with me.

I only hope that Nicolette someday feels the same.

But if she does? She's falling for the idea of who she thinks Royce McIntyre is. And while the man I am when I'm with her *is* who I am, there's so much I've kept from her because I was afraid of running her off.

From the beginning, I was convinced she'd take off the first chance she got. But after tonight... I finally know what Nicolette was hiding from me.

Maybe it's time to come clean about what I've been hiding from her.

Holding onto her hand, I lead her toward the leather couch in my living room. I sit down, then tug on her, guiding her to sit right next to me.

Not my lap. Hours ago, I was ballsy, inviting Nic to perch on my lap before I worked her panties over, giving her my cock. So her dress is gone and it would take more effort to shimmy off her borrowed sweatpants. That's not why I don't do it. If I'm going to come clean, I need to do it now—and not be distracted by her ass on my lap.

"Royce? What's up?"

I know she's gotta be exhausted. Part of me is, too. But I don't want to be a pussy. I don't want the excuse to skip out on this conversation.

I squeeze her fingers. "You were with a Dragonfly." I almost want to grab a drink to wash the taste of saying *that* out of my mouth. "Do you know anything about Heather Valiant?"

I'm not sure what I want her answer to be. There are so many stories, so many rumors about what happened that night... no matter how hard Link tried, he could never get them all straight. Not with our crew, not with Damien's. The most he could do was back me up, threatening that anyone who came after me would have to go through him first.

Maybe it would be better if she doesn't—and then, as my heart sinks, she nods.

"Actually, yeah. She was Danny Valiant's sister. I know him because he was an enforcer, like Kieran. She got involved with this guy... let me remember. I know this. Was it Josh?"

"Jake," I correct.

She nods. "Right. Jake something. She wasn't a Dragonfly, but her brother was, and this Jake guy wanted to take her away from the Family and share her with a Sinner. Danny told her to break it off with both of the guys. That maybe Sinners do that shit, but Dragonflies don't. But Heather... we weren't friends."

Nic lets out a soft, unamused chuckle. "Kieran didn't let me have friends. But we were stuck in the same spot. Dragonfly property who couldn't get out. She thought the Sinner would save her, but before he could, a different enforcer decided to take him out. Or her. No one really knows... but he shot Heather, and she died." Shaking her head, her braid falling down her back, she adds, "That was my wake-up call. Even if Kieran didn't kill me, staying in Springfield might. It took me another three years to finally get the balls to break it off with him, but I did it so I didn't end up like Heather Valiant."

That's a gut punch I didn't fucking need. Because, after hearing all that, once she hears *my* confession? She might decide that fate has a twisted sense of humor because, in a way, she *has*.

She waits a moment while I stay quiet before she asks, "Why? I haven't heard anyone bring up Heather in years... so why did you?"

"Because I'm the Sinner."

Roll 'em...

EIGHTEEN
SEAHORSE

ROYCE

Nicolette screws up her face. "What?"

"The guy you were talking about... I was the one who was there when we got shot at. You're right. I'll never know who that prick was trying to fire at, but the bullets found Heather that night." I take a deep breath, then admit in a stoic voice, "I held her as she died."

"Oh, Royce... that's fucking awful." She lays her hand on my thigh. "I didn't know... they only mentioned the Josh—the Jake guy. But it was you... Shit. That must have hurt so bad. You must have really loved her."

If only I had.

I shake my head. "I barely knew her."

She blinks. "I... I don't understand."

"Part of what you said is right. Jake... he was obsessed with this woman he met at college. He followed her here, discovered she was the sister of a Dragonfly, and decided to pursue her anyway. She wasn't interested. She wanted nothing to do with him, but Jake... he's *different*. He didn't understand. He wanted her, and he did everything he could to take her. But before he could wear her down, she came to me to get him to stop."

"Because you're the Sinners' underboss?"

"Because Jake is my younger cousin."

Nicolette's mouth parts.

Yeah. I know.

"She had no idea I was in the life when she found me at the Playground. To her, I think it was a perk. When she saw me, she saw her way out. Heather thought I could get Jake to leave her alone *and* get her overprotective brother off her back. I'm a fixer, right? She wanted me to fix her. She told me she loved me. She wanted me to love her, too."

Nic rubs my thigh with her palm. She's not drawing away from me, which is a plus, though her face has shadowed over. "Did you?"

"No."

"Oh."

"I'm sorry. I know I'm an asshole. When I say I couldn't care less about this woman I didn't know... it was my responsibility as family to keep an eye on Jake. Once I learned she had Dragonfly ties, I got him to back off. He's not in the life. I didn't want him getting involved. But, somehow, she convinced herself she was in love with me instead... and it got back to her brother anyway. Like me with my cousin, he had eyes on her. When she called me and begged me to meet her that night, I did because I was going to tell her there couldn't be anything between us. If she didn't want one McIntyre, she didn't get to trade him for another. But then... she died."

And I've spent the last six years wondering if I'd shut her down sooner, if I hadn't felt bad and gone to meet her on neutral territory that night, if she'd still be alive.

It was a Dragonfly who killed her. I was still shot at, though I'll never know if I was a target. The only way we avoided full-out war was because it *was* neutral territory, and the triggerman confessed to Damien that he took out a fellow Dragonfly's property.

Because, like Nic, that's all Heather Valiant was.

She moves closer, so close that she actually is almost on my lap. "Why are you telling me this?"

Good question.

"Because you trust me," I tell her honestly. "And I need you to know what kind of man you think you do."

"Oh, I know what kind of man you are."

"And what's that?"

"The one who brought me to see one of my favorite shows, and who made it an evening to remember before Kieran tried to fucking ruin it. But I won't let him. I was his property once. I'm not now." Nicolette reaches for my belt. "I'm *yours*."

I'm struck speechless as her nimble fingers start to undo it.

I don't normally wear a belt. Our syndicate doesn't have an exact dress code. Link insists that the face of the Sinners—guys like me, him, Luca, Killian—we all have to wear suits so that we can go against our early, thuggish reputation. Pressed pants, button-downs, and a jacket are common, though some guys wear ties and belts, some don't. No tie for me, but I'm hit or miss, usually more miss, with the belt.

And then, a couple of nights ago, Nicolette bought me one.

She noticed that some of the crew at the Playground used them. Though she knows damn well it's not because I can't afford it, she still took money of her own—money that she's determined to earn and keep—and bought me a belt in case I needed one.

I've worn it since, and the hungry look on her face whenever I began to unbuckle it these last few nights makes me wonder if she bought it more for me or for her. It doesn't matter. I'll do anything if it excites my Nic, including fiddling with the fucking thing whenever I get dressed.

Luckily, it's a lot easier getting it off than on, some-thing Nicolette proves as she easily undoes it for me right now.

I watch her curiously. I sure as hell don't stop her, and I'm rewarded when she unzips my pants next. Reaching for my cock, she takes a firm grip of it, then eases down to her knees.

I love pussy, but Nicolette? She's got a thing about cocksucking. Once we became intimate—once I proved to her that nothing will stop me from pleasuring her with my mouth—she showed me that she's just as eager to give me oral.

I don't expect it. That would be a dick move, and I'd rather have her come on my face than force her to her knees. But when she's offering...

Only one problem. Considering the conversation we just had, I'm not so sure *why* she's offering.

Because she thinks she's my property now?

Because I'm *hers*?

Maybe it's not that... and I decide to just let her show me affection this way as she swirls her practiced tongue around the head of my cock, strangling any answer from me the moment I feel the heat of her mouth on my skin. I shudder, taking a deep breath as Nic sucks me in a little deeper, taking the first two inches while gently grazing my dick with her teeth.

I was limp when she grabbed me; sorry, an asshole I might be, but reminiscing about a woman dying in my arms just doesn't get me going. Nicolette taking over? Nicolette grabbing me like she has every right to—and she *does*?

Nicolette nibbling on the underside of my cock, fisting it, stroking it, doing anything she can to make me feel good?

I'm hard in no time, and grateful for the distraction.

That's what she's doing, isn't it? Took me a second, but I got there eventually. Ripping me out of the past, thrusting me right into the present with her, she swoops her braided hair over her shoulder, cocks her head slightly, and takes me as deep as she can before hollowing her cheeks.

My sac tightens. I lean back into the couch, clutching the cushions as she worms her way closer. Nic is bobbing her head now, doing all of the work while I sit there and let her.

This is for me. She doesn't have the words to tell me—and since that means she'd stop blowing me in order to do so, I'm fine with that—but the message is clear. Heather might be gone, but it wasn't my fault. I was the poor guy who got stuck in the middle of it, all because I wanted to help my cousin and the woman he was convinced he loved.

It was obsession, plain and simple. What he has with this Simone woman now? That's probably obsession, too, but... *fuck*. That's not my problem anymore. Jake got himself into this mess. He can get himself out of it, too. I'll help him if he really does need me. But if he doesn't? I'm not worried about him.

I was obsessed with Nic. No denying that. I was obsessed, but the more I've gotten to know this woman, the more I'm convinced it *is* love. I love her, this magnificent creature who went to her knees for no other reason than because she knows I needed this connection.

Heather died, and I couldn't save her. I spent six years dealing with the guilt—and I barely fucking knew her.

But Nicolette... if anything ever happened to her? I don't know what I would do.

I'm not so sure I want to find out, either.

Grunting under my breath, I force myself to focus on the now instead of the future or the past. I try to hold out as long as I can, but it's been a stressful twenty-four hours and I'm wrung out over thinking about my past, plus everything I learned about Nicolette's.

She's certain that Alfieri won't come after her right away. In the three weeks since she caught him sneaking around her house, there's been no sign of him until tonight, and she doesn't think that's going to change.

She's also absolutely certain that he didn't buy the fact that I'm just her boss for a single second.

Good. Because I'm *not*. I'm hers, just like she's mine, and I prove that by shooting my load into her mouth with an anguished cry of her name.

Nicolette takes every last drop, swallowing it completely before wiping her mouth with the edge of her thumb. There's something in her soft brown eyes I can't quite understand when she glances up at me, but there's also lust and affection and, unless I'm completely making it up, *love*.

"You're such a good girl," I murmur, even more satisfied when she preens at my praise. "Now come on up here, baby." I pat the cushion next to me, gesturing for her lay down. "It's my turn. Let me make you feel good."

Let me make you remember that you're here with me, that monster is your *past, and I won't let him hurt you ever again...*

I need this. I need her surrender, and maybe I should have realized my mistake before I did, but I don't as I reach the bottom hem of her t-shirt and start to push it higher.

When the shirt goes up halfway, she circles my wrists with her fingers. "Royce," she murmurs. "You know I don't like that."

I do know. But it's been weeks since the first time we fucked, I've sucked and licked and played with every other part of her, she's done the same to me, and she *still* won't let me remove her shirt?

I don't get it. It doesn't make sense. Maybe before she came clean about her past with Alfieri, I'd understand being uncomfortable, but I've made it clear: I'm not Alfieri. I won't hurt her. I want her to trust me.

Why can't she trust me with this?

"You know you don't have to hide anything from me, right? There's nothing about you that I don't like."

I press a kiss to her navel, tonguing her belly button before rubbing my nose against the gentle swell of her lower abdomen. She writhes beneath me, enjoying my caresses. Taking heart in that, I skim my hands up her sides.

Her shirt is bunched up beneath her tits now, her full midsection on display. She seems comfortable enough like this. Why not go a little further?

Slipping my fingers beneath the cups, I shove her bra over her tits so that I have full access to them.

That's all I wanted. I love her body, but after fantasizing over the cleavage she had on display down at the Playground for months now, I've been dreaming about getting my palms on her breasts without anything coming between us.

They're gorgeous. A perfect handful, perky just the way a twenty-seven-year-olds are when they're not sagged down after having kids, with pretty pink nipples that have my mouth watering.

"See? I told you there was nothing about you that isn't fucking beautiful. Look at these tits." I lower my head, just about to suck one of those perfect nipples into my mouth—

—and that's when I see what she *was* hiding from me. "What's this?"

Nicolette suddenly pales. Sitting up quickly, her hand

cups the curve of her breast, slapping over the ink, but there's no point hiding it anymore. I know what I saw.

I just don't know what I'm supposed to do about it.

"Royce, I..."

That's all she says. Scooting away from me, covering the tattoo with one hand, tugging down her bra awkwardly with the other, she mouths wordlessly as I stare, half-disbelieving.

It's a *dragonfly*.

OVER THE YEARS, BOTH WHEN THE LIBELLULA FAMILY WAS just starting out, and once they were firmly our rivals, I've seen a shit ton of dragonfly tattoos.

I always thought it was hysterical. One of the things Damien sniffed over when me and Link split off from him was how Link decided that anyone loyal to our local mafia would have a devil tattoo in honor of him. And, yet, what did Damien do?

Insist that anyone in his Family be marked with a dragonfly.

I get it. Libellula is literally the Italian translation for the word 'dragonfly', and god knows that Damien is insanely proud of his heritage. He formed his crime family to protect his birth family—including his younger sister, Genevieve—and used the dragonfly as both the name and symbol for his gang.

Unlike Devil's specific design—the devil horns and tail that nearly all Sinners have—Damien's dragonflies don't necessarily look the same. They come in different shapes and sizes and colors, but they're as professionally done as anything Cross can do.

The tattoo that is drawn just below the curve of Nicolette's right boob? That one definitely isn't.

The lines are shaky. I'm no artist—I leave that to Cross—but even I recognize a shit job. I'd chalk it up to the positioning since it couldn't have been easy to start on her side, then curve up around the tit itself, but a pro could do it.

And that tells me a pro didn't do it.

So, who did?

Deep down, I already know the answer. Because this? This isn't a tattoo that marks the wearer as a proud Dragonfly.

Oh, no.

This is a brand that marks a woman as a Dragonfly's property.

I swallow the rush of anger threatening to gag me. If what I suspect is true... it's not Nic's fault. Yes, she hid it from me, but wouldn't I do the same thing? My tattoo is where it is, not because I'm ashamed of it, but because it means something to me. Anyone who doesn't think I'm a Sinner only has to ask me to prove it and I'd start unbuttoning my shirt gladly.

Not Nic. Poor girl... she spent the last few weeks clinging to her shirts because she didn't want me to see it.

Cool it, Royce. Don't give her any reason to think she made the right decision, hiding it from you.

I've only just found out about Alfieri. If I hadn't known the truth of her past... if I hadn't known she had a tie to the Dragonflies... how would I have reacted to seeing that the woman I was obsessing over was a member of my syndicate's rivals? Truce or no truce, I know the answer to that.

I'd feel tricked. Betrayed. Like I fucked up again, and it was like falling in with Heather all over again.

But she isn't Heather. She's Nicolette, and I take a deep breath and ask one question: "Did Alfieri do this to you?"

She gulps. "Yes."

I wait a beat, then ask another: "Did you want him to?"

Nicolette shakes her head. "No." It's a whisper. More than that, it's a *confession*. "I told him not to. He... he didn't like me saying no. I wasn't allowed. And then... he did it himself."

He marked her. Prison-style, if I'm any judge, with a needle and some ink and no way to keep her safe from infection except a hope and fucking prayer.

Okay. *Okay*.

I move to the next cushion, closing the gap between us. I don't want to push her, so I keep my hands to myself, though I do turn my body so that I'm all she can see.

"Do you want it gone?"

Her head bobs, loose hair falling like a curtain into her face. Before I can push it away, she shoves the strands behind her ears. "I looked into getting it removed. I couldn't afford that. Covering it up would be better, but even that was too pricy. Trust me. I'd do anything to get rid of it, but I've just kept it covered up with clothes the last ten years instead."

Ten years...

223

Fuck that. She spent ten years with a tattoo she didn't want?

I can fix that. "Have you thought about it? If you could cover that shit up... what would you put over it?"

For a moment, I see hope written on her face. Like she honestly believed that tattoo might be the thing that pushes me over the edge, that sends *me* running... and she's both surprised that it isn't, while also taking a moment to believe that I might be able to do something for her that she hasn't been able to.

Of course. I'm a fixer. That's what I do.

"Go on, Nic. Tell me."

"It's silly."

I take the chance to sidle up next to her on the couch. Laying my hand on the edge of Nicolette's jaw, I angle her head so that she has no choice but to look straight into my eyes.

"It's not. So tell me."

An impish grin. "A seahorse."

Okay, then.

Seahorse it is.

NINETEEN
CROSS

ROYCE

Talk about fucking déjà vu.

Almost two hours ago, I was in the back offices of the Playground, having a meet with Tanner and Link. Tanner's l long gone by now, Link hurrying back to be with Ava, but while the sound-proofing means it's quiet as I let Nicolette in, I know we're not alone.

Tanner's set-up is here, but another one of the offices belongs to Carlos 'Cross' da Silva. The artist for our crew, it's his responsibility to ink any Sinner with Devil's mark. Like a right of passage for each of our members, once you're a Sinner, you get branded with the devil horns and the tail.

My tat is different. When Link lined me up to be his second, I wanted to show him that I was loyal to him and his vision. I didn't just get the horns and the tail. Oh, no. I had Cross draw me a full-on devil that stretched from my left hip up to my pec. It's detailed, with a swarthy face, black hooves, and even a pitchfork. Then, because I'm 'Rolls', I had him add a pair of dice beneath it, showing off snake eyes with the words 'Roll 'em' written in a gothic-style font beneath the dice.

It fucking *hurt*. I decided then and there that I would never get another tat, and I haven't. Besides, with the devil and the dice, it's got the two most prominent facets of my personality right there: the life and gambling. What else would I need to ink on my skin?

So while I don't visit Cross in his office often, I'm usually the one who brings new recruits down to get branded. I've also known Cross since we were in high school together, long before either of us ended up in organized crime. I was the popular golden boy, he was the loner artist, but we lived on the same block and developed a fast friendship.

I'm the one who brought him into the gang when Link was building it up. Because of that, he's in the inner circle with us, even though the only reason he stays a Sinner is because it gives him plenty of canvases to practice his craft on.

When I texted him and told him I needed a cover-up tat done *stat*, I didn't expect any excuses. I didn't get any, either. He told me to head on over and he'd be ready to take care of it.

Cross is a quiet guy. He's not the type to ask questions, or show any hint of curiosity. So when I lead Nicolette into the room, he nods at me, looks her over, nods at her, then gestures to the chair.

"So, Rolls tells me you're interested in a cover-up. Where is the old tat?"

Oh, fuck.

Why is it just occurring to me now that, in order to get rid of the old tattoo, Cross has to have full access to her chest?

I know I'm being irrational. I know I'm being jealous and overprotective.

That doesn't stop me from snapping, "She keeps the bra on."

Cross nods. "On the boob. Got it. Still gonna need to see it, and if that means the bra comes off—"

"The bra doesn't come off."

Nicolette reaches out, laying her hand on my arm. "It's okay, Royce."

Cross glances over at me before turning his attention to Nicolette. "For you maybe, miss. I think Rolls is having a hard time thinking of me looking at your chest." His dark eyes are back on me. "You've seen one rack, you've seen 'em all. It's just skin to me, buddy."

I wish I could believe that.

"Royce," murmurs Nicolette, taking her hand back, folding her fingers together in her lap. "I don't have to do this if you don't want me to."

Damn it. Can I really deprive Nic of something she so desperately wants—and that I *need*—because I don't want Cross getting a peek at her tits?

I glare at him, then soften my expression as I face Nicolette again. "Sorry. Don't mind me. I'm being an ass. You're the one who has to be topless for him to do this. If you're okay with it, I am."

I'm *not*.

She nods. "If he's willing to get rid of the fucking thing on me, I don't care." Then, to prove it, she shrugs off her jacket, slips off her t-shirt, and unhooks her bra in quick succession.

Cross, to be fair, barely notices. He's busy prepping his station, and when Nic murmurs, "Ready," he grabs a tube of something from his tray and wheels his chair closer to her.

He reaches out to get a look at her old ink.

I growl under my breath.

"Rolls," he says, more patiently than I probably deserve, "I can't do the cover-up if you won't even let me touch her."

Does he think I don't know that?

I wave my hand at the tube in his, buying time to get a hold of myself. "It's a tat, Cross. What do you need that ointment for?"

"It's a numbing cream," Cross answers, and I know him well enough to tell that I'm testing his last nerve. "I find it's good for clients not used to getting ink. I put it on, wait about twenty minutes, then when I start the outline, they don't feel anything."

I tap my side. "You didn't offer it to me when you did mine."

Sometimes, Cross has this tiny smile of his that says he finds the whole fucking world funny. I get that now as he says, "Because I only offer it to those I don't want to watch squirm."

"Dickhead."

He shrugs. "Fair enough. But I like to think of it as payback."

"Payback? For what?"

"For stealing my fruit cups senior year. You don't even like peaches, Rolls."

I glance over at Nic, who is currently watching this exchange between me and my old friend with rapt attention. I wink at her. "True, but you can definitely say I love me some *cream*."

Cross rolls his eyes as he opens the ointment and plops a dollop of that shit on his glove. "Stay classy, sunshine," he mutters.

To his credit, he quickly and efficiently swipes the cream over the tattoo. Only a small amount goes on her actual tit, and Cross gets it done, then scoots his rolling chair back toward his station. After wiping his gloved finger off, he picks up an iPad and an Apple pencil.

"Rolls told me you want a seahorse. I'm going to draw you up a mock-up here, see if that's what you're thinking. We can make adjustments as we go, talk about coloring and shading... but give me an hour, hour and a half, and that dragonfly will be history."

"Thank you," she breathes out, her chest rising and falling with the motion. "I appreciate it."

I nod at Cross. "Can she put her shirt back on while you do that?"

"Only if you want to wipe the cream off. Kinda defeats the purpose of putting it on, and then she'll feel more pain than necessary."

I mutter a curse under my breath.

Cross peers up at me. "You want to wait outside while we do this?"

And leave him alone with her? "No."

Nic shifts in the seat. She gives me a small smile of her own before saying, "I've got an idea. The cover-up is on my right side. If you don't want my tits hanging out while he's working, why don't you come on over here and cover my left one for me."

Hang on—

"You mean hold it in my palm so Cross can't see it?"

"Hold it. Fondle it. Play with my nip... whatever you feel comfortable with."

Cross snorts as he sketches away on his iPad. "No sucking," he says, not even bothering to look up. "Probably no fondling, either. Last thing you want is her wiggling when I got my gun going."

He's got a point. Dropping my mouth next to Nicolette's ear, I murmur, "When we get back to my place, I'm making up for lost time," before I move to the other side. The weight of her tit is perfect against my palm as I take it, firmly grasping the swell as I cover her nipple from view.

This time, Cross does look up from his drawing. "You don't have to do that yet. I haven't even finished the outline."

I shrug, and don't let go of Nic. "That's okay. I'm perfectly happy to wait."

BY THE TIME CROSS IS DONE WITH NICOLETTE'S TAT, IT'S closing in on three in the morning. That's nothing to the syndicate's artist. I've never known a guy who runs on less sleep than Cross does. Poor guy's the poster child for insomnia and energy drinks, and it's a fucking miracle how he can keep a steady hand with how little he gets of one and how much he downs of the other.

I bring Nic back to my place when he's done. Thanks to the cream, she's not hurting now, but Cross told me it would wear off soon, and she was yawning as he finished giving us the instructions on aftercare. From experience, I know that the ribs are a tender spot to get inked, too. Add in the fact that he really made sure to cover up that dragonfly, and she's gonna feel it later. It's probably better for her to go home and rest.

Of course, to me, 'home' means my apartment.

She doesn't argue. On the way to the Playground, she repeated that that was the last of the secrets she held close. Afraid that I'd believe that she was a willing Dragonfly all along—and ashamed that she let Alfieri brand her like that—she didn't want me to see it when we first got together. After that, it just never seemed like the right time, and I got that.

I was the one who waited weeks to mention Heather, wasn't I?

But now it's all out there. She knows my demons, and I'm prepared to help her fight hers. Covering up Alfieri's mark on her was a step in the right direction. Keeping her secure in my place so that he can't get to her again is a no-brainer.

She has a problem. I'll fix it.

That's what I do.

I tuck her into my bed, laying on top of the comforter next to her until she's snuffling gently.

Somno might be another one of Link's kinks, but it's not mine. So while I can't help but look at this woman and want to bury my dick so deep inside of her that she'll never get rid of me, I won't do that while she's sleeping.

Besides, I need my dick kinda clean for what I'm about to do.

I won't be gone long. I make sure to lock up my place, typing a quick text to Cross as I head back out to my car. He said he planned on having a drink or two at the Playground before he headed back to his place, but I let him know as we were leaving that he'd better be sober for the next hour. Now I shoot him a message that I'm on my way back and to be ready for me.

He's in the same small studio when I let myself into the back offices, playing a game on his phone. He holds up a finger when I enter, muttering, "I almost got this level done."

Two seconds later, he snaps a 'fuck' under his breath before tossing his phone to the side, then grabbing a pair of gloves.

I raise my eyebrows at him. "Lost?"

"I'll beat it next time. I got your message." Gesturing at the tray set-up, he shows he has the tattoo gun ready, new ink poured out, and the outline all prepped for me. "I'm ready when you are."

I remove my jacket, tossing it over the chair. Then, daring him to say something, I flick open the button on my pants and pull the zipper down just enough to reveal my groin. I purposely went commando once I decided to do this, so there's a patch of skin and a few stray pubes greeting him and that's all.

Cross just grabs the numbing cream from the tray. "You want this, sunshine?"

"Fuck you."

The artist laughs. "Just checking. You seemed so put out that I didn't give you the stuff when you got your devil tat done. Believe me, the needle digging into your dick is gonna hurt a lot more than your ribs."

He should know. Despite being buds with him for almost fifteen years, I've never seen Cross naked, but rumors run that he's almost completely covered from the neck down. Well, except for his hands, which are unmarked, and a spot on his chest next to his trademark cross that gave him his nickname.

"Don't put that tattoo gun anywhere near my junk. That belongs to Nic now." I tap the spot near my pubic bone. "Right here. Give me the seahorse right here."

"You got it, Rolls."

And when he finishes coloring it about forty minutes later, I have only my second tattoo ever.

It's a piece for Nicolette Williams, and my way of showing the world that I'm *her* property.

Hopefully, that makes this lovesick idiot one step closer to being just hers.

Roll 'em...

TWENTY
TEARS

NICOLETTE

I never thought a seahorse tattoo would make me cry.

Kieran hated tears. He would tell me that they were a waste of his time and mine, that I couldn't manipulate him by crying. I never was a big crier or anything, but one of the things he 'trained' me out of was tearing up at the slightest inconvenience. Of course, that meant I refused to shed a tear when the hypocritical bastard decided he *wanted* me to.

Now, though? I think of the seahorse, and my heart aches—in a good way.

It's not even the cover-up by my boob that Cross did for me. I love it, and it's such a relief to know that, for the first time in years, I don't have Kieran's handiwork on me. It's a piece of art *I* chose, from the style to the colors, and it doesn't matter that it's a silly tattoo without any 'real' reason behind it other than I've always kind of liked seahorses. To me, it represents my freedom. That last tether to my abuser that I finally cut loose.

But when Royce dropped me off at my house the next morning at my request and stayed, insisting that he didn't have anything other to do than spend the day with me, he waited until he'd checked on the healing process of my tattoo before showing off *his*.

I didn't even realize that, after I passed out in his bed the night before, he went back to see Cross. He promised that I was locked up tight, that there was no way Kieran could reach me; after the long discussion I had with Ava earlier about what exactly it meant to belong to a Sinner, I believed him. His tattoo is smaller than mine—his is about the size of a half-dollar, while mine needed to be closer to a tennis ball to completely cover up Kieran's dragonfly—so he wasn't gone long. By the time I woke up the next morning, he was lying in his oversized bed with me.

Hell, considering his bed is fucking huge, with black satin sheets that seem to suit my lover, if I woke up and didn't sense him next to me, I might've even thought he was just on the other side.

Nope. In another sweet gesture that is so typically Royce McIntyre, he got a matching tattoo. I didn't ask him to. I blubbered like an idiot when I saw it, and kinda freaked him out, but what else could I do? I went from being marked by a man I want to forget to sharing a tattoo with one I don't think I'll ever be able to.

Do I think this is it? That he's my forever? I hope so, but I haven't been that naive since the first time Kieran shoved his bare foot between my legs under the table while Mom and Dave were talking about who knows what. There's no denying that Royce has this 'savior' thing going. I thought that before I discovered he was the Sinner who was there when Heather Valiant was shot. Learning the truth about that tragedy only confirms it for me.

If Royce is looking for someone to rescue, he can't do any better than me. It's like I was tailor-made for him. I see it. Odds are he does, too, even if he won't admit it.

Do I believe that he cares for me? Since I'm head over heels for him, yeah. He's attracted to me, we get along great, and we have a lot of fun together. Whether it's resuming our ongoing banter about who Christine should have chosen in *Phantom*, teaching each other how to cook—and *that's* going as well as you'd think—or licking chocolate off of each other after another baking disaster, I can see myself spending forever with this man.

The question is: can he see himself spending forever with *me*?

We don't talk about that. The future? We both conveniently avoid talking about it.

We do the same thing when it comes to Kieran.

That's on me. I just... I want to enjoy whatever time I have with Royce. It's not as much as I like. The underboss spends all of his free time with me, but he doesn't have a lot of it. The Sinners keep him busy, and I've lost track of how many times since we've been sleeping together that he's had to get up from bed, throw on his trademark dark suit, and disappear to do something for Devil.

I wouldn't say I've moved in with him, but that's only because most of my stuff is still stored at my mom's house. The morning after everything that happened in Riverside, I was slightly surprised when Royce so quickly agreed to bring me home. I thought that was his way of getting rid of me—until I saw the tattoo by his dick that he told me got so that, when he looks at his cock, he remembers that it only belongs to one woman.

Me.

That should have tipped me off that Royce is serious about us. At the time, I thought he was just saying that to make me feel better about the whole Kieran situation. I've known we were exclusive since he wore my mom's neon pink apron and told me that he was my lover now, and it was like Royce felt this need to confirm it.

I'm his. He's mine. For as long as we're together, there is no one else. I know he was just making it clear that—despite rumors in the East End about Sinners sharing their women—Royce won't share. As far as he's concerned, Kieran can fuck off, and if my ex ever tries to come between us, Royce will take care of him.

He promised.

I believe him.

I want to say it's not his problem, but my lover makes it his problem. I find that out that same morning after when, once I finally stop sniffling over the seahorse tattoo by his pubic bone, he tells me to pack up what I'll need for the next few days.

I haven't moved in with him—but that's only semantics, really. I sleep at the Suites with Royce. I either go to work at the Playground, spend the evening with Royce at his place, or visit Ava upstairs when she's not snuggled up close with her terrifying husband. If only because, this way, Kieran won't be able to find me, Royce keeps me close.

I just... I wish he had another reason why he wanted me near.

It's been a little more than a week since Kieran 'bumped into' us in Riverside, and I'm still having a hard time believing that he gave up no matter how I try to convince Royce otherwise.

I know him. Sure, it's been almost three years since I saw him last, but I don't think he changed all that much. The only reason why he didn't follow me to Willowbrook was because I made an escape plan. Knowing it wouldn't be easy to leave him, I had everything set up before I told him we were over. Money. A new apartment. A new number that no one knew, not even my mom.

I was going to make a clean break until I could figure out a way to explain why I had to go. It wouldn't be easy, and I've never felt financially stable since I walked out on Kieran, but if I wanted to get out, I had to *go*.

He laughed when I said that's what I was doing. I remember that so vividly. He laughed and told me that we'll never be over. That I would always belong to him. And, to prove it, he disappeared for three days on a kill mission for Damien Libellula.

Kieran absolutely expected me to be waiting for him when he got back. My only regret is that I didn't have cameras up in the apartment I shared with Kieran before I left. I'm sure his reaction to finding out I'd done just what I said and slipped out into the night with nothing but the clothes on my back, my ID, and the dollars I squirreled away over the years would've been a sight to see when I was safely two states away.

I was careful in Willowbrook. I stayed to myself. I worked two jobs to make ends meet, and often went hungry when I couldn't. Fresh out of an abusive relationship, I wasn't eager to start a new one. Dating was off the table, though I did react the same way I did when I basically pounced Royce: to prove to myself that I was free of Kieran, I was willing to fuck anyone who seemed like they were just looking for a good time.

Honestly, that's what I thought I was getting out of Royce. One night, right? He won me for one night. It was a delightful surprise that that one night has turned into more than a month—and if I wasn't worried about Kieran coming after me, I'm sure I would enjoy these honeymoon days with Royce a lot more.

I guess I should've been grateful that I made it from August to February without Kieran knowing I was back in town. It's why I specifically didn't go near the East End, or why I reluctantly agreed to work in the Sinners' nightclub. Some part of me knew he would eventually figure out I was back... but now that I have proof he has, it's like he's vanished off the face of the planet.

I don't trust it. I don't trust *him*. I can't shake the feeling that he's planning something, and if I chafe against some of Royce's overprotective measures, I remind myself that he's just trying to keep me safe from Kieran the only way he can.

If only we remembered that Kieran isn't the only one who might be pissed off that the two of us are together...

Tonight, Royce is having a hush-hush dinner with Devil, Damien Libellula, and the mayor of Springfield. From what he told me this afternoon while I was getting ready for my shift at the Playground, the two leaders of the local mafias meet with Mayor Harrison once a month to discuss 'things'. He left it at that, and I didn't push. Because he would be occupied until at least halfway through my shift, he wanted to know if I'd rather stay home.

'Home' he called it, and my heart warmed. At the same time, I lost out on too many tips this week. I can't live off of the ten grand that Royce insisted I deposit— and that I sure the hell did—forever, and I took off more time than I liked. I needed to work. Besides, Royce assured me that there's no way Kieran will get past the bouncers that work the Playground's front door.

Kieran didn't.

Miles Haines *did*.

Later, I'll admit that I completely forgot about that guy. An obvious sore loser, once Royce beat him at poker and Miles started crowing about how Royce cheated, he seemed to also disappear. There was no sign of him at the Playground, and part of me wondered if he earned himself a ban for questioning the manager's integrity. That, or he was just so stinking pissed at losing his bet *and* that I started seeing Royce after the poker game, that he didn't want to show his face around the club. I tried to keep our relationship under wraps in case it didn't work out, but yeah... that didn't last.

Then my shifts were cut, I barely spent any of my time at the Playground, and the only one I was looking over my shoulder for was Kieran.

That was a mistake. Because, no matter his reason for vanishing for a couple of weeks, Miles showed up when I least expected it.

The Playground is hopping. It's a good thing that Royce is busy since I wouldn't have had time to stop by his personal booth to say 'hi' between all of the tables Jessie assigned me. Even when I didn't have a table, she told me to work the casino so that I could get some extra tips. I'm sure Royce put her up to it, but I didn't care. Halfway through my shift, I was feeling a lot better about how much money I'd have in my pocket.

Like most of the downstairs girls, I keep my purse in the back. I don't keep all of my tips on me at all times. Once I have a good amount, I excuse myself so that I can drop the bills into my purse. At the Playground, to steal from a fellow employee means you end up in front of the Devil of Springfield himself. Since no one wants to do that—or see what kind of punishment he'll throw out— no one steals. Simple as that.

I head to the backroom, dropping off a bundle of singles, fives, and a couple of twenties—and it's when I'm on my way out again to see if Jessie has more tables for me that Miles waylays me.

"There you are," he says, that slimy voice of his catching my attention. I was distracted, doing the math in my head about how much more I could hope to make tonight, and I don't see him until he steps in front of me, grabbing me by my upper arm. "I've been looking for you."

I shake him off. "Well. You found me. But I'm in the middle of a shift, so—"

"You owe me, Nicolette."

"Sorry," I say, trying to move around him. Impossible when the corridor toward the backroom is narrow, but I try anyway as I add, "I'm not interested."

At the Playground, that's all I *have* to say. All of the customers know the rules. They can cajole. They can offer whatever they think will make a girl say yes. They can beg if they want... but as soon as any of us say we're not interested, that's the end of it.

Up until now, Miles played by the rules. He got to the point that he offered me ten thousand dollars to sleep with him—when I finally broke down and agreed—but he lost that money to Royce. Royce won. It's over.

Not, apparently, for Miles.

"You cost me ten grand. You owe me."

"Sorry—"

"Real quick. I'll even go upstairs with you. What do you say? Ten minutes with me, and we can call it even."

And cheat on Royce? No way. "Like I said. I'm not interested. Now, if you'll excuse me..."

Miles stays firmly planted in my path.

I huff. "Look. I'm trying to be nice, but you lost that bet—"

"He *cheated*."

I'm not arguing about this. "Then take it up with Royce."

He moves quicker than I would've thought. Before I

know it, the sleazy bastard lunges at me, snatching both of my arms this time. He squeezes them, trapping my arms at my side, then shoves me hard. My back hits the wall, my head slamming into it next. For a split second, I'm stunned, and he takes advantage of that.

He takes advantage of *me*.

TWENTY-ONE
MISTAKE

NICOLETTE

One hand goes to my throat, pinning it in place as he squeezes just enough that I go immovably still. As soon as he sees that I have, he releases my right arm. Before I can break free, he shoves his hand down my shorts. I gasp, and he grabs my whole damn pussy. His middle finger jabs me repeatedly, digging for my entrance as I do nothing but take it.

He places his cheek against mine. "Someone paid ten grand for this pussy. I'm gonna see for myself what makes it so fucking special. And you? You're going to let me."

No I'm fucking *not*.

Thanks to Kieran, fourteen-year-old Nicolette would have.

Sixteen-year-old Nicolette would have.

Even twenty-year-old Nicolette would have.

But the Nicolette who finally broke it off with her abuser? Who finally got a taste of what it was like to be with someone who saw her as a person and not just a pussy?

Going still as he violated me is instinctive. Fucker thinks that means that I'm welcoming this, welcoming *him*, and he pays more attention to fingering me than he does to my expression.

That's his mistake.

At this moment, I'm reminded of the first time I was ever intimate with Royce. How he kissed me in the supply room, squeezing my ass before we ended in a position fairly similar to this. There's one big difference, though. Even when he was just my boss, I was with him the whole way. He checked in with me before he touched me, and when he did? He was gentle. Seductive. He didn't just jam his hands down my shorts and try to fuck me with his finger like this asshole did.

And that's why I didn't rear back my leg and knee him in the fucking nuts like I do this handsy bastard.

His nails scratch the side of my throat as he rips his hand back, body folding up like a metal chair. Miles lets out a howl as he drops, cupping his cock as he starts screaming unintelligible threats at me.

For a moment, I rub my neck, glaring at him through a sheen of hate-filled tears.

I'm so fucking pissed that he made me cry. That he cornered me at my place of work, and that I naively thought that the big-shot customer would give up on his fixation with me just because Royce beat him at poker.

If anything, that's *more* of a reason why he'd come after me again. After harassing me for weeks, I finally relented enough to give sex work another try. There was no connection. He's handsome in that blandly, mani-cured way that older men with money have, but I wasn't attracted to him, either. Whether I used one of the rooms upstairs like the other girls or went to a hotel with him instead, I was fucking him for money. When he didn't have it, I didn't go home with him—and he's probably been stewing over it ever since.

Royce won me. Since then, I've found myself falling deeper and deeper for him. He went from being my boss and my savior to my lover. I *choose* to be with him. There's not enough money in the world to get me to cheat on him because this is the relationship I've waited my entire life to have.

And this asshole tried to ruin it for me.

It's not about me anymore, though. This is revenge, plain and simple. Royce won. He won that poker game, he won a night out with me, and though he never cashed it in the way that Miles would've expected, he won my heart. Big shots like Miles feel like the world owes them everything. Royce won, but Miles thought he should.

Once he recovers, he's coming after me. I can see it on his face. Only the force of my knee into his crotch is saving me right now, and I'm not about to stick around and let him get back to his feet.

I don't even bother grabbing my bag. My phone's in there, so is my money and the key card that would let me into Paradise Suites. Just now? I don't give a shit.

If I jog, I can make it to my mother's place in twenty minutes. I have a spare key hidden where even Kieran won't find out, and an alarm system that should keep anyone out.

And, calming myself just enough to tell the first waitress I bump into that I was puking in the bathroom and need to go home sick, I bolt from the Playground.

ROYCE

As I speed across downtown Springfield, I'm about to lose my fucking mind.

Nicolette didn't go home, and by that, I mean no one at the Suites has seen her since I brought her to work earlier. And that's a problem because she left her shift abruptly about an hour ago. With her purse, phone, and wallet left behind at the Playground, I have no way to reach her—and no idea where she is.

I knew I should have blown off my duties today. I never do, and when I watched Nicolette pull on her Playground uniform earlier today, something in my gut told me I should—but I didn't listen. Instead, I dropped her off at the club, then went out to take care of business.

It's been a day from hell already. Part of this 'truce' we have going on means that, when I catch a young Dragonfly peddling their shit on the West Side, I grit my teeth and turn my head. At the end of the day, customers will buy their dope whether I try to stop them or not. Breeze is the drug of choice this winter. Like a hopped-up E, it's for partying, making its users loose and hot and reckless.

Link thinks we can take advantage of that. Our girls need johns. The Playground needs partiers. Breeze has boosted business, which is habitually slow this time of year.

But it also makes some of our wallets super fucking stupid.

Burns tipped us off about something that happened in the bathrooms the other night. One of the officers on Link's payroll, he let us know that the handful of straight-and-narrow cops looking into Breeze have traced it to the Playground. Some sergeant's kid took too much and found himself in an compromising position before his buddies dragged him out of it. Burns was chuckling when he described the kid bruising his cock by trying to fuck a urinal, and I'm just glad that none of the Playground's staff had to deal with that.

Of course, that means I had to fix that problem. The kid's dick will heal, but the sergeant was pissed off when he discovered Breeze was flowing freely in one of our main establishments. He threatened to bring in a task squad to clean us out, and I had to smooth things over to get the cop off our backs.

Adding him to Link's payroll helped, but it was annoyingly tedious.

The vice mayor was waiting for his monthly pay-off, and I had to deal with that, too. I checked in with Jake. Went to the dinner with Link, Damien, Mayor Harrison, and the twink he's currently fucking—oh, sorry. I mean, his *aide*.

By the time I was done for the night and I got to the Playground, all I wanted was a stiff drink and a second alone with Nic. She was on schedule from six to two, so my midnight arrival meant she should've been there.

But she wasn't.

Jessie thought I knew. When I arrived and Nic wasn't

there, she figured that I had to know. Chloe was the one who tipped her off. Something about how Nicolette was puking in the bathroom and had to leave early, but she was in such a rush that not only did she sidestep informing the floor manager she had to go, but she abandoned all of her belongings in the backroom.

One look at my face and, fuck. I didn't hide it. I'm usually so good at keeping a straight face—that's the gambler in me—but when she said Nicolette left her stuff behind... her *money* behind... I didn't hide it all. Jessie chased me all over the club as I checked to see if anyone had seen Nicolette leave—and if she left alone.

The guys at the door confirmed it. She left by herself, heading down the street. They assumed she was going to get her car, but how could she? I dropped her off. Her car's parked in the Suites' parking deck, and her keys were in her purse.

So was her key card to my place, but that didn't stop me from dashing home anyway to check once I got confirmation that Nic had walked out of the club alone. Not only that, but everyone on staff knows better than to let Kieran Alfieri in. I'll have Tanner check security footage just in case—but, first, I needed to find my girl.

She wasn't at my home. Hoping like hell that meant she returned to the only other place in Springfield where she felt secure behind her cameras, I headed right for her mother's house.

My heart skips a beat when I see the living room light on through her slightly askew black-out curtains.

I park my car in the middle of her street, instead of tucked away, out of sight. I'm usually a lot more careful than this. When I was watching over Nic... I did everything I could to keep from catching her neighbor's attention.

Not tonight. Not when I've spent the worst fucking forty minutes of my life, worrying about her. Even if what Chloe said was true, even if Nicolette got food poisoning from lunch or something, it doesn't matter. She could've contacted me.

She didn't.

I thought I made it clear. From the moment I called her mine, I meant it. It doesn't matter how fucking busy I am or what I'm doing. My phone is on. Even if I missed a call, the second I was free, I'd get back to her. But I didn't have a single missed call from Nicolette, and she vanished on me.

Maybe if I wasn't waiting for Alfieri to test my hand. To leave the safety of the East End and try me. I specifically didn't mention the little problem I'm having with one of his enforcers to Damien over dinner today. I figured, if the head of the Libellula Family knew what kind of game his enforcer was playing, he might slip up. If not, I don't want to fill him in in case I have to take care of Alfieri.

I should've known better. Damien didn't give anything away, and my hands are still tied when it comes to that bastard.

And now, while I was busy playing nice with our rivals and the mayor, something set off Nicolette...

I'm a fixer. Goddamn it, I'll fix *this*.

I leave my car at the curb, right in front of her house. It's in direct view of her surveillance cameras, so if she's watching them, she'll know I'm here before I get to the door. The air bites as I slide out of the car. It's only as I stalk toward the front door that I realize I left my suit jacket behind somewhere.

Oh, well.

I grab the doorknob. I'm not super surprised that it's locked, though I had hoped Nic saw me coming and left it open. It's not. I rattle it to get her attention, then wait a few seconds. When she doesn't call out that she's coming, I raise my voice and shout, "Nicolette? I know you're in there. Open up. It's me."

No answer.

Fuck no. I slap the door with the flat of my hand. "Nic, baby? I'm not playing. Open this door, or I'm going to open it for you. Okay? Don't lock me out. Not me."

Still nothing.

Well. She can't say I didn't warn her.

"On the count of three, I'm gonna kick the door down. I'll replace it, but if you're in trouble, I'm not staying out of it. Yeah? Yeah. Okay. One. Two—"

The doorknob rattles from her side. "Holy shit, Royce. Don't kick it. I'm trying to get it unlocked."

I clench my teeth and step away from the door, waiting for it to open.

When it does, I walk right inside before she can stop me, then whirl around on her. My mouth opens—and not a single damn word comes out.

Up until the moment I arrived at her house, I knew there had to be a different reason behind Nic cutting her shift short. Whatever happened, it wasn't what she told Chloe. I was sure of that. But when I see her red, puffy eyes—signs that she's been crying—and her damp hair, fresh from a shower, my gut twists.

She's trembling, hugging her middle, and while I could maybe try to pretend she really did come down with a stomach flu or something, it's in the way her bottom lip quivers. It's not because of the way I came storming in here like a bat out of hell, either. Something happened. Something bad.

And I must've made it so much worse by acting like a fucking maniac.

"They told me you were sick. I was worried. I'm sorry—"

"Miles Haines assaulted me," she blurts out. Four words that stop me dead in my tracks as she lifts her hand, covering her mouth.

"He *what*?"

She gulps, and her trembles turn to undeniable shakes. At first, she doesn't say anything else, just gestures at her throat. Before, I only paid attention to her puffy eyes. Now? I see marks on the side of her neck that are obvious scratches. Beneath them, a few bruises are already beginning to form. Assault... he obviously hurt her.

But when I reach for her, and she flinches, I know the truth.

"He touched you. Where?"

Nicolette uses her pointer finger to gesture below.

No.

He's dead. Simple as that. Miles Haines is dead.

Nicolette must see the answer in my face because she tries to explain. About how he cornered her where there were no cameras and no witnesses, how he accused me of cheating, how she tried to get away before he grabbed her, basically choked her, then raped her with his finger.

"I'm going to kill him." I already was, but now? I promise her, "He's dead. "

"Royce?"

I shake my head. If I repeat myself, she might ask me to spare him, but even for Nicolette, I can't be that merciful.

And then she says, "I wish I had killed him," and that settles it even as she says, "but my only thought was to get away."

That's okay, baby. I'll fix this.

"I understand that. And, don't worry, it's going to be okay. I just... why didn't you tell anyone?"

"Honestly? For a minute there, it was like I was back with Kieran. That's when he did it. I couldn't stop him, but then I kneed him, and he went down... and I had to run." Her eyes flicker up, meeting mine. "But you came after me."

I take a step toward her, bracing myself in case she flinches. I won't blame her if she does... but it does a little to thaw me out when she doesn't. Instead, throwing herself at my chest, clinging to me as she shakes, I vow to her, "I will always come for you, Nicolette."

Just like I'll do anything to protect her.

Roll 'em...

TWENTY-TWO
HUNTER REED

ROYCE

Now, my first instinct is to grab my Beretta, find Miles Haines, and eliminate him. He's not a Dragonfly; that wouldn't be going against our truce. But then I remember that it actually *might*. Haines is a well-known patron of not only the Playground, but also East End properties. A big spender who made a big mistake, I can see how taking out Haines might complicate matters in these trying times.

Good thing this isn't the first time when, as the fixer, I needed someone taken care of without implicating any other Sinner.

Alfieri is too high up for an accident like I have in mind for Haines. Especially once his former relationship with Nicolette came out, if anything happened to Alfieri, it didn't matter who eliminated him. It would fall back on us.

But Haines... if no one knows that I have a reason to take him out... well. Look at that.

I wait until she stops shaking before I drop a kiss to the top of her damp hair. Then, pulling away from her just enough so she can see the look on my face, I clear my throat.

She gazes up at me.

"The Sinners protect our own." I take Nic's hands in mine, squeezing them. "But you're mine. And I'm going to protect you. I just want to make one thing clear about what happened. You said he cornered you in the corridor, you got him in the balls, then left. No one saw it happen?"

She shakes her head. "We were alone."

That's what I thought. Good. I'd have bigger problems on my hands if someone at the Playground knew Nic had been assaulted and kept it from me. What probably happened is that Haines hobbled out as soon as he recovered, never telling anyone he passed that the blondie waitress got him good.

Of course, if he didn't try to use his money against her —trying to get the Playground to side with a wallet over a waitress—it's probably because he plans on getting revenge on Nic some other time.

Good luck, asshole.

Still holding tightly onto Nicolette, I lead her over to the couch. Once she's seated, I take out my phone. It isn't often that I need Nicholas Reed's services, but over the last few years, I've had enough reason to that I keep the shadowy businessman in my contacts.

I stumbled upon the true nature of the Reed twins by accident. We had this waitress a couple years back. She obviously used a fake name, running from something, but just like I did with Nicolette, I gave her a chance. It wasn't long before I figured out she was running because she was a witness to a murder.

Well, no. She was accused of being a murderess, and though she knew the true identity of the killer and refused to squeal, it was hard to prove her innocence. After a while, the cops gave up, but because the killer was actually her former student turned young lover, she was hiding out from him.

I forget what name she went by then, only that her real name is Tamryn Carlisle. Up until this past Christmas, she lived in Springfield, though she's originally from this small, secluded town called Shadowvale. It's about two hours away from Springfield, and I know that because, when I heard rumors of a hitman operating out of Shadowvale, I looked into it.

The Reed twins—a pair of brothers about my age—basically run this town. This Shadowvale. On paper, it's because they own the two largest businesses: the sanitation company and the sawmill. In truth, Nicholas Reed takes hit jobs, and his brother, Hunter, sees them out.

It's late. Almost one in the morning. Just because I'm up, it doesn't mean that Nicholas will be up—but I could give a shit. Men in our line of work are used to late hours, and if I can hire him, he'll surely make me pay for it.

After making sure that Nicolette is comfortable, I call up Nicholas's contact. I tell myself I won't be annoyed if he doesn't answer, but I'm fucking relieved when his gruff voice says, "This better be worth it, McIntyre."

"It will be," I assure him. "I got a job for you."

"From your tone of voice and the late hour, I assume you mean Hunter."

"Yes."

"Interesting. For our usual fee?"

I look at Nicolette. She's folded her legs beneath her, hands tucked in her lap, eyes looking away from me as though perfectly aware what sort of conversation this is.

A muscle tics in my jaw. "For triple."

"When do you need this job done by?"

"As soon as Hunter can get here to take care of it," I tell Nicholas solemnly.

"E-mail me the details by morning. For triple our fee, whatever you need done, it'll be done by tomorrow night."

I don't doubt it. Just like how I don't ask questions about Tanner's skills, I definitely don't doubt Hunter Reed. He's aptly named all right. Even if Haines goes under, assuming that Nicolette came and told me what he did to her? Hunter will find him—and no one else will ever again.

"Sounds like a plan."

"Good. I'll talk to you in the morning. As for now, I'm all tied up." Over the phone, I hear a laugh. Considering it's a woman's laugh, I know it's not Nicholas—though I'm pretty sure who it is, especially when he amends his comment to, "Well. Someone's tied up."

He ends the call abruptly, but after dealing with Nicholas before, I'm used to it. Instead, I prepare myself for Nicolette's curiosity. I know that, if I explain to her what my intentions are, she'll understand. After all, she spent a decade as an enforcer's property; me not liking that fact doesn't change it. That's part of the life, and if I thought she couldn't handle it, I would never have gotten this involved with her.

But I have, and I meant it when I said I would do anything to protect her.

Only... I was right. She's not curious.

She's *fuming*.

"Nicolette?"

"I'm so stupid," she mutters. "I should've known there was something wrong with him when he tried to pay me ten grand for sex."

Oh, no. I absolutely refuse to let Nicolette blame herself. Besides, that prick had a perfectly good reason why he would do that, and I tell her so.

"It's because you're beautiful, baby—"

She scoffs. "You're just saying that because you *are* the one sleeping with me."

"No. I'm saying that because I love you. Even if I didn't, I've got a good eye. I know a beautiful woman when I see her. I also know a good-hearted one who has been dealt a shit hand, who bluffs when she has to, folds when she has to, and will do anything to win."

I thought that would be enough to get her attention off of what happened and onto me where it belongs.

I was *wrong*.

After a couple of heartbeats where she just gapes at me, she turns away, avoiding my earnest expression.

And I realize... I've lost her.

Why? Is it because of the way I came blazing in here? Or how I made it clear in no uncertain terms that I was taking care of Miles Haines the way a Sinner would?

Even if I didn't grab my gun and hunt him down myself, she obviously heard enough of my conversation to guess that that would be his fate.

Is that what's upsetting her?

She knows who I am. She knows *what* I am. So I'm not as in-your-face possessive as Link is when it comes to Ava. I won't beat the shit out of a guy just for looking at Nic funny, but Miles didn't just look. He touched... he *took*... and he brought her back to a place she never wanted to be again.

He deserves everything the Reed twins do to him.

"Oh, come on, Nic. I whipped up the best metaphor to gambling and all you could do was stare at me? I thought that was pretty good."

Looking back at me, she blinks once. Twice. Then, in a shaky voice, she says, "You said you love me."

I did. "Haven't I told you that before?"

She shakes her head.

Huh. "I could've sworn I have."

"Saying 'I love you' when you're inside of me doesn't count, Royce."

"It should. When you trust me with your body, that's the time I feel closest to your heart. Why wouldn't I feel love for you?"

Nicolette is still staring at me as though she *wants* to believe what I'm saying, but is struggling to. And I get it. I do. I don't remember the last time I've told a woman I loved her and meant it—if I ever have—so I'm not so good with the declaration thing. But I do love her, and when I thought something happened to her earlier, the realization that I'd kill anyone who hurt her made me admit that I was only fooling myself by not telling her with words.

So I tell her with my actions. I should've remembered. Nicolette... she needs the words.

"I love you," I tell her again, using the second knuckle on my pointer finger to tilt her chin back so that she can see the honesty in my face.

I don't need her to tell me it back. As far as she knows, we've only been aware of each other for such a short amount of time.

But when her face splits wide open with the first grin she's had since I saw her earlier tonight, I hold my breath. And then she throws her arms around my middle, burying her face in my chest before murmuring into my jacket, "I love you, too," and the last bit of the knot deep in my gut finally unravels.

For now, at least.

AS LATE AS IT IS, I STAY WITH NIC AT HER PLACE. THE NEXT morning, I'm done with pretending she doesn't live with me. I help her pack up even more of her shit, set the alarm to protect her mom's place, and drive her home.

I verified that Nicholas got all the information I sent him. I stayed up long after Nic finally relaxed against me, sleeping on my chest. I composed that e-mail to Nicholas, then let Link know what happened so that he was in the loop.

He offered to hunt Haines down and make an example of him. All he had to do was claim that a wallet hurt one of Devil's girls, and there isn't a person in Springfield who would care that Link shot Haines's cock off before putting a bullet through his brain.

But then Nicolette would be considered one of Devil's girls. And maybe I'm being even more irrationally jealous, but she's *mine,* and I want to handle the situation the way I best see fit.

Link agreed with me, and that was that.

Nicolette doesn't ask for details. If she did? I'd offer them, but once she reads between the lines and asks if she won't have to worry about Haines coming after her again, and I promise her that she won't, she—like Link— lets it go.

That day, we go to the Playground after dinner. A few of the waitresses stop by, waving at Nic, and I encourage her to let them know she's survived her stomach flu. She even apologizes to Jessie, promising she won't do that again before we sit in my favored booth.

It's imperative that we're seen. When Miles Haines goes missing, someone will notice. Someone will care.

I won't, but just in case? I cover all bases and enjoy an evening with Nicolette as—somewhere in Springfield— Haines is getting what's coming to him.

Around eleven o'clock that night, a shadow falls over our table. A good-looking guy with eyes even bluer than mine, a stubbled jaw, and a wicked smirk appears silhouetted against the teal neon that decorates this part of the club.

Hunter Reed, in the flesh.

Hunter and Nicholas are identical twins. At first glimpse, it's impossible to tell them apart. Luckily, their clothes give them away. Like most Sinners, Nicholas Reed prefers expensively tailored suits. His brother? He has a leather jacket, dark jeans, heavy boots, and a cocky look that says he knows he's caught the eye of most of the clubbers.

Not that he'll care. He has a dainty little blonde wife of his own, and she's all he cares about.

Well, that and Nicholas, but considering how twisted these twins are, that's a given.

With a *clunk*, I see the second thing that tells me I'm dealing with Hunter. Though I know he's armed—his weapon of choice being a switchblade—all I can see is the motorcycle helmet that he just dropped on top of our table. It has a skeleton emblazoned on the front of it.

I asked him why once. Hunter told me he likes the idea of being death personified, chasing whoever it is in his sight.

Yeah. He's a disturbing fucker, but he does good work.

I raise my eyebrows at him. I've been expecting him. I told Nicholas where I'd be if his brother needed to find me, knowing that Hunter has a tendency to show off in front of anyone who knows his serial-killing secret.

"How's it going, Royce?"

My gaze slants toward Nicolette. "Good. You?"

"I've had a most... thrilling night, you could say. Chase didn't last as long as I like, but the hunt was highly satisfying. Thanks for that. Nicholas hasn't let me have any fun since Halloween, so this was worth the drive. Speaking of... if you want to lend me your van again, I got a spot where no one will find your guy."

I know exactly where that is, too. The Reed twins have

their own private cemetery behind their big house in Shadowvale for the rapists, abusers, and molesters that they target to get out their own bloodlust.

It's a perfect resting place for Miles Haines.

Dipping my hand in my front pocket, I avoid my rigged coin, reaching for a set of keys instead. With a smirk, I toss them at Hunter.

He catches them one-handed. "Thanks."

"Just make sure you get it back to me this time. After Christmas, we were down a van for three whole weeks."

"Sorry about that," Hunter says, not sounding sorry at all. "We had a lot of snow this year. But Nick said 'thanks', too." He chuckles to himself. "He sure appreciated your help in delivering his Christmas present."

Considering I agreed to help Hunter Reed bring Tamryn Carlisle to visit with Nicholas for the first time since she left Shadowvale years ago, I'm sure he did.

Huh. Tied up, indeed.

Lifting his helmet, Hunter gives me a mock salute. "Pleasure doing business with you, Sinner. Until next time."

Nicolette waits until Hunter has vanished among the throng of dancers before she takes a sip of her cocktail, then asks, "So... do I want to know what any of that was about?"

Probably not. I lift my own drink up, tipping the shot glass in her direction. "Just know that I upheld my promise, yeah? You won't have to worry about Haines bothering you ever again."

Now, if only I could get rid of Alfieri as easily...

Roll 'em...

TWENTY-THREE
IT'S NOT OVER

NICOLETTE

Royce was right. It's been a week since Miles Haines 'disappeared' and it's like no one gives a shit.

I'm sure *someone* does. A wife, some kids, parents... there had to be someone who loved him. If not that, then the fact that he was more than happy to blow cash at both the Devil's Playground and properties on the East End. Money talks, and there has to be someone out there who notices that one voice has been silenced.

It hasn't gotten back to us, though, and that's all I care about. Whether it's because, as Royce explained, he 'contracted out', or because we had an obvious alibi—being seen by everyone visiting the club that night—when he went missing, it doesn't matter. We're free and clear.

Well, when it comes to Miles, we are. I don't have to worry about him cornering me in a hallway or trying to take what he thought I owed him.

But what about Kieran?

I want to convince myself that our 'chance' meeting the night I saw *The Phantom of the Opera* with Royce was just that: a coincidence. Too bad I know Kieran Alfieri better than that. If he let me see that he was out there, watching me, it's because he *wanted* to.

Is he watching me now? I know he had the house under surveillance because of the dragonfly figurine he left in my mailbox and the obvious camera he left behind. That's one good thing about basically moving into Royce's place. Even if Kieran figured out that this is where I've been staying lately, the Paradise Suites has a doorman, an elevator with a key card, and security vetted by the paranoid Devil himself.

There's no way to know which floor belongs to Royce unless someone told him, and when I'm not hanging out with my lover in his place because he's too busy to keep me guarded? He shuffles me off to the penthouse to keep Ava Crewes company.

Now, I like Ava. It was easy to form a quick friendship with her once I realized that, when it comes to any possible relationship she has with Royce, I have nothing to worry about. They're close because he's Devil's right-hand man, and Ava is Devil's coddled bride.

And despite being a coddled mafia queen, she's so sweet and down-to-earth that I couldn't help but like her. Besides, it's not her fault that she gets stuck with me because, in his way, Royce is just as overprotective as Ava's husband. Especially since she's going on seven months pregnant, Devil refuses to let Ava leave the penthouse. I'm not forbidden to go myself, though Royce has 'suggested' that I stay upstairs where it's safe while he's busy with Syndicate business.

Like tonight.

The top Sinners seem to be busy, busy fellas. There's always some deal going down, some business that needs to be taken care of, some meet that needs to be made. More often than not, Devil has to be there—as the head of the mafia—with Royce acting as both backup and the voice of reason for him.

However, when Royce received a phone call two hours ago, it wasn't a Sinner who needed his help. It was that cousin of his. Jake. The guy who got involved with Heather Valiant all those years ago, then got poor Royce mixed up in it, too.

I don't know what he did. From Royce's expression as he kept the conversation short and clipped, it's not good. It was important enough to have him deciding to send me up to the penthouse so he could go out and handle it, though he swore he'd be home for dinner.

Ava's husband is gone, too. Where? Who knows. Unlike me, Ava doesn't want to get involved with the Sinners. At first, that surprised me. I mean, she has the devil brand on her inner forearm, just like the rest of the gang. When I pointed that out, she actually smiled and said she got that to piss her husband off.

Okay, then.

A lot of the wives and girlfriends don't have the mark. They don't do 'property' on the West Side, though Royce told me he could arrange for that guy, Cross, to give me one if I want it. I'm thinking about it. Part of me really wants to say 'fuck it' and get it done. It wouldn't even be a knock against Kieran, either, like erasing his dragonfly with my seahorse was. It would be my way of saying I was going all in with the man that I love.

The Sinners are his life. If I take their brand, telling all of Springfield I'm one of them, I'm telling Royce in one of the only ways I can that I'm *his*.

He loves me. He told me so. He says it in words, in the matching seahorse tattoo he got just for me, and definitely in the way he'll kill to protect me, even if he doesn't do the actual dirty work himself. He loves me—and I just wish that was enough.

It's so soon. That's all I keep thinking about. It's the end of March, I haven't been with him for two full months yet, and I want to believe this whirlwind relationship means *forever*... but I thought that about Kieran once, and got stuck with him for way longer than it should have taken me to get out.

I don't want to leave Royce. But I have baggage, and he has never committed to anyone before... so, despite the seahorse, I just don't understand why would he choose *me*?

He says he's protecting me. When he kisses me on the forehead, leaving me with my friend, I can't help but feel like I'm being passed from babysitter to babysitter.

In frustration, I mention that to Ava. She actually smiles, her green eyes bright as she shakes her head and says, "Welcome to the West Side."

She seems to think it's normal. I guess, when she's married to the head of the Sinners Syndicate, expecting his baby early this summer, it *is*.

I let it go. Instead, since it's just the two of us in the

living room—with the housekeeper in the kitchen, and Ava's personal guard milling around the front hallway—we decide to spend the afternoon planning her upcoming baby shower.

I'm honored when Ava asks me for my help. A little less than honored when she admits that she has no one else to ask since she cut ties with her old life when she chose to marry Link—like Royce, she calls Devil 'Link' though I'll never dare—and the other Sinner wife is child-free. I don't know shit about baby showers, but thinking like Royce, I decide to help her research how to throw the best one possible.

Around mid-afternoon, we take a break. I'm still holding out hope that Royce will bring dinner home like he promised, but when Ava murmurs something about craving tacos, I think that sounds like a great idea.

"I had these really awesome tacos from Jay's last week," she tells me. "Link picked them up for us when he was coming home for the night."

"I've heard of that place, but never ate there. They're good?"

"Very. But they don't deliver."

That's okay. I shrug. "I'll go get you some tacos."

"What? No."

"Why not?"

Ava leans back into her seat, cradling her baby bump. "Seriously, Nicolette. I mean it. You don't have to do that. If I'm hungry, I can get something from the kitchen." She pauses for a moment, then chuckles. "Well, no. Mama Mona will insist on feeding me—"

"And she makes a mean taco?" I ask.

I've met the Crewes's housekeeper-slash-cook-slash-honorary grandmother. A stern yet friendly Polish woman in her late sixties, she lived in the same apartment building as both Devil and Ava back when they were teenagers. When Devil became, well, *Devil*, he hired Mona to work with him. Ava admitted to me that Mona was facing homelessness when he did, and that Ava's husband wasn't as much of a dangerous gangster as his reputation suggests, but even serial killers can love their mamas.

Kieran certainly does. With a leaf tattooed down the back of his arm for every life he takes as a Dragonfly, he might boast that he's an enforcer for the Libellula Family, but I know better. He's a sick and twisted killer who'd kill a hundred men if he thought it would bring Maizy Alfieri back from her grave...

I shake my head, knocking that thought loose. I'm safe. Royce promised. Besides, I'm not afraid that Kieran will turn his gun on me. He doesn't want me dead. Oh, no. He wants me on my knees, worshiping him again the way I did when I was sixteen and I didn't know any better.

Ava watches me curiously. She didn't say anything in response to my comment—and, for all I know, with as much experience in the kitchen as Mona has, she *can* make a taco—but, instead, leans forward as though trying to see into my brain and get a glimpse at where it's gone.

Sorry, hon. You wouldn't like it in here.

I grin, getting up to my feet. "Jay's Taqueria is, like,

two blocks away. I can pick up a snack for us and be back in fifteen minutes at the most."

My purse is sitting on the couch. It has my wallet in it, and I toss my phone on the top so it's within easy reach. "Text me what baby Crewes feels like chowing down on. See if your bodyguard is hungry, too. It's on me."

It's the least I can do for their company while Royce is occupied.

Who knows? Maybe then I won't feel like the annoying kid he leaves behind with the babysitters.

I'M NOT BEING FAIR. I KNOW THAT, AND THE WAY I DON'T let Ava try to talk me out of leaving proves it.

Royce is worried about me. He has been since our run-in with Kieran in Riverside, and after Miles cornered me at the Playground, he's made it his point to keep me safe the only way he knows how. Part of that was taking me off the schedule when he didn't think he could watch over me at the club. The other part was making sure I wasn't alone whenever he couldn't be with me.

I know how important he is in the syndicate. I should be grateful for the amount of time he *does* spend with me. The more I've gotten to know Devil's wife, the more I see what there is to expect when your lover is high up in organized crime.

I thought I knew. After all, I was considered Kieran's for so many years, but I'm beginning to see there's a huge difference between being the underboss and an enforcer.

One's the second-in-command to the top guy; the other is a glorified serial killer. The Libellula Family has a bunch of enforcers. The Sinners Syndicate only has one underboss.

He's a busy fella. I get that. And I should accept that his overprotective nature is a product of being in organized crime and seeing how dangerous Springfield can be. But that's the thing. Kieran used to be overprotective, too. Possessive. Controlling. There are times when I see hints of him in the heavy-handed way that Royce handles situations, and though he's quick to correct them when I point them out, it still bothers me.

Maybe it shouldn't. The fact that I'm comfortable enough with him to let him know when he's going too far is something I *never* had with Kieran—and that was after ten years of knowing him. Royce? It's been six weeks since the night that changed my life. I'm not the silly little girl who looks at the world with rose-colored glasses anymore. I see what kind of man Royce McIntyre is— and, for good or for bad, he's *mine*.

But I'm not willing to sacrifice my hard-fought independence yet. If that means I'm going to run out and get tacos for me and my new friend, I'm going to. I need to prove that I'm worthy of his affection. That he doesn't need to be my 'white knight'. He just has to be the man who loves me and who I love in return.

The Sinner prowling around the penthouse is *Ava's* guard. He gives me a curious look when I pass him on my way to the elevator, staying silent as I walk out of the penthouse. If he thinks that I'm heading downstairs to Royce's place, that's fine. He'll figure it out when Ava asks him his order.

My phone buzzes as I'm stepping out onto the street. A quick peek at the screen reveals that Ava caved: she wants three chicken tacos, extra cheese, no tomatoes. No order for the guard, and I wonder if she asked him. Deciding I'll order a couple of steak ones when I get there, just in case, I toss my phone back in my purse and start toward the taqueria.

I know it's close. Because of that, I'm not really paying attention. I don't know... it could be that relying on Royce has lulled me into a false sense of safety because, when someone bumps into me, knocking me aside, I wasn't expecting it.

Once upon a time, Nicolette would've mumbled an apology even though it wasn't my fault. Right now? My head shoots to my left, looking to see who it was who basically *shoved* against me. The streets aren't really that crowded right now. My first instinct is that it had to be on purpose because why else were they *that* close?

As I pause on the corner, all I see is the wide back of a man with dark hair. Bastard barely missed a step as he stormed away, leaving me behind.

Annoyed, I flip him the bird with my right hand—and that's when it happens. A sudden hand comes out of nowhere, lashing my wrist from around the corner, yanking me with such force that I'm nearly pulled to the ground.

I wasn't expecting that, either, and I'm knocked almost completely off-balance this time. I start to scream, but the second I open my mouth to let the shout out, I hear a *cracking* sound.

Pain explodes in my face as my head snaps over my

shoulder. It takes a second for me to comprehend what happened. I've been slapped. No. Not slapped. The man holding tight to my wrist in one hand, yanked me toward him, then backhanded me dead across the face with the other.

He lets go now. Putting everything into the followthrough, he lets go and, next thing I know, I'm on the ground. I have just enough time to throw my hands out to break the fall, another round of pain slamming into me as the asphalt of the empty road digs right into my palms.

It all happens so fast. My purse spills all over the ground, but I barely notice. My first instinct is to curl up into the fetal position to protect the rest of my body as my cheek *burns*, but then a pair of dark winter boots move in front of me, and I can't stop myself from looking up.

Kieran hikes up his jeans, crouching down in front of me. A stray curl crosses in front of his forehead. "You okay, darlin'?"

No.

Roll 'em...

TWENTY-FOUR
DARLIN'

NICOLETTE

Panic flares up inside of me. I don't even think about screaming. It's all about getting away from him, and if that means crawling, I'll fucking *crawl*.

And that's when he rises up, then steps down *hard* on top of my right hand.

I gasp, and he warns, "Don't scream, Nicolette. This is just between me and you. Don't you scream."

It's been three years since I've heard that tone from him. Quiet and threatening, but with enough pleasantness to it that he can gaslight me into thinking I misunderstood how he meant it... when I hear Kieran's soft voice drift down to me, I'm sixteen again, he's sliding into my bed, running his hand down my sleep pants, telling me to be quiet, that I don't want to wake our parents up, that it's *just between me and you*...

I freeze. There's nothing else I can do. I'm on the

285

ground, he's standing over me, and twenty-seven-year-old Nic disappears.

Kieran smiles. "That's my girl."

I whimper, scraping my palm against the gravel as I try to pull my hand out from beneath his boot.

Ignoring me, he reaches inside of his long coat, pulling out something that he keeps concealed against his palm. His duster fans out behind him, and he drops to one knee. His hand goes for my throat, and I don't know what he has in his hand, but he jabs me with it at the same time as he hooks his hand under my pit, helping me off the ground.

The whole exchange took maybe two, three minutes.

Whatever Kieran jabbed me with? It works even faster.

My eyes start drooping as he drops my arm over his shoulder. His hand shoots around my waist, supporting me as he half-drags, half-carries me toward a car parked nearby. I never even saw it there, and when I do see that he has two doors open for an easy exit and entrance, I tremble.

"Shh. Don't worry. I got you." He gooses my side before pulling his arm back, pushing against me so that I have no choice but to topple down onto the passenger-side seat. "I'm bringing you home."

The last thing I remember is flopping over. I have no control of my body at that point as I fall onto the driver's seat while Kieran chuckles darkly to himself as he slams the door closed behind me.

By the time he walks around his car and slips in through the other side, I'm already out.

MY CHEEK IS TENDER, MY HEAD THROBBING, AND MY WHOLE damn body feels like it weighs a thousand pounds when I wake up.

The ground beneath me is chilly and *hard*. My lower back and hip are stiff, too, but it's my upper body that warns me that something's wrong. Though it's been years since I've had a hangover, this is exactly what I remember it being like.

What the—

That smirk. That goddamn smirk as he stepped on my hand before hoisting me up, moving me around like his own personal doll.

How could I have forgotten that *smirk*?

My eyes spring open and, as though I could sense it while coming to, there it is.

Kieran is sitting on top of some kind of wrapped pallet. The room I'm in is gloomy enough that it doesn't bother my eyes, though I can make out his silhouette against the wall opposite of where I'm sprawled on a cement floor.

His jacket is gone. Wearing nothing but a black t-shirt that shows off the trail of his tattooed leaves, black jeans, and black boots, it's hard to pick out details from this angle... but I see the smirk and know that, whatever happened since he grabbed me, I'm not going to like it.

"Impressive," he says, pushing off the pallet before standing up on his feet. "The drug I shot you up with was supposed to keep someone of your height and weight out for at least another hour."

"You... you drugged me?" That would explain the woozy feeling. I'm outraged enough that he would do something like that to me that I snap past my growing fear. "With *what*?"

"Doesn't matter. I got a guy who hooked me up. Not as decent as that geek Devil's got working for him, but it does the job. It kept you quiet while I moved you."

"Moved me? Moved me where?"

"If I wanted you to know that, darlin', I wouldn't have bothered with drugging you. But it'll be fine. You were only out for about a half an hour. I'm glad. I was getting bored, waiting for you to wake up."

My heart is racing. Panic knocks aside some of the fatigue that came along with whatever he gave me, and as I pull myself up to a sitting position, I look around.

There's not much to see. Besides the two lamps on opposite sides of the small space, all I see is a set of stairs, countless pallets of what's obviously stacked cash now that I can see a little better, and *Kieran*.

Oh, no. Oh, no, no, no.

Dragonfly turf. There's no way I'm not on the East End. The cash gives it away—since the Libellula Family is famed for their counterfeiting operation—but the fact that Kieran felt comfortable enough to abduct me from the West Side and lay me out down here tells me he's on his home territory.

I'm pretty sure I'm underground. The cold has seeped in past the cinderblock wall, and the grey cement floor screams 'basement' to me. There aren't any windows, so I can't see outside at all, and I can't deny that that's not on purpose.

"How did you... *why*?"

"Oh, Nicolette... I know you know why."

I do. I don't want to admit it, but I *do*.

"Kieran—"

"Do you know how much trouble you've caused me?" he asks conversationally. Then, as though he just had a sudden thought, he asks, "How is your mom? Still recuperating?"

I'm not feeling so great, but I'm not so out of it I don't hear alarm bells clanging against my skull. "What? She's fine. Why? Why did you ask me that?"

"Just checking." Kieran shrugs. "I mean, I didn't *want* to kill her. I already lost one mom when I was young. Dad was only with your mom for a couple of years, but I thought of her as mine, too. I didn't want her to have to die to get you back to Springfield, but a little car accident? I didn't think that was so bad."

Wha— *no*. "You're the one who ran into her with your car? She said it was a hit-and-run!"

"Well, obviously. I wasn't going to stick around and get caught. You think I'm new here or something?" He snorts under his breath. "Fucking *Haines* did."

My stomach jolts. "What do you know about Miles Haines?"

"That he's a fucking idiot who didn't know how to follow simple orders. He's lucky someone else took him out before I got the chance to." He pauses, a knowing look on his handsome face. "I'm assuming it was McIntyre."

"I— I don't know what you're talking about."

"Of course not. He probably didn't want to scare you

off with what being in the life's really like. Not me, darlin'. I want you to know my dark side. You can only love me if you love all of me. Just like I love all of you."

He's insane. This... this is *insane*.

"You don't love me!"

"If I didn't love you, I wouldn't have cared when that idiot informant came nosing around the East End, selling info about the pretty blonde that just started up at the Devil's Playground. Fuckin' Fink. He should've taken the money I offered him and shut up, but he wanted more." There's that laugh of his that haunts my dreams. "Just because I offered good money for anyone who could tell me anything about Nicolette Williams, didn't mean he could try to extort me, you know? I had to shoot him. Even a goody-goody like you would agree with that."

Okay. I'm fuzzy and I *hurt* and I have no idea what he's talking about. Did... did someone hear my name at the club and realize that Kieran had a price on my head? That's what it sounds like to me, but Fink? What's a Fink? Well, who, since he's dead... and Kieran's right. If he sold me out, he *deserves* to be dead.

Still, I'm so lost. I'm in so much pain, too, I'm fucking *terrified*, and he's. Still. Talking.

"And then, after I hired Haines to follow up on Garrett Fink's intel, the fucker tried to double-cross me. I gave him that ten grand to bring you to me. What does he do? Blows it against Rolls fucking Royce. So no Nicolette. No cash. I'm telling you, darlin', this would have been so much easier if you just returned to me like you were supposed to."

I shake my head. It only exacerbates the throbbing headache I can't deny, but I have to. He needs to know.

I would *never* willingly return to him.

He sighs, ignoring my ill-disguised panic.

"And then, just this last week alone... I had to park outside Sinners' territory and wait for you to crawl out of their rathole. And all because you thought that pretty boy could keep you from me. But he can't, darlin'. Not when you're *mine*."

Holy shit.

I swear, there is such a difference in the way that Royce claims me and when Kieran does. Royce... his possessiveness warms me to the bone. But Kieran? My skin crawls, and not just because he admitted that he hurt my mom.

That he killed the guy who told him I was back in Springfield, working at the Playground.

That he hired Miles Haines to basically *kidnap* me.

That he knows all about Royce and me, and he's spent the last week stalking me outside of his place...

It's in the way that, after all of his easy admissions, his hand drops to his crotch, eyes shining bright with lust and hate and *murder* as he looks down at me.

I get the lust; he's looked at me like that since I was fourteen with no boobs, no ass, and he saw easy prey. The hate, too. For walking away from him, from abandoning him these last three years, for fucking anyone else... oh, he *hates* me. Any love he might have convinced me he once felt is long gone.

And that's why, when he peers through the shadows

down here, there's no denying the murder in his eyes, either...

That's who Kieran Alfieri is. He's been coddled by the Libellula crime family since he was twenty-two. They took him in ten years ago when he proved himself to them, looked the other way when he kept me as his property when I didn't want to be with him, and gave him the outlet to be the murderous psycho he's always been.

And, lucky me, he decided when I was a kid that I belonged to him.

TWENTY-FIVE
DEFIANT

NICOLETTE

Sick asshole still thinks I do. Why else would he look down at me with a slight curve to his lip after he drugged me, kidnapped me, took me captive... and then, without breaking eye contact, unbutton his jeans?

He doesn't stop there. To my growing horror, Kieran unzips his pants, shoving them down past his ass before dipping his hand beneath his jeans and pulling out his dick.

No surprise that he's hard. He'd deny it, but he was always more turned on by my fear than anything else.

Like now. As he shows off the erection, complete with pre-come already beading at the tip, I know that this is his way of proving to both of us that he'll always consider me to be his—and if I know what's better, I'll give him what he expects.

Of course. As a teen, I learned to give him what he

wanted because he'd get it, one way or another. He wouldn't rape me—or, at least, because he never got that consent under constant duress could ever be considered *rape*, he wouldn't think of it as that—but that's because he did everything he could to make me agree. When I was young enough not to know better or understand that a twenty-one-year-old shouldn't be fucking his sixteen-year-old stepsister, he'd push and nag and cajole until I gave in.

Later, Kieran would punish me if I acted out. He'd make me go without food for a couple of days, and when that didn't work, he had no problem hitting me, knocking me around to get me to behave the way he wanted me to.

But no matter how he treated me, and what I let him have, there was one thing he couldn't do: he could never stamp out the last bit of defiance in me.

I show him that now. I'm at his mercy, no purse in sight, my phone gone, and the realization that no one probably has any idea what happened to me... but when he grabs my arm roughly, forcing me into a kneeling position, then shows me his cock, there isn't anything on earth that will have me obediently sucking him off like I've done a hundred times before.

He expects me to be the naive girl I was. To show that he owns me, that he *controls* me, he'll shove his cock in my face and wait expectantly for me to worship him.

I *won't.*

"I waited too long for you, darlin'. Now be a good girl and open up."

I clench my teeth, keeping my mouth closed.

Kieran moves closer. Spreading his legs, bracing them

against the cement floor, he bumps his cock against my lips.

I shake my head.

He blows out a rush of air. Then, as though I'm being unreasonable, he sighs, then digs his thumb into the underside of my jaw, cutting off my breath.

Fuck. Panic makes me stupid. I forget I can breathe through my nose and, instead, gasp out a breath.

As soon as I do, he shoves the head of his cock past my lips. Once he's in, he assumes that I'll give up. I'll stop fighting.

For a moment, I *do*.

His hand goes to my hair to keep me in place. He tugs on the strands, making sure I can't go anywhere as he rocks on his heels a few times. It's obvious to him that I'm not going to start out willingly licking him, nibbling him, sucking him... but he wants a blowjob, and knowing Kieran, he'll do whatever he thinks he must to get it.

It's not just a blowjob, though. This is showing me that I was fooling myself with all the time I spent with Royce. Kieran probably thinks that he was being magnanimous, giving me a few days with my 'boss' to get it out of my system—but the way he spat out 'pretty boy' like that before, plus knowing where I've been... he knows way more about my relationship with Royce than he should.

Enough that he's being even rougher than usual to *replace* him.

That's what he's doing. It's not about pleasure for him. It's ownership, and he shows me that again and again as he begins to flat-out fuck my mouth.

I'm gagging now. Choking. Tears fill my eyes as he forces himself in and out, the head tickling the back of my throat as my stomach lurches. My gag reflex just about triggered, I'm so close to hurling.

I snap instead.

This wasn't my choice. None of this is. I told Kieran three years ago that it was over. I meant it then, and now that I have Royce in my life? I know what I was missing, wasting all that time with a bastard who treated me like property instead of a person.

No. He treated me like a *pet*.

Well, this bitch is about to bite back—and that's exactly what I do.

I bite his cock, a broken part of me being reforged as steel as Kieran *howls*.

Of course, I knew he wouldn't let me get away with that. I wasn't thinking that far ahead, but I should have because his reaction is worse than anything I might have expected otherwise.

He punches me at the same time as he tears out a chunk of my hair. Not once, either, though it takes the one close-handed hit to get me to release my teeth. As he pulls his cock out of my mouth, his punch sending me to the floor, he kicks me in the side with his boot, then punches me dead-center in the face at least twice more before he stalks away, cursing under his breath.

This time, I do curl up in a ball, trying to protect myself from the rage I unwittingly let loose.

I say unwittingly... I fucking knew what I was doing. It took a lot to provoke Kieran to violence—the manipulative monster preferring to convince me that I *wanted* everything he ever did to me—but he also wanted me to believe that when he *did* lose his temper, it was something only I could do.

Because he loved me, right? And because he expected my love—and obedience—in return.

Not this time, bro.

"Damn it, Nicolette!" His voice is further than before. Squinting through the pain, I see he's storming around the other side of the space, cock out, pants just below his ass as he fumes. "You shouldn't have done that!"

He shouldn't have tried to force me into going down on him.

It was worth it. I don't know how bad he beat me for biting him, but it was *worth* it.

Almost reluctantly, but knowing I have to, I bring my hands to my face. One touch. One touch to feel that my crooked nose isn't the right shape before the pain has me nearly blacking out from it.

"You broke my nose," I gasp. I figured... but, wow. It *is* that bad.

"You bit my cock," Kieran snarls, marching closer again. "You're lucky that's all I did to you. Look at it, Nicolette! I see fucking teeth marks!"

I wish I could. The slap on the street left me with one swollen eye. He backhanded me then, but his cruelty is unmatched. He might want me to think it was an instinctive reaction, striking me because I took the chance to make him hurt, but he couldn't have landed a better punch. He smashed my nose, following through right to the other eye, and I can barely see anything but shapes— not details—through the tears and the haze of pain.

He slugged me with my teeth digging into his cock. If only I'd snapped down and bit the fucker completely off.

I finally realize that hot blood is streaming down my face. My broken nose is bleeding, heading right into my mouth. I choke when I get the first rusty tang against my tongue and lips, sputtering it out.

Even in this state, I know better than to hike up my shirt and use it to stem the flow of blood. If Kieran hasn't noticed that his brand on me is gone yet, that I replaced his tattoo with a seahorse... he's already pissed. I don't really want to make him any angrier.

Shit. My sudden burst of adrenaline from before is beginning to wane, and while I don't regret what I did, I definitely set him off way easier than I used to.

I remember the *murder* I saw... if I'm not careful, I might be his next leaf.

Just as I have that thought, Kieran proves that he really is one scary fucking bastard. Pulling back his obvious fury, he blows a breath out through his nose, and when he walks over to me again, he's as calm as he was the night he 'ran into us' in Riverside.

Standing over me again, he tucks his cock back into his pants. "Fuck. What a waste of time. All I wanted was a little head, but I make you suck me off again, you'll choke on that blood. I went to a lot of trouble to get you back, darlin'. I'm not gonna let you die on me now."

No. Kieran's just going to make me *wish* I was dead.

"It's fine," he says in a tone that tells me it's *not*. "You'll make it up to me. And if you don't? When I go after McIntyre, I'll make sure to cut off his dick first so you have something to practice on. You like that, darlin'?"

Damn it. *Damn* it. I'm not surprised in the least that he'd immediately jump to threatening Royce, but if I'm careless with my own safety, Kieran knows me well enough to guess that I won't be with Royce's.

I collapse to the floor, all of my defiance sapped out of me at the thought that he would target Royce because of *me*.

I'm so *tired*. Whatever he did to me outside of the Suites, I could just lay down, close my eyes, and fall back asleep. It wouldn't help me escape the nightmare I've found myself in—would probably only make it *worse*—and I know better than to give in.

I have to stay awake. If anything, to prove to him that he's not going to control me so easily... I *will* stay awake.

But I won't fight him again. Not until I can figure out a way to convince him to spare Royce. I'll give him whatever he wants if he does, though I'm careful not to tell him that. In this mood, sacrificing myself for my lover would only give my abusive ex all the more reason to go after him.

For now, I have to bide my time and hope like hell Royce cares enough to find me.

Whether it was his threatening Royce or because of the damage he did to my face, Kieran accepts it when I go quiet and still—until he crouches down again and, instead of trying to feed me his cock, tries to take my chin in his hand so he can eye his recent handiwork.

I can't help it. I jerk my head out of his reach. It sends another wave of unbearable pain flashing through me, but I just can't help it. To have him lay those brutal hands on me... I'd rather the pain.

Kieran sighs. "This isn't the way I thought our reunion would go, darlin'."

"Fuck you," I spit out, spraying blood with it. He'd expect the venom, and I'm glad to give it right now.

Tsk-ing, he says, "Bad girls get soap. Is that what you want? I'll wash that fuckin' mouth out with soap and see if that changes your tune."

Hypocrite. Kieran's always been such a goddamn hypocrite—but he doesn't bluff. I remember that. If he says he's going to shove a bar of soap in my mouth, he'll hold me down and make me suck on that the same way he expected me to blow him to make his point.

"Don't make me be the bad guy, Nicolette. I don't like it when you make me the bad guy."

Then maybe he shouldn't *be* the bad guy.

He taps my cheek, sending even more agony through me. At my hiss of pain, he asks, "Maybe you want water instead, hm? That's a good idea. I'll get you some water, you can wash out that blood, and we can start over. What do you think?"

He doesn't want to know what I think.

"That's my girl." He presses his lips to my forehead. "Don't go anywhere, darlin'. I'll be right back. And in case you get any idea of leaving me again?"

Kieran pulls something out of his back pocket. When he jangles it, I squint. It's a key ring with a single key on it. Smirking down at me, he twirls it on his pointer finger. "Door has an automatic lock from the inside so that we can get in, but it takes a key to get out again. Walls are soundproofed, too. A perfect place to keep you until you remember that we're meant to be."

Oh my god. I'm going to die down here, aren't I?

Especially since, when I force myself to my knees, ready to chase after him to see if the door really *did* lock behind him, I don't make it more than a wobble before I collapse back onto the floor.

After that, I can't do anything but drift between unconsciousness and the new nightmare I've found myself in.

Roll 'em...

TWENTY-SIX

SPRINGFIELD WASH

ROYCE

East End.

The goddamn East End of Springfield.

As my eyes keep darting over to the app on my phone showing off the blinking green dot I've been following for the last hour, I'm torn between worrying over Nicolette's fate and cursing my cousin to hell and back.

If I'd been at home or the Playground, I could have made it across town in twenty minutes. From the moment Link got through to my cell, I was already racing toward my car. There isn't a cop in Springfield who'd try giving me a ticket once I told them who I was, so with my lead foot to the pedal, I might've even made it in fifteen.

But I wasn't in Springfield. I was in the middle of bum-fuck-nowhere—okay, it was Merrill Grove, a small town over an hour out of the city—when I got word that Nic was missing, and my heart nearly fucking stopped.

Because this isn't like when Link would sneak off from the Playground or an evening meet so that he could sit outside of Ava's house. Nicolette went a few blocks away from our apartment building, right in the heart of Sinners territory. She was supposed to go get tacos, there and back again, but when a half an hour passed and a call to the taqueria revealed she never made it, it became obvious to Ava that she wasn't just missing.

She was *taken*.

Ava called Devil, who cut short his meeting with the Valdez crew to rush home and be with her. Once he arrived at the penthouse, he sent Ghost out to see if he could find any sign of Nicolette.

He did. Courtesy of calling her phone nonstop as he searched, he found that, her purse, and her wallet shoved in a trash can on the corner of 6th Avenue, two blocks away from Paradise Suites—and conveniently next to a narrow side street that could pass as an alleyway.

I don't blame Ava. I don't blame her for waiting so long before alerting the boss that Nicolette was gone, just like I don't blame Nic for going out on her own to pick up some chow. I made it my point to tell her that, when she's with a Sinner, she's safe. I wanted her to believe that, and she *should* have.

So, no, I don't blame them. I blame the fucker who waited for me to be gone for the evening before he took the first opportune moment he could get to snatch up Nic.

There's no doubt in my mind that that's what happened. Unlike when Ava was snatched up by the

Libellula Family last summer, there aren't any witnesses to what happened to her. No Sinner who sold her out, either, as far as I know. Just her tossed purse, and my certainty that she wouldn't leave me behind if she had the chance.

To keep me from losing my mind as I race toward her, I have to believe that.

I blame me, too. If I'd been in Springfield...

Fuck. A rare show of repressed temper, I slam the flats of my hands against my steering wheel, then take a sharp turn, hoping to shave off a few minutes as I head toward the East End.

It's common knowledge that I don't often leave the city. I'm Springfield-born and bred, and before I joined the syndicate that rules the West Side, I'd spent my formative years running all over these streets. It takes a lot to get me to head out of town. Usually, it's just orders from Devil—something he needs me to do, something I have to take care of in his name—but tonight, I actually had to get the boss's permission to do some clean-up on my own.

Fucking Jake. I knew how badly he was chasing after this new girl. After seeing what happened with the first two, I've picked up on his M.O.

First, he plays the nice guy. He might bump into them at the store. Hold a door open for them. Remark about the weather.

I got a face that makes people want to see if they can beat me at the casino, maybe knock me down a peg or two. I'm probably too pretty for my own good, and while that made finding willing bed partners easy enough, I had to prove myself when other gangsters thought I'd be an easy mark myself.

Just because I'm not fast to draw my weapon, doesn't mean I'm a pacifist. Fuck no. Lincoln was one of the best brawlers in Springfield. As an impressionable eighteen-year-old weakling, I looked up to him. That's how our friendship started out, with him beating the shit out of guys, and me watching in amazement—and jealousy. Eventually, he took me under his wing, teaching me everything he knew.

Games of chance have always been more of my thing. Three-card monte at first, then poker. Blackjack. Craps. The roulette wheel. I get a thrill out of being the most competent, smooth-talking fucker around, but a pretty boy like me won't last long on these streets if I couldn't throw a punch or take one. With Devil as my teacher, the punches I threw became harder, and I dodged faster so that I barely had to take them.

Link kills those who piss him off. I prefer to knock them around to teach them a lesson first, then arrange for them to disappear if they don't. As the underboss, I have at least ten enforcers who stand out from the rest of the soldiers. One word from me, and anyone testing the Sinners Syndicate gets their second—and final—lesson. That's not even counting when I've outsourced, calling on professionals like the Reed twins whenever I'd rather it *not* be traced back to our crew.

Then there's Jake. My cousin isn't like me. He has a face that's pleasant yet nondescript. What color is his hair? Brown. His eyes? Brown. He has an average build, with an average height, and the best way to describe him if you had to is *boyish*. He's twenty-six, could pass for younger, and absolutely no one would think he was a threat... until he goes from being interested in a girl to deciding that she's his.

When that happens, the only person in this world that's safe from him is her—and, damn it, *me*.

Family, right? I'm family, and if I wasn't, if I wasn't trying to protect my idiot cousin from his mistakes, this never would've happened. But when Jake called, I had to go. I've spent years doing my best to rein him in, keeping a short leash on him so that Link doesn't decide he's more trouble than he's worth. As long as Jake understands that any consequences—like what happened after Heather—are not anyone's problem except for his, I'll be there for him.

I thought he got that. After passing along Link's message a few weeks ago, Jake promised that he would do better this time. If Simone wasn't interested, he'd accept that. Considering I had Tanner run Jake's new obsession and I found out she was married to some guy named Will, I figured he'd get the hint that this was another lost cause.

I should've known better. Understandably, I've been a little distracted lately with falling in love—and, okay, obsession—myself. Jake was quiet, Link wasn't pushing me to get rid of him, and I was happy to focus on Nicolette... until I got the call from Jake earlier that he needed my help.

There was a reason why Jake's been quiet. My cousin followed Simone out of Springfield two weeks ago—and had a fatal run-in with her husband. Will Burke was killed in some back alley in a small town I'd never heard of until Jake needed help with clean-up.

He's never gone that far before—but he did early this morning. I went because I had to, and I'd brought a couple of my crew with me to clean up my cousin's mess. We were just finishing up when I felt my phone vibrating in my pocket and answered it to hear Link snapping at me to get my ass back to Springfield.

Killian and Bruno stuck around to make sure nothing could be traced back to Jake; a favor to me, and one I know they'll definitely call in one day since I basically abandoned them in bum-fuck-nowhere in my haste to get to Nic. I had to hurry. One peek at the app at my phone, and I knew exactly where she was.

Dragonfly territory.

I don't tell Link. Just in case I got it all wrong and Nic betrayed me, choosing to return to her grooming bastard of an ex, I keep it from my boss. He'll understand. It's like how when Ava was nabbed and Damien wanted a meet with Link. Link went alone.

For Nicolette, I'm going to do the same damn thing.

Is it insane? Yup. Should I rely on my brothers in the syndicate to back me up? You'd think so.

Will I?

No.

I promised her she'd be safe. Whatever is happening to her, it's on me. Besides, the only one who knows that I injected a tracker in Nicolette after that fucking wallet got his hands on her and it took me longer than I liked to find her is Tanner. He created the microchip and the injector that buried it beneath her skin, and unless Link asks him, he won't offer up the info.

Link will figure it out. For one, I only got the idea to chip Nic because Link insisted on doing that to Ava a couple of months ago. Seeing her be taken by Damien's Family really did a number on him, which is why he had Tanner come up with a sub-dermal tracker in the first place. Her overprotective, possessive husband needed to know where she was at all times after that.

She wasn't the only one he got chipped, though. He did it to himself—making my days of guessing where he went over—and then, as his underboss, jabbed me next.

Once I don't head straight to the Suites to figure out our next step, he'll track me—and that's assuming he doesn't have the app on his phone open the same way I do.

I don't care. From the moment Link told me she was gone, all I want is to get her back. That's it. So it might be suicide, walking into Dragonfly turf when our truce is shaky at best. One of those assholes has Nic.

And I'm getting her back.

THE TRACKER INSISTS THAT NICOLETTE IS SOMEWHERE close by.

It led me to the back exit of a laundromat. At first, I'm not sure if that could be right, but then I think about it. Sinners deal with guns, girls, and gambling. Dragonflies do drugs and dough. Simply put, the Libellula Family gets their wealth and power from the illicit drug trade and a massive counterfeiting ring.

To make fake bills look used, I've heard his pros wash the bills, then put them in a dryer with some rocks. Why wouldn't the Dragonflies do their business as blatantly as possible, in a joint called Springfield Wash?

There are two doors back here. One has a window that peers into the busy laundromat. The other? It's solid metal covered in chipped white paint and a crooked **EMPLOYEE'S ONLY** sign.

The green dot turns red when I move in front of that one.

It's open. I don't know what I would've done if it wasn't, but when I grab the knob on the outside, it turns under my hand. Before I yank on the door, I pull out my nine-mil. Disengaging the safety takes a second, but I do it. I don't have any idea what I'm walking into. Could be nothing, could be an ambush. Just in case, it's better to be prepared.

My gun up, I use my left hand to pull open the door. It's gloomy, a pair of cement stairs leading me underground. Over the blood pumping through my veins, thudding in my ears, I think I hear... whimpering.

I tip-toe down the stairs, ducking my head as soon as I can to get a peek at what's below.

On the floor, I see fabric. Laundry bags? Maybe. Pallets of fake cash line the walls, fresh from the printer, I bet. And there, curled up alongside one of them, is a head of golden blonde hair I'm intimately familiar with.

She's turned away from me, and if I didn't hear the

soft cries coming from her, I would've feared she was dead.

Regardless, my gut tightens, fingers twitching on the trigger as if she *is*.

A quick sweep reveals that she's the only one down there. I spare two, maybe three seconds to make sure of it, then murmur, "Nicolette? Baby?"

At my voice, she starts, then slowly moves. No. She rolls over, and when I get my first look at her, I have to clamp my jaw down so I don't howl.

What the fuck did he do to her?

Roll 'em...

TWENTY-SEVEN
FLIP A COIN

ROYCE

N icolette's face is covered in blood. Both eyes are swollen shut, mere slits now, and her nose is crooked. The tiny diamond stud is missing, like someone pulled it out—or *punched* it out.

She struggles to go from lying on her side to rising up on her knees. "Is someone here?" she whispers.

Fucking hell. Can she not see me? There are two weak lamps down here and no windows, but that's light enough that I can see her... but I don't look like someone took a barbell to my face.

That realization gets my ass in gear. I don't even finish walking down the stairs. I jump down the last four.

"*Nic.*" The sound is ragged, torn from my chest. I immediately shove my gun behind me, tucking it in my waistband as I drop to my knees on the cement floor. I could give a shit if the gun goes off and I shoot myself in the ass. All I care about is getting to her—and finding out what the hell happened. "It's me, baby. I got you. I'm here."

"Royce." Her bottom lip is split, dried blood welling in the corner while the gash in the middle is shiny and red. When she fights to smile at me, my heart breaks at the same time as pride joins the other parade of emotions marching through me. Whoever did this to her tried to break her—but that will never, ever happen, and her strength fucking amazes me as she fumbles for my hand, squeezing it tightly. "You came."

Of course I did. I'd walk over fucking glass and hot coals to make it to this woman.

Her battered face screws up, free hand scrabbling against the hard floor as she tries to scoot closer to me.

"How did you... how did you know where I was?"

My first instinct is to grab her face, to hold her steady, to witness every mark blooming on her skin because someone has to take it in. I don't want to cause her any more pain, though, so I settle on laying one hand on her shoulder, tightening my fingers around hers with the other, giving her a connection so that she knows I'm here with her.

What I don't do is tell her that I tracked her through a microchip. She'll need to hear that eventually, but in this state? Knowing Nicolette the way I do, it'll only agitate her more.

She can hit me with another frying pan if it makes her feel better later. Now? It doesn't matter how I found her.

All that matters is what happened to her while I was racing to get to her.

So, in a voice stifled with an ice-cold anger I can't deny, I ask her softly, "Who did this to you? Who hurt you?"

She gasps, choking on a breath that I quickly realize is a sob. That's answer enough—as is the fact that we're in a Dragonfly hidey-hole—but I wait with as much patience as I can scrape up for her to finally whisper, "Kieran."

Alfieri.

The bastard who stole her innocence before stealing the last thirteen years of her life. First, because he'd trapped her in an abusive relationship. Later, because everything he did left its stamp on her, including her need to have her independence to the point that she almost *lost* it.

I'll get her out of here. I'll get her safe, get her help, and then I'm coming back to deal with her nightmare.

I start to scoop her up. It doesn't even occur to me to see if she can walk. She's still on the floor, and I'll gladly carry her.

I don't get the chance. Before I can figure out how to lift her up without aggravating her injuries, I hear the door behind me open. One step, then another, jaunty fucking steps that are ten times worse because whoever is coming down here is *whistling* merrily as he does so.

Nicolette starts to tremble. And that? That seals it for me. When I walked down those steps, my only plan was to find her and get her back where she belongs: with me. But the way he whistles, jogging down the stairs as though he didn't leave Nicolette in pain and whimpering on the floor fucking *infuriates* me. It takes a lot to push me; my even-keeled temper is the foil to Devil's rage. But now?

I finally understand what could cause one man to hack off another's head the way that he did all those years ago.

An hour and a half. Alfieri got his paws on her, tossed her in this basement, and fucked her up this bad in an hour and a half—and the motherfucker is *whistling*.

I try not to think about how much worse off she would've been if I'd been any later. I got lucky Alfieri wasn't down here when I arrived, but my luck just ran out. Before I could get Nicolette out of here, he's *back*.

Swearing to her that I won't let him hurt her again, I'm on my feet, facing the stairs as Alfieri appears without ever thinking about grabbing my Beretta.

That was my mistake. So used to my fists being my weapon of choice, I balled my hands tight in barely restrained fury when I saw the look of surprise on Alfieri's face. He recovered quickly—quicker than me, goddamn it—and he dropped the glass of water he'd held in his hand, trading his surprised expression for one of pure murder the same time as he went for his gun.

I don't flinch. It hits me a second too late that I fucked up, but I do what I always do in situations like this: I pull a half-smile to my face and hope he'll underestimate me. That's all I need. One second, and I'll take care of this.

And then the bastard snorts, lowering his gun to his gut, and I want to think I have him right where I want him... until he says, "Rolls fucking Royce in the flesh. Shit. You got here quicker than I thought. Good. That'll save me time."

I don't give anything away. I'm sure of it, but Alfieri laughs.

He laughs. I want to rip his tongue out of his mouth and his lungs out through his chest so that he can't say another word, and he *laughs*.

"Oh, yeah. I know who you are. When I saw you with my property, I made it my mission to learn everything about you." Alfieri gestures at my curled-up *empty* fists. "What are you thinking, fixer? You don't get your hands dirty. You use your mouth for Devil." He curls his upper lip. "Pretty boy like you, I wouldn't be surprised if you give him your ass, too."

Oh, *come* on. A woman-beater and a homophobe, too? Could this guy be any more garbage? I know there are some fellas in the syndicate who have a problem when it comes to who a couple of 'em love, but that's never been me. As long as the adults are consenting, who gives a fuck, right?

Nicolette loves me. She *chose* me. I didn't have to throw her in a basement for her attention after preying on her when she was a kid.

He deserves to die for that alone. Hurting her. Making her bleed... making her *afraid*... if he wasn't already a dead man when I pulled my car up to the door, he is now. No need for outsourcing, either, not like I did with Miles Haines.

I was still trying to take care of Nic and the Sinners at the same time. Now? At this moment, I know exactly which one owns my loyalty more than the other.

And I'm not making Nicolette spend a moment longer in this hellhole than I have to.

I move my left hand from hanging at my side to the top of my thigh.

"Hands, asshole," barks Alfieri. His smarmy bastard act disappears in the blink of an eye as he trains his gun on me again. "Let me see your hands, or I stop fucking with you and just take you out now."

Will he shoot me? Oh, definitely. I don't have a doubt in my mind that he's doing exactly what he said: believing he has the upper hand, he's fucking around, taking his time before I become another leaf on the back of his bicep.

Dumb fucks. They always underestimate me, don't they?

"I just want to reach in my pocket. Come on, Alfieri. You don't think I got a piece in here, do you?" I throw my suit jacket away from me just enough to reveal my empty holster while still keeping the gun hidden behind my back concealed. "You were right. I came as quick as I could. I forgot my gun, but I do have this."

He doesn't stop me from slipping the fingers of my left hand into my pocket, retrieving one of my coins. I show it to him.

"A quarter?" Suddenly amused—and still not thinking I'm capable of doing anything other than rolling a pair of dice—he lowers his piece. *Good.* "What the fuck do you think you can do with that?"

"Let's flip it. Heads, you get Nic. Tails? She's mine, and you never bother her again. We walk out of here and forget this happened," I lie. "Same as if you win. Come on, Alfieri. I know your kind. A Dragonfly first, yeah? You gonna fuck up Libellula's truce with the Devil of Springfield over some pussy?"

If he won't, I definitely am.

I hope to fucking hell that Nicolette knows better than to believe anything I'm saying. Alfieri was right. I'm a walking mouth. If I can use words first, I will, but sometimes they're just not enough.

I raise my eyebrows at the fucker who thought he could take the only woman I've ever loved like this.

He shrugs. He's as much of a liar as I am, but I let him think I'm dumb enough to be fooled as he says, "Sure. Go on. Flip it."

I do.

The cocky bastard's eyes trace the arc of my quarter. I know he couldn't care less which side it lands on. The proof is in how, even as the coin spins, he's lifting his gun once more, aiming it back at my chest. There's no way in hell he'll let me have her.

Fair enough. I don't plan on letting him have her, either.

Will he shoot me the second the coin hits the ground? Probably. Good thing I started to react before he did.

He's watching the coin, so sure he has the upper hand that, for a split second, that's the only thing in this basement that has his attention.

Fucking moron. Alfieri never should've taken his eyes off of me. He also never should've taken my word that I didn't have a gun just because my holster was empty.

His gun is still only halfway to position when I reach behind me, yanking my gun out and aiming right at him.

I'm not a marksman. I don't have the practice with my

Beretta that Link has with his Sig Sauer. When he made an example of Twig Mathewson, shooting him in the cock first, then the head... that was for an audience. Fuck that. Alfieri hurt Nic. Just when I promised her that she was safe, he shattered that illusion, stealing her away from me—and he *hurt* her.

A Beretta M9 holds fifteen rounds. Despite rarely firing it, I spent the last ten years in guns. An irresponsible gun owner is a *dead* gun owner. I take care of my shit, and that includes checking how many bullets are in my magazine.

I empty five of them into Alfieri. Right to the chest so that there's no hope of him surviving. One of the first lessons I learned when I started out in the life was that a sharp mind and fast tongue might get me far, my quick fingers even farther, but if I decide to fire my piece?

I'm no cop. I'm not trying to incapacitate anyone. Sinners shoot to kill.

And that's exactly what I do.

Blood sprays everywhere when the first bullet tears straight through his chest and out his back, and I'm grateful that Nic is crumpled up on the floor, far enough away from the spatter that it barely hits her. His chest so much fucking Swiss cheese, Alfieri flops upon impact of each bullet. He's dead with the first hit—a chest shot that hit his heart—but his body takes a few seconds to catch up. The other four bullets are simply a mix of insurance and revenge.

Tough guy thought I was an easy mark. Like so many others, he was wrong.

I don't often let my rage out of its cage, but I make an

exception for the monster who hurt my girl. Shit, I would've made him suffer more if I could. If Nic didn't have her hands over her ears, blocking out the deafening gunfire that echoes around the empty room he kept her captive in, I'd take out the last of my aggression on the worthless corpse sprawled out on his belly.

I spare a quick assessing look over Alfieri, verifying that there's no surviving the damage my gun did or the blood he's lost. The quarter, I notice, landed about ten inches away from his shoulder. Tails.

Of course. I needed my right hand to pull my gun. My 'heads' quarter was in the other pocket.

Oops. Oh, well.

Now, if she didn't have her hands over her ears... but she does, and despite how loud it is, I can still make out the sound of her sobs over my ringing ears.

Once the threat to her is gone, I go right on autopilot. Stopping only to engage the safety on my gun, holster it, then snatch up my bloody quarter, I'm immediately at Nicolette's side. Crouching down low, I scoop her up, lifting her onto my lap as the first tremors run through me.

If she struggled, if she made it clear that she didn't want anything to do with me at this moment, I don't know how I would've reacted. It would be totally understandable, but just like I had to off Alfieri, I need to make sure that Nicolette is okay.

"I got you," I swear again, and this time I fucking mean it. "He can't hurt you anymore. Never again, baby. You hear me? Never again."

Instead of stiffening or trying to get away from my hold, she collapses into my embrace.

"I thought... I thought... Oh, Royce." She buries her face against my chest, jolting when she hits her obviously broken nose. Yanking back, Nicolette glances up at me through her swollen eyes. "I thought you— shit. I got blood all over your shirt."

Fuck the shirt. I cradle the back of her head, guiding her down so that her cheek is pressed to my chest. I'm careful not to bump her nose. I want her to know that her comfort is the most important thing in the goddamn world to me right now. Let her bleed all over me so long as it's blood she can spare.

"Shh..." I stroke her hair, doing my best to be soothing—and not think about the last time I was crouched low, a bloody blonde in my arms. A Dragonfly hurt her then, too, but I wasn't able to avenge her—or save her. With Nicolette, I'll *do* both. "I'm gonna move you. Is that okay? I'm gonna carry you up the stairs. I got my car. We're getting you home."

Her fingers dig through my shirt, into my chest. "I thought you were going to let him keep me."

"*Never*," I vow. "I will never let anyone take you away from me."

It's as though that's all she needed to hear. Still clinging to me, she nods, shudders out a breath, and closes her eyes.

TWENTY-EIGHT
DAMIEN LIBELLULA

ROYCE

My heart lodges in my throat. Holding her in place on my knee, I free one hand, placing it under her nose. She's still breathing. A thumb lifting up her eyelid reveals the whites. Her eyes have rolled back in her head.

She's out. From panic, exhaustion, *relief*... I don't know what it is, but she knows she's safe with me. She waited until she was safe in my arms to let herself go.

I don't know what Alfieri managed to do to her. The mess he made of her face is enough, and only now that he's dead do I acknowledge that the zipper on his jeans was down. Button was done up, sure, and there could be a bunch of reasons why his zipper wasn't... but the worst of them have me squeezing Nicolette tight before I rise up to my feet.

Right now, it doesn't matter. In time, I'll get her to tell me what went down after she left the Suites. And if I don't, that's okay, too, so long as she understands that I won't let that happen ever again.

It's a bitch, carrying her bridal style the same time as I have my gun out. Worse when I get all the way to the top of the stairs and realize the door's locked. I give myself a moment to curse under my breath before figuring out my next move.

I could call Link. Assuming he hasn't tracked me here, I've got my phone in my pocket. I could call the boss, but I'd rather get the fuck of Dragonfly territory before I loop him in.

I make an executive decision. Still holding onto Nic, I go back into the gloomy basement. She doesn't stir with all the jostling of her that I'm doing, and I'm glad. I don't want her to watch as I rifle through a dead man's pockets.

There isn't anything that Alfieri has that I want. I leave his weapon on the floor, don't bother with his cash or his wallet, and only take the single key ring that I hoped he'd have. Figuring that he had to be able to come and go to leave Nic down there, it made sense this would be the key to the inner lock.

It is. Since there's no way in hell I'll ever willingly come back here, I toss the key after I unlock it. Here's hoping no one else in the Libellula Family has a key to the basement because, if you ask me, it would be poetic justice if Alfieri was left to rot beneath a front for his mob. I doubt it, not with all those pallets down there, but a man can dream, yeah?

My gun makes it hard to shove open the door without moving Nic too much, but I refuse to walk out of this place empty-handed. I don't know who might have seen me walk in here—or if any of the Dragonflies know that Kieran Alfieri had earlier—and the last thing I want to do is walk out and face one of our rivals.

It's the last thing I want to do... and yet, that's exactly what happens.

Looking as though he decided to take a stroll in the wintry dark, there stands Damien Libellula, wearing one hell of an expensive jacket over his immaculate suit. The collar is up, hugging his sharp jaw. His hair is parted perfectly on the left, combed precisely so that every dark strand is in place.

He has a shark's smile and a pair of shrewd eyes, though his voice is pleasant as he calls out a greeting to me before he nods at my drawn weapon.

"You gonna put that away, Royce?" He shows me his hands. His empty hands. "I think we can hash this out without any guns. Don't you?"

I could shoot him. I could shoot the head of the Libellula Family dead where he stands, and I'm pretty sure no one could stop me. Sure, he probably has bodyguards just out of sight who'd turn me and Nicolette into Bonnie and Clyde at their end, but I *could*.

I don't.

It takes a moment for me to maneuver the woman in my arms so that I can slip my Beretta back into its holster. Not because I want to talk to him at all, but because I can't risk Nic getting caught in any crossfire.

However, before I can tell Damien that, his smile widens.

"There. It's just you and me—"

Is it? As though me putting my gun away was a signal,

someone moves their head around the corner of the building. I only see two cars—mine, and a flashy red one that must belong to Damien—so I doubt it's someone who is actually is trying to wash their clothes.

"Really?" I ask wryly. "No backup?"

"I was already coming to see what one of my top enforcers was doing at another one of our operations after asking for a week's leave. Personal business, he said, until my cameras caught him with a woman over his shoulder as he carried her into the cellar. Imagine my surprise when one of my guys said he saw one of Lincoln's arriving ten minutes ago. I'd hoped to catch you on your way out. I don't think there's any need for backup, though, do you?"

That's the thing about Damien Libellula that always rubbed me wrong. Even when he was running guns alongside me and Link, he had this attitude that he was better than most crooks. Not only that, but he's so damn *rational.*

Of course, if you cross him, you're dead. If you insult him, you're dead. If you so much as look at his baby sister wrong, you're gutted with his trademark stiletto knife— and then you're dead.

He hides his brutal side behind a gentile veneer that I'd buy if it wasn't for the fact that I was on the streets the same time as he was. He might be a decade older than me, his salt-and-pepper hair making him seem older than his forty years, but I know the real Damien.

He prides himself on his honesty. If he says he didn't bring backup, he didn't *bring* backup.

But someone is still watching us from a distance. If it

wasn't for the way the lamplight falls on them, I'd think it might be a coincidence—until I notice the way they're watching Damien specifically.

I look closer. It's a woman. A pretty woman, maybe late twenties or so. She doesn't seem curious, or in awe that the head of the Libellula Family is out for a stroll.

Oh, no. She looks *furious*.

"You sure," I ask, a tiny jerk of my chin in her direction. "Looks like we're not alone."

He doesn't even turn around. "If it's a gorgeous brunette staring daggers into my back, don't you worry about that. She's not here for you. She's gunning for me." A low chuckle, as though he said something funny. "Probably because she's pissed off I took her gun."

I blink. "What?"

Damien waves his hand. "It's personal. Like I said, don't worry about it. I'm here because I want to know what went on in my cellar."

He does, does he?

I don't want to disturb Nicolette, and I only hope she's so out of it right now that she doesn't realize I'm taking her chin gingerly between my fingers before I turn her so that Damien can see what Alfieri did to her.

"This," I bite out. "This is what happened."

Damien sucks in a breath. "I was afraid of that. I'm sorry, Royce. Listen, I have a doctor on call. If you'd like, I can have her come down and tend to Ms. Williams."

My fury was already building up. That just adds fuel to the fire. "McIntyre."

"Pardon?"

"Her name is McIntyre."

Or it will be. First fucking chance I get, I'm making this woman mine legally. Even Link knew that a wedding license and a ring were enough to make his lover think twice about trying to get away. He even had a second wedding, showing her off in front of half of Springfield down at St. Pat's. She'll be my wife, and I'll spend the rest of my life making sure no one can ever hurt her again.

Damien hesitates. I see his eyes slide to the side, and I realize that he's checking to see if that woman is still watching us. I follow the direction of his gaze only to see that she's gone.

He sighs. "I know what you must think of my Family," he begins, frowning when I scoff. Clearing his throat, he tries again. "Our women only get involved with the business when they choose to. Otherwise, they're protected—"

"And called 'property'."

"We need to know who is being protected," he responds with a tight smile. "If you're not a Dragonfly, then you need to belong to one. But, I assure you, it's consensual. Or it's supposed to be." He purses his lips. "I assume I'm down one enforcer."

I tilt my head toward him. "You assume right."

"I told him to leave the Williams girl alone. That she traded her loyalties from our Family to Lincoln's syndicate. That's not a crime, is it? But he didn't listen." Damien *tsks*. "If you hadn't handled him, I would have. He should be glad about that."

Considering the rumors I heard about what Damien does to Dragonflies who betray him or disobey, I'm sure he's right.

"I thought I made myself clear years ago. Even when we didn't have our truce, civilians should never get mixed up with the syndicates."

Heather. He's talking about Heather. "Being on the wrong side of town shouldn't be a death sentence, Damien."

The mafia leader doesn't disagree, and even goes one step further by admitting: "What happened to Heather Valiant was and will always be a mistake. A tragic mistake, but one that I readily corrected. I would have done the same thing tonight if I had to. I want you to understand that."

I do. It's for the same reason why the prick who shot Heather was dead within twenty-four hours, while I just had to carry the guilt with me that I couldn't stop her from getting mixed up with the syndicates.

I nod. "I'm glad you see it that way." And that he doesn't seem pissed that I offed Alfieri. "Now, if you'll just move over, I'm getting Nic—"

Before I can finish my demand, another car turns the corner. For a second, I think Damien was stalling, that he was waiting for more of his mafia to show up, but then I recognize Luca sitting behind the wheel of the luxury town car as it stops by us.

The door to the backseat flings open. Bursting at the seams of his suit from his obvious temper, Link comes stalking toward us.

Damien smiles at him. "Ah... Lincoln. So nice of you to join us at last."

"Fuck you, Damien. I was already on my way before

you called me and told me my underboss might need a hand."

So he didn't bring any backup... but he arranged for me to have some?

Fucking hell. Just when I think I have Damien Libellula figured out, he does something like this.

"Lincoln—"

My old friend takes in the unconscious woman in my arms. He points. "You found her. Great. But what the fuck happened tonight?"

I can answer that.

"One of his enforcers took Nicolette. He hurt my wife." I swallow and purposely meet Link's dark gaze. "I killed the fucker."

I don't have to tell either of these leaders who was responsible for it. Damien had his cameras that showed Kieran carrying an obviously drugged Nicolette into the basement—that had to be the case, and depending on what he gave her, that might also explain why she passed out again—and Link knows because I talked to him about Nic's ex before.

Damien doesn't say anything now. Link, however, looks confused for a moment.

He wipes the corner of his mouth with the back of his hand. "Did I miss something? Wife?"

I nod. "We haven't had the wedding yet, but she's my wife."

Link's dark eyes light up. "Ah. Gotcha."

I don't have to explain—and I wouldn't have the chance to if I wanted to give it a try. Slipping away from where the rest of us are gathered, Damien crosses the small parking lot. A high-pitched *beep* as he disengages his car's alarm catches both mine and Link's attention.

"In honor of our truce, I hope to be invited to your wedding," is the last thing Damien says before he slides into the flashy red car parked next to my boring black one and closes the door, leaving me and Link alone behind his counterfeiting operation.

I take that as our cue to get the hell out of the East End. Despite what Damien said about understanding why I had to eliminate his enforcer, I'm sure he'll have his own clean-up crew coming to take care of his soldier's body.

As for his request... I don't say anything to that since he wouldn't be able to hear me anyway, but I make a mental note. If Nicolette is okay with me inviting the head of the Libellula Family to our wedding in the future, sure, I'll send him a save the date.

I just got to get there first—and that includes taking Nicolette back to the West Side where I can get her checked over.

We wait for Damien to leave. Once his car disappears from our sight, Link turns to me.

"Luca's gonna drive you. I know you won't want to put her down until you're somewhere you trust, so let's do that. Give me your keys, okay? I'll bring your car back to the Suites."

"Link, I don't know what to say—"

He claps me on the shoulder. "You're my second, Royce. You've stood by my side even before we were Sinners. It's about time I return the favor. I got this. You take care of your girl."

I nod, ignoring the lump in my throat. Link... he gets it—and he proves that he gets me, too, when he says, "Listen. My second biggest regret is not putting a bullet in Joey Maglione's skull before Ava was forced to. You did what you had to. Don't think about the bastard you blew away. Just focus on your wife, okay?"

I don't ask what Link's *first* biggest regret is. It's obvious. If he could turn back time, he'd never have walked away from Ava in the first place. He had fifteen years to regret willingly giving her up because he was convinced he wasn't good enough for her.

I know I'm not good enough for Nic. I come with baggage—but, then again, so does she. And if there's one thing I take out of Link's words, it's this: I won't let it haunt me. Not like Heather. He's right. I did what I had to do, and if my wife—my soon-to-be wife—struggles with watching her past die in front of her, I'll deal with that, too.

That's what I do.

I deal with the Devil. I clean up the Sinners' messes.

I love Nicolette Williams—*McIntyre*.

And I will do anything to protect her.

'Til death do us part.

EPILOGUE

NICOLETTE

When Royce told me to pack for a weekend getaway, I didn't hesitate.

It's been a month since everything happened with Kieran. Sometimes, I'm surprised at how quickly it went from the end of March to the knocking on May's door. It feels like I blinked and, suddenly, the time was gone.

It's a stress response. I know that. From the trauma of being assaulted by Kieran again, followed by the absolute relief that slammed into me when I watched Royce blow that sick bastard away. He doesn't think I saw it. He believes that—thanks to my broken nose and busted eye —I was too out of it to witness the five seconds that changed my life.

I let him. My protective lover—and, yup, one of my former stalkers—has always wanted to save me any way he could. To spare me from watching him execute my abuser... it's better if Royce thinks that I didn't gasp in gratitude as I watched as the first bullet found its home in Kieran's chest before the relief—the absolute *relief*—had me crying the first tears I shed since my twisted ex abducted me.

A little white lie for my white knight.

I don't really remember a lot about what happened after he was dead. One moment, Royce was squeezing me to him, making promises that fluttered into my ear, then out again. I clung right back, like he was a mirage that would disappear if I so much as closed my eyes.

But I did. I'm not sure why, only that it wasn't my choice. When I woke up again, I was stretched out in the back seat of a car, lying on Royce's lap. He was stroking my hair with trembling fingers. He didn't stop when he noticed me quirking open my good eye, only gave me that crooked half-smile of his before telling me that I was safe.

This time, he was right. Even as I drifted back to sleep —or unconsciousness—I looked up into those blue eyes and knew that, with Royce McIntyre, I will always be safe.

There's no more pretending I haven't moved into his place. After Devil's driver, Luca, brought us back to Paradise Suites—and the leader of the Sinners Syndicate himself drove Royce's car home for him—he carried me into his apartment and, for the next few weeks, I didn't leave. One of the local doctors on the syndicate's payroll gave me pain pills that had me flying before resetting my nose and patching up the rest of me. I wasn't trapped with Kieran long enough to do that much damage, though A for effort, asshole, considering how much he worked me over in such a short amount of time.

I'm on leave from the Playground. Royce promised that I could go back when I was feeling better. I didn't push it because a) I'd be lying if I said I wasn't still a little shaky from being assaulted twice in two weeks and b) the double shiners and obviously broken nose might buy me some sympathy, but it was better to wait to pull my uniform back on until the bruises finally faded.

The last of the mottled green and yellow skin is hidden under a face of make-up tonight. It's the last bit of physical evidence left from Kieran's attack, and while I know the emotional wounds will take longer to heal, having this weekend with Royce is a starting point.

The man's a fucking godsend. I wake up each morning, wrapped in his arms, wondering how the hell I got this lucky. And maybe, when I was still doped up on pain meds, I might've mentioned that if he's sticking around because he feels guilty about what happened, not to bother, he quickly proves me wrong.

If anything, Royce blames himself for not being there in time to keep Kieran from doing what he did. Bullshit. I knew when I started this thing with Royce that he was a high-ranking member of the syndicate. Now I know just how high he is in the organization. There will be times when he has to do his job. I get that.

I also know that, if I'd listened to Ava and not tried to prove that I was meaningless in the grand scheme of things, I wouldn't have gotten caught by Kieran. So sure that Royce was going to get tired of me and move along like he's done with every other woman before, I stubbornly clung to the one thing I recovered after my time with my ex: my defiant independence.

CARIN HART

I'm learning. Just like Ava did, and the other wives and girlfriends. In the Libellula Family, women were property. In the Sinners Syndicate? I only have a few examples to go by, but they're treated a hell of a lot better on the West Side than on the East End. These men might be possessive and overprotective, but every moment I spend with Royce, I feel appreciated, too.

Loved.

Worshiped.

And it's fucking amazing.

This impromptu trip is one example. He just woke me up with a kiss this morning, asked me if I was up to taking a quick flight, and grinned wickedly when I told him I was. I didn't even have to pack. He did that himself: a suitcase for him, one for me, and a large black bag that hung from a hanger that he loaded into the limo.

Devil let us borrow Luca again. He drove us to the small hangar where the syndicate has its own private plane, murmuring something to Royce as he got out to help retrieve our luggage from the back. Royce had another smile for Luca as he accepted the hanger from him, and then we were off.

It was a three-hour flight that went very quickly once we were allowed to move about and my lover pointed out the bed. Seriously. Devil's private plane has a *bed* on it, with clean sheets that were more than a little rumpled by the time we were touching down again in...

Las Vegas.

I don't know that that is where we are until I'm sitting next to Royce in a car waiting for us at the airport we flew into. It's a rental, which makes me question his "spur of the moment" excuse when I think about flight plans for the private plane and available rental cars that he could get at a moment's notice.

He claims it's part of being a fixer. No matter what, he can get his hands on anything, and if his eyes slide over to the large, black bag hanging on the grab bar behind the driver's seat... well, I was definitely curious.

Then we drove forty minutes through the desert before eventually passing the iconic *Welcome to Las Vegas* sign. My heart rate kicked up as I saw the neon lights of the Strip for the first time, but Royce barely reacted to the glitz and glamour of it all.

Figured. A habitual gambler who was *good* at it, plus access to his boss's private plane... this probably isn't his first trip to Vegas. He confirms it when I ask, but then, in that sly way he has, says, "But I've never been where we're going."

Color me intrigued. Leaning back against the leather interior of the flashy car he rented, I alternated between gaping at the various buildings, casinos, and people I saw and trying to get a good read on Royce's features.

Damn poker face. He's not giving anything away.

It's another twenty-five minutes, thanks to the congestion; it's about nine by the time we pull off the main road, following the GPS on his phone to a crowded parking lot. Luckily, we find a spot, and if I have no idea why this one particular lot is so important, I go with it.

"Don't worry about the luggage," Royce says, pocketing the car keys. "We won't need that until the hotel."

Okay. So we're not at the hotel.

Hmm.

I wait in my seat as Royce climbs out. I learned my lesson about allowing my chivalric gangster to open my door for me. It's such a small thing for me, but it makes him happy to do it, so why not?

He's holding onto the black bag's hanger with one hand, offering me the other to help me out of my seat.

At my curious look, Royce chuckles. "This we *will* need, Nic. Trust me. I did my research. It's better if we bring our own."

Yeah... he's really got me stumped now—and I stay that way as he throws his arm over my shoulders, tucking me into his side and guiding me down one street, then another.

Within a couple of minutes, I'm staring up at two words made up of block letters and shining light bulbs: **WEDDING CHAPEL.**

I blink. Doesn't matter. Doesn't change what I'm seeing, either.

It's hard to tear my stare away from the entrance to the sandstone-colored building. I do, though, and—*wham*—now I'm looking at a gaudy sign that looks like it belongs in front of a shopping center. It also says 'Wedding Chapel' on it, with a drawing above it. Then, above *that*, are three worlds written in a thick, italic font:

Viva Las Vegas

I'm a big musical freak. That doesn't just extend to Broadway and showtunes. Any media that has singing and dancing in it will catch my attention. I've watched plenty of classic Elvis films—mainly because of my affection for musicals and my mom's affection for Elvis... who got it from my grandma—so I'm familiar with *Viva Las Vegas,* both the song and the movie.

They get *married* in that movie.

Over my stunned silence, I hear a zipper being tugged down. I spin back in time to see Royce opening up what I realize now is obviously a dry-cleaning bag...

"Holy shit," I whisper. "That's a wedding dress."

"Correction, Nic. This is *your* wedding dress."

My mouth falls open.

Royce pushes aside the garment bag, showing off the dress inside. Which is, quite obviously, a wedding dress. It's more than that, though, as I take in some of the details. I don't know how he fit it in that bag. Once free of it, I see the thick, ruffled skirt, the intricate bodice, the closed sleeves that end in even more ruffles, and I know exactly what I'm looking at.

It's a replica of Christine's wedding dress, the one the Phantom forces her to wear during the finale of the Broadway show.

Which means it really is *my* wedding dress, isn't it?

Moving into me, Royce hoists up the dress, measuring it against my body. His smile has a self-satisfied edge to it as he nods. "Just like I thought. It should be a perfect fit."

"How did you... where did you... what—*why*?"

"Remember, Nic, I'm intimately aware of every inch of your body. It was a snap to figure out the right size for you. As for why... that's pretty obvious, don't you think? A bride deserves the wedding dress of her dreams for her special day. Night. You know what I mean."

I *think* I do. "Are you trying to tell me we're *eloping*?"

Royce nods. "Did I ever mention that, when I was a kid, I looked up to Link? To Devil?"

I have no idea where he's going with this, but I nod.

"Think of this like me following his lead again. He had a wedding just for him and Ava to make sure she was his. After that, he did the whole shebang. Church wedding, tons of guests. Big reception down at the Playground. I thought he got it right. Tonight's for us. Tonight, I make you mine officially. You want to get hitched at St. Pat's and invite your mom and your friends? We can do that this summer. But I wasn't waiting any longer than I had to to keep you, Nic." He reaches out, brushing his thumb along the height of my cheek where the whispers of my bruises are. "Just long enough for you to heal a little."

"I... I don't know what to say."

"I do." His blue eyes gleam beneath the shining lights of the sign. "Say 'yes'."

Yes.

It's not even a question. Do I love Royce McIntyre? Of course I do. Would I give anything to be his wife? Yes.

But am I going to bust his chops a little?

Oh, definitely.

"'Yes' to what?" I ask him. "You didn't ask me anything." When Royce arches his eyebrows, I prod a bit more. "Like, I don't know, something about *if* I'll marry you."

"And risk you thinking you can refuse? Yeah, right."

I can't help it. I laugh.

You think I wouldn't. I spent years trapped in a relationship where I was expected to do what I was told, and

I couldn't refuse *anything*. Even joking—and I'm not so sure Royce *is* joking—I'd be punished if I did.

But I don't have to worry about that with Royce. So it's only been a couple of months. So I'm going to have to hide the fact that I eloped with him until after I get that big church wedding he's talking about, otherwise I'll break my mother's heart. That's nothing new—but the way I feel about Royce is. The way he makes me feel when I'm around him is.

If I laughed at Kieran, he'd slap me. But Royce?

He grips the back of my neck before I even see him move. With a gentle squeeze, my head tilts up, giving him full access to my mouth. He swallows the last of the laugh with his kiss, turning it deeper until I'm clutching at his suit jacket.

Royce pulls back first, though he doesn't let go of me with his free hand. The other is hanging on to the wedding dress for dear life as he bows his head, pressing his forehead to mine.

"There's no asking, Nic. Far as I'm concerned, you're already my wife. I've thought of you as such since... well, fuck. I can't really tell you how long it's been. The beginning, maybe? When I was sitting at the table with that fucker, watching Julio look over his shoulder so he could signal what cards Haines had... you were already mine."

Hang on—

Signal what cards he has...

I gasp, jerking back just enough so that I can get a good look at his full face. "You did cheat!"

"Correction," he says again, a hint of a tease to his

voice as he straightens. "I'm a Sinner, baby. I always play to win."

And then, as if to prove it, he gives the perfect wedding dress just enough of a shake for the wind to catch and carry the ruffles.

"You're serious. You... you really brought me here just to get married?"

"Yes, and we don't have much time. Our reservation is at ten. They were very clear. Miss it and we lose out." A small shrug, and again the dress is beckoning me. "Money talks in Vegas, but they have their own syndicates here. I can't expect them to fall at my feet and do what I tell them because I work for the Devil of Springfield."

This time, I snicker. "Poor thing."

Royce sniffs. "I know. It's a hardship, but what are you gonna do? Besides, Devil only gave me the weekend away. He has Killian standing in for me while we're gone, but two days is about his limit. He needs us back. Ava, too."

"Her baby shower is next week," I remember. And she's so close to popping, I hope we get to have it. "I can't miss it."

"We won't. We'll get the whole weekend to celebrate getting married, then once things settle down back home, you can pick what we do next. A big wedding where I can show you off... a destination thing where it's just you and me, Devil, Ava, and I can meet your mom... a honeymoon for me and you, and that's it... you decide."

"Really?" It feels so good to be able to let sarcasm slip into my tone instead of policing it. "Little ol' me gets to pick?"

"Hey. Marriage is a compromise."

He sounds so put-upon, I can't even be annoyed at his heavy-handedness; after all, I knew what I was getting into when he finally admitted to being my stalker... and I stayed. It never even occurred to me not to. And that's why, all sarcasm gone, I smile up at him instead: "So long as I marry you first, right?"

"You got it." Then, as if Royce honestly believes I need a little more convincing, he adds, "Did I also mention that the best part of this place is that it has themed weddings? I found one that has a theater-style stage, fog, props, and a sound system so I can crank out whatever showtune you want to walk down the aisle to... so long as you're walking right to me."

Holy. Shit.

I don't say it out loud this time. I can't. His thoughtfulness has temporarily struck me speechless. Sure, he arranged all of this without consulting me at all—or, you know, *asking* me—but, for one of the first times in my life, I feel seen. I feel *loved*.

My silence has him taking a step back of his own, watching me closely. After a few seconds, he clears his throat. "What do you think? It's better than saying 'I do' in the middle of the night in a crooked judge's office, yeah?"

Definitely.

I know what he's referring to, too. During one of my chats with Ava, she brought up her first wedding. I already knew she had two—with the second one coincidentally happening the day she discovered she was pregnant—and if Royce wants to follow Devil's lead there, that's fine with me.

Especially since, instead of getting married in a judge's office, he brought me all the way to Vegas to do a quickie wedding in the Viva Las Vegas Wedding Chapel, where I can be the star of the show with my gorgeous husband-to-be standing beside me.

I think someone needs to pinch me because I might just be dreaming.

I can't believe this is happening. I want so badly to snatch that dress from him, tell him to lead the way, then find out if it really is a perfect fit for me. So my hair's not done. So my make-up probably wore off during our in-flight entertainment. I didn't bother re-doing my face after I cleaned up in the tiny bathroom on the plane, but when Royce looks at me in the Vegas lights, I feel like the most beautiful creature alive.

And he wants to marry me.

I nod at his pockets. I shouldn't, but that doesn't stop me from saying, "Aren't you going to flip your coin? Heads, we do this. Tails, we don't?"

He rigs his tosses. Depending on which one he picks, that will tell me exactly how he feels about all of this.

Only...

Royce pulls one from his pocket. I can't tell if it's the one with a pair of heads or a pair of tails, and I don't get the chance to see before he palms it. It's gone in the next moment, his right hand free to gently cup the edge of my jaw.

"When it comes to forever with you, Nic, I won't leave that up to chance."

My heart swells inside of my chest. He couldn't have given me a better answer. "'All I Ask of You.'"

His brow furrows.

I grin. "That's what I want to walk down the aisle to. 'All I Ask of You' from *Phantom*." Reaching out, I run my finger down the silky material of the nearest sleeve. "Fitting, right? With the dress?"

"So it's a 'yes' then? You'll marry me?"

As if there was any doubt about *that*.

I slide my hand from the dress, laying my palm over his chest.

Over his *heart*.

"Like you said. Sinners play to win."

He might have won me in a bet. But me?

I got the biggest prize.

I got Royce McIntyre as mine—and as the opening chords to Christine and Raoul's promise to each other lead me toward my forever with him, I'm not sure if I ended up with the possessive stalker or the golden savior... but it doesn't matter.

He's both, and like the dress he brought for me, that's *perfect*.

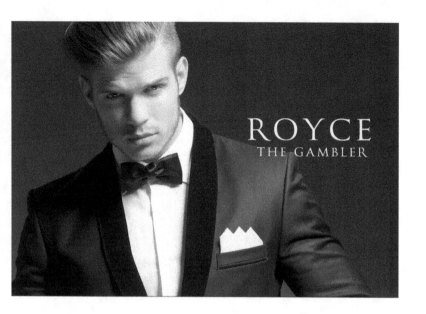

ROYCE
THE GAMBLER

The Devil's Playground

NICOLETTE
THE PRIZE

AUTHOR'S NOTE

Thanks for reading *The Devil's Playground*!

It was so much fun to get inside of Royce's head. He's still the—*ahem*—devil-may-care, smart ass of a gambler readers met in book one, but his loyalty to Link, the Sinners, and Nicolette was important to me—as well as showing how he can hide his possessive side behind a half smile and a coin toss. He and Nicolette deserve their HEA, and I look forward to checking in with them again in the future.

Speaking of the future... if you were interested in what was going on with the subplot featuring Royce's cousin, Jake, his book is coming out next. Called *Silhouette,* it delves into Jake's past, as well as how far he'll go to get his most recent target of affection. It's a stalker romance—with a heavy emphasis on the *stalking* part—and it's out on April 16th!

After that, readers finally get to see what the East End of Springfield is like with *Dragonfly*. Featuring Damien

Libellula as the hero—and the woman stalking *him* as his heroine—*Dragonfly* is out in June!

And if you liked the quick mentions/appearance of Nicholas and Hunter Reed, the murderous twins have their own duet already released: *Close to Midnight* (Hunter & Sally) and *Really Should Stay* (Nicholas & Tamryn).

One last thing: if you purchase a physical copy of this book—paperback, discreet paperback, or hardcover—send me your mailing address via email (carinhartbooks@gmail.com) and I'll mail you a free bookmark and a signed bookplate.

Keep reading/scrolling/clicking for a sneak peek at the covers & blurbs for both *Silhouette* and *Dragonfly*!

xoxo,
Carin

**Don't look out your window
—because you might not like
what you see...**

SIMONE

I can't escape him.

I thought I did. When I
slipped off one night, leaving
everything in my old life
behind, I was ready to sacrifice
it all if only to leave *him*
behind, too.

But, like always, my ex chases after me. That's what he
does, after all. Holding to the vows I was too young and
naive to understand, William Burke will have me 'til
death do us part.

And then, almost immediately, it does—when Will is
slaughtered in a back alley.

He haunts my dreams. Stars in my nightmares. I see him everywhere, hear his voice in my head. I look out my window and he's there. Even dead, I can't escape him...

And that's when I look out my window and realize that it isn't Will watching me from the shadows.

It's another man. A stranger.

A silhouette.

And a *killer*.

Because he's not just watching me. He wants me more than Will did... enough that he'll kill *for* me.

Stalk me.

Take me.

JAKE

They say the third time's the charm—and whoever they are, they better be right.

I lost Casey. Heather... that was a tragedy.

And now I want Simone.

I refuse to give up on Simone.

So she wears another man's ring. He torments her, and she's in need of a hero.

I can be that for her, but when she doesn't seem quite that impressed with my gift, I realize I need to get to know my sweet vixen a little better before I make her mine.

And that's exactly what I do.

***Silhouette is a standalone dark stalker romance that is set in the same universe as *No One Has To Know* and *The Devil's Bargain*.

Releasing on April 16th— pre-order now!

PRE-ORDER NOW

WHEN DEEP HATE TURNS TO EVEN DEEPER LOVE...

Revenge is a dish best served cold—but what happens when your target has you blazing up inside?

SAVANNAH

Five years ago, the Libellula Family ruined my life.

It doesn't matter who was responsible. I blamed the man who created his gang of thugs: Damien Libellula himself. If it wasn't for him giving free rein to his soldiers to pass their funny money through my store, I wouldn't have been accused of money laundering —and counterfeiting.

I was a naive twenty-five-year-old then. Four years in a minimum-security prison later, and I'm out for revenge.

I changed my name. My hair. My accent.

My *life*.

And I did that all because my plan to get revenge on Damien? I'm going to stalk him. Infiltrate my way into his life in any way I can. I'm going to make him trust me.

Maybe even love me.

I'm going to seduce him—and then I'm going to kill him.

At least, that was the plan. But Damien, he has a different one.

Before I can do any of that, he makes me his *wife*.

DAMIEN

I thought it was amusing at first. The gorgeous brunette who followed me everywhere, too stunning to hide in any crowd.

Then, when I grew impatient to see what it was she wanted with me, I approached her—and she stabbed me in my side.

Another man might be put off by something like that. Not me. I've always liked my women feisty, and Savannah's murderous side was so refreshing in a world where everyone bows down to me.

At that moment, I decided I would do everything to bring her to her knees.

Following a page out of my old rival's book, I made her a deal: she goes back to prison—and that's assuming she survives my Family long enough to be charged for attempted murder—or she gives up her freedom and becomes my bride.

I know she only chooses the second option because she thinks she can get close enough to kill me again.

I must say, I'm looking forward to her trying... especially when I'll certainly enjoy showing her just why she shouldn't.

Dragonfly is the third book in the **Deal with the Devil** series, a collection of interconnected standalones set in the fictional crime hotspot of Springfield. It tells the story of mafia leader Damien Libellula and the one woman who will trade revenge for something more, Savannah Montgomery.

Releasing June 18, 2024!

KEEP IN TOUCH

Stay tuned for what's coming up next! Follow me at any of these places—or sign up for my newsletter—for news, promotions, upcoming releases, and more:

CarinHart.com
Carin's Newsletter
Carin's Signed Book Store

facebook.com/carinhartbooks
amazon.com/author/carinhart
instagram.com/carinhartbooks

ALSO BY CARIN HART

Deal with the Devil series

No One Has To Know *standalone

Silhouette *standalone

The Devil's Bargain

The Devil's Bride *newsletter exclusive

The Devil's Playground

Dragonfly

Dance with the Devil

Ride with the Devil

Reed Twins

Close to Midnight

Really Should Stay